Be sure to catch the next segment
in the Crown and Glory series,
Her Royal Husband by Cara Colter,
coming in July 2002 in Silhouette Romance.

* * *

Harrison wasn't sure he was a man of honor himself.

Not at the moment. He'd had no intention of touching her. He'd deliberately kept himself from it, in fact. Yet, he could feel the taunting fullness of her soft lips beneath his fingers. Her warm breath trembled against his skin.

It would be so easy to slip his hand around the back of her neck, lower his mouth to hers and find out what it was about her that tested his control. But now wasn't the time to cave in to temptation.

She stepped back, looking very much as if she didn't know why she hadn't moved before now. He confused her. But he figured that made them even. She was confusing the daylights out of him.

Dear Reader,

June is busting out all over with this month's exciting lineup!

First up is Annette Broadrick's *But Not For Me.* We asked Annette what kinds of stories she loved, and she admitted that a heroine in love with her boss has always been one of her favorites. In this romance, a reserved administrative assistant falls for her sexy boss, but leaves her position when she receives threatening letters. Well, this boss has another way to keep his beautiful assistant by his side—marry her right away!

Royal Protocol by Christine Flynn is the next installment of the CROWN AND GLORY series. Here, a lovely lady-in-waiting teaches an admiral a thing or two about chemistry. Together, they try to rescue royalty, but end up rescuing each other. And you can never get enough of Susan Mallery's DESERT ROGUES series. In *The Prince & the Pregnant Princess,* a headstrong woman finds out she's pregnant with a seductive sheik's child. How long will it take before she succumbs to his charms and his promise of happily ever after?

In *The Last Wilder,* the fiery conclusion of Janis Reams Hudson's WILDERS OF WYATT COUNTY, a willful heroine on a secret quest winds up in a small town and locks horns with the handsome local sheriff. Cheryl St.John's *Nick All Night* tells the story of a down-on-her-luck woman who returns home and gets a second chance at love with her very distracting next-door neighbor. In Elizabeth Harbison's *Drive Me Wild,* a schoolbus-driving mom struggles to make ends meet, but finds happiness with a former flame who just happens to be her employer!

It's time to enjoy those lazy days of summer. So, grab a seat by the pool and don't forget to bring your stack of emotional tales of love, life and family from Silhouette Special Edition!

Sincerely,

Karen Taylor Richman
Senior Editor

Please address questions and book requests to:
Silhouette Reader Service
U.S.: 3010 Walden Ave., P.O. Box 1325, Buffalo, NY 14269
Canadian: P.O. Box 609, Fort Erie, Ont. L2A 5X3

Royal Protocol

CHRISTINE FLYNN

SPECIAL EDITION™

Published by Silhouette Books

America's Publisher of Contemporary Romance

Special thanks and acknowledgment are given
to Christine Flynn for her contribution to the
CROWN AND GLORY series.

To all the wonderful ladies who helped create Penwyck.
Thanks!
Chris

SILHOUETTE BOOKS

ISBN 0-373-24471-1

ROYAL PROTOCOL

Books by Christine Flynn

CHRISTINE FLYNN

admits to being interested in just about everything, which is why she considers herself fortunate to have turned her interest in writing into a career. She feels that a writer gets to explore it all and, to her, exploring relationships—especially the intense, bittersweet or even lighthearted relationships between men and women—is fascinating.

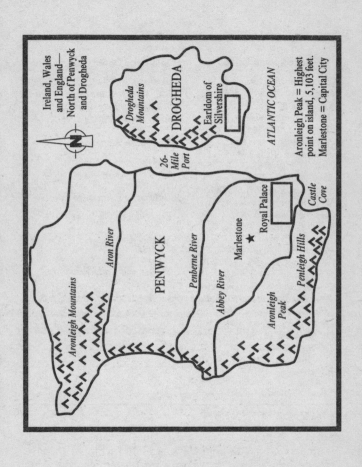

Ireland, Wales and England— North of Penwyck and Drogheda

Drogheda Mountains

DROGHEDA

Earldom of Silvershire

26-Mile Port

ATLANTIC OCEAN

Aronleigh Peak = Highest point on island, 5,103 feet.
Marlestone = Capital City

Aron River

PENWYCK

Aronleigh Mountains

Penberne River

Abbey River

Aronleigh Peak

Penleigh Hills

Marlestone

Royal Palace

Castle Cove

Chapter One

Admiral Harrison Monteque moved with the silent aggression of a nuclear submarine as he strode down the gilded main hall of the royal residence. Uniformed guards snapped to attention in his wake, doors opening to allow him entry without question as he moved toward the queen's private apartments.

Not one of those young guards made eye contact with him. A fair number held their breath. No one wanted to draw his attention for fear they weren't standing smartly enough, weren't looking alert enough. He wasn't even their commander. Not directly, anyway. Yet every one of them knew that the formidable man in the impressively decorated navy-blue uniform held the respect of every officer in the military and that he demanded the best of anyone who served the crown.

The best was nothing compared to what he demanded of himself. Rumor had it that he constantly pushed his own limits, asking even more of himself than he did of others.

Lately he'd been pushing himself more than many would have thought humanly possible—had they known the pressures and responsibilities he and a handful of his peers had secretly undertaken.

For nearly two months he had lived on four hours of sleep each night. Five at best. He spent his nights poring through reams of diplomatic communiqués, stacks of ministerial requests and reports usually meant only for the eyes of the king—all to keep the government running smoothly and protect the interests of the kingdom of Penwyck's citizens.

He spent his days in briefings with his three counterparts on the king's Royal Elite Team—each of whom had spent the night with piles of paper of his own—and overseeing the fleets of ships, the aircraft and the fifty thousand sailors under his command.

His caffeine consumption had doubled.

So had his intake of antacids.

If he'd still smoked, he didn't doubt that he'd be up to a couple of packs a day by now. If not before, then certainly after this morning.

Prince Owen, one of the king and queen of Penwyck's twenty-three-year-old twin sons and a possible heir to the throne, had been kidnapped.

A note to that effect had been delivered to the royal offices two hours ago. The prince's absence, along with the signs of struggle the guards had found in the prince's bedroom, proved the note hadn't been a hoax.

Harrison had been in an intelligence meeting when he'd received the call. As head of the Royal Elite Team, he had immediately ordered full security for the rest of the royal family. Those he could find, anyway. Prince

Owen's vagabond twin, Prince Dylan, was still off trekking Europe, deliberately ignoring the need for security for someone of his stature. Or perhaps escaping it. But Harrison had taken full measures to protect those he could. He'd then had the king's personal secretary break the news of the prince's kidnapping to the queen.

He would have told Queen Marissa himself, but there had been other security measures to implement, questions to ask, answers to demand. Aside from that, he never did well when it came to breaking upsetting news to a woman. Where females were concerned, he definitely lacked training when it came to offering emotional support.

He had no choice but to speak with her now. As he understood it, Her Majesty had been at breakfast with two of her three daughters, the Princesses Megan and Anastasia, when the note had been received. Security precautions demanded they be separated. The princesses had been escorted to their rooms on the second floor of the east wing. The queen had retired to her chamber.

The thud of Harrison's polished black shoes echoed off the marble floor as he approached a set of carved double doors. His only hope was that she would remain as calm and serene as she always appeared to be.

A baby-faced lieutenant in the Royal Guard's red-jacketed uniform and red beret jerked his rifle to parade rest and snapped a salute. "Admiral."

"Lieutenant," Harrison returned, and walked past the door the soldier held for him.

The queen's drawing room was as ornate as the rest of the palace: ceilings and cornices were coffered and curved; walls were covered with hand-carved plaster and gilded wainscoting; the marble fireplace was graced by marble columns. Except, here rich colors of royalty gave way to frankly feminine shades of cream and yellow. Other than the pale velvet sofa framed by a sheer-curtained window, the furniture was all dainty chairs and chaises covered in silk damask and totally unsuitable for use by any male with muscle on his bones.

The secretary's desk, tucked against a far wall, was unoccupied. A guard had called ahead, so they'd known he was coming. The queen's personal secretary, however, the gray-haired and very proper Mrs. Ferth, was nowhere to be seen.

Impatient at the thought of having to wait for the woman to announce him, he started back for the guard. He'd barely turned when the tall, carved doubled doors at the far side of the room swung inward. A slender woman in a pale-pink wool suit, her gleaming blond hair restrained in a tight twist, stepped out and closed the doors behind her.

Impatience turned to an inward groan.

No one saw the queen without going through her secretary or her lady-in-waiting. With the secretary obviously unavailable, that left him stuck with the woman he'd come to think of as the ice maiden, Lady Gwendolyn Corbin.

"Lady Corbin," he said, acknowledging her with a nod of his dark head. He knew there were those who found the woman walking toward him quite charming. Where they got that impression was beyond him. From the cool formality she'd always exhibited around him—on the rare occasions he had been around her—Lady Gwen had struck him as possessing about as much warmth as the marble statues in the garden.

"I must speak with Her Majesty."

"She's coming. Can you tell me what's going on?" With her hands clasped tightly enough to whiten her knuckles, she moved closer, her blue eyes searching his. "Sir Selwyn would say only that Prince Owen had been kidnapped and that the queen is to remain in her rooms. Do you know what happened? Is he hurt?"

Gwen anxiously searched the ruggedly carved features of the tall, powerfully built man before her. Harrison Monteque had always reminded her of a Scottish warlord, that breed of male who had defended his highlands with nothing but brute force and a sword of hammered steel. The hard angles and planes of his face were framed with deep-auburn hair cut close, she assumed, to tame any hint of curl rather than to meet military code. His eyes, the amber brown of a panther's, held hers with disconcerting ease.

He was over six feet of commanding, demanding male in an admiral's uniform. But even without the gold braid trimming his cuffs and epaulets, the five stars denoting his rank and the slew of ribbons decorating his chest, his authority was unmistakable. Power radiated from him like heat.

She had never felt comfortable around the man, never cared for his iron-fisted methods and his overbearing manner. Yet, as she stood waiting for him to shed light on the awful events of the morning, she wouldn't have cared if he'd marched in with trumpets and his troops, as long as he could tell her what was happening. Her concern for the royal family and her friend the queen totally overrode everything else.

"I'm afraid I can't answer that."

"Because you don't know? Or because you can't say?"

Harrison heard no challenge in the question. Only disquiet and a hint of totally unexpected vulnerability.

"Because what I have is only for the queen."

"Can you at least tell me if the news is positive?"

He had never seen her look at him so openly before. Without the polite-but-cool facade she usually wore around him, he couldn't help but notice the flecks of turquoise in her lake-blue eyes, the delicate curve of her cheek, the soft part of her lovely mouth.

He'd never before noticed the poreless quality of her skin, or the intriguing, tantalizing fullness of her bottom lip.

He noticed now—along with a distinct and unmistakable pull low in his groin when he caught a hint of the surpassingly erotic perfume she wore.

Caught completely off guard by her, unaccustomed to being caught off guard by much of anything, he banished his body's betraying reactions beneath military bearing and watched her openness fade.

"I'm sorry," he said, though the tightness in his voice hardly made him sound it. "I really must speak with the queen." Wishing she wasn't standing so close, he nodded over her shoulder. "If you would please get her for me?"

"No need," came the cultured tones of Queen Marissa's voice. "I'm here."

As Gwen had done moments ago, the queen of Penwyck stepped through the double doors that led from her salon and bedchamber. A tall, slender woman of grace and breeding, her dark hair was knotted at her nape and held with a filigreed gold clasp. Her cashmere slacks and silk blouse were as flawless as the diamonds on her fingers and the thick gold chain draped around her neck.

Gwen dropped a quick, automatic curtsy. Her Majesty's striking features bore the strain of the morning as she acknowledged her with a nod and continued toward the man dominating the decidedly feminine room.

Harrison's air of command suggested that he deferred

to no one. Yet he immediately offered a respectful and amazingly gallant bow.

"Admiral Monteque." Lifting her hand to indicate that he should rise, she stopped by a small chair beneath a surprisingly casual portrait of the royal family. In it, she and King Morgan were in hunting clothes, their five children surrounding them with their horses. "Please, let's dispense with formalities. What can you tell me of my son?"

His incisive glance cut toward the woman quietly waiting ten feet away. "May I speak with you alone, Your Majesty?"

"I would prefer that Lady Gwendolyn stay."

"This is a matter of security, Your Majesty."

"We all realize that, Admiral," she replied, too tense to sit, too refined to pace. "Please, what do you know of Owen? I heard a guard say that his room has been searched. There was a struggle." Her hand clutched the back of the chair as she took a deep breath. "Was there any sign of...violence?"

"There was no blood," he replied, fairly certain that was what she was asking. "At least none that was immediately visible. We have forensics people in there now."

"Doing what?"

"Dusting for prints. Searching for physical evidence. Royal Intelligence is on top of it."

"But what are they doing to find him?"

"What they're doing right now will help find him," he explained, taking her insistence as a merciful sign that she was holding her own. "They need clues to know where to start." He paused. "The best one we have right now was in the ransom note."

It was against his better judgment to continue in the

presence of the woman watching him so intently. He had no idea what Lady Corbin's security clearance was, but he knew it wasn't anywhere near high enough to be privy to the events now taking place. He also knew he wasn't in a position at the moment to do anything other than as his sovereign instructed.

"The contents of the note will not be made public," he continued with a pointed glance toward Gwen, "but we know why he was taken. Whoever took the prince is demanding that Penwyck withdraw from the treaty we are about to sign with Majorco."

"That's the ransom demand? That we not sign?"

Harrison's confirming nod was as tight as the muscles knotting his gut.

Majorco was an island thirty miles southeast of Penwyck. Like the island of Drogheda to the east, it was a principality. At least it had been until the last of the ruling family died off last year and left them without an heir. The existing parliament had taken over quickly enough to form a democracy, but their military had fallen apart.

The country's new leaders had asked Penwyck for protection and proposed an alliance that had quickly become part of a larger agreement the king had been unable to refuse.

"You know that withdrawal from the alliance isn't an option," he carefully reminded her. "The treaty with Majorco has become crucial to our trade agreement with the United States. That alliance must go through at all costs."

The queen visibly paled. "Not at all costs, Admiral."

"You know how important this is to the kingdom."

"You will not sacrifice my son."

Even as the queen spoke, Gwen moved toward her, graceful in her silence, and stopped protectively a few feet from her side. He didn't at all appreciate that she was looking at him as if he'd snatched the prince himself.

"I assure you that is not our intention. We will find him," he insisted, because the alternative wasn't one he was willing to accept. "Our analysts are already working on the note to see where it came from. Intelligence is also profiling every radical and subversive organization that might feel threatened by that alliance."

Gwen's glance caught his. "Who brought it?" she quietly inquired. "The note. Who delivered it here?"

"Please answer her," the queen asked when he hesitated.

"A commercial courier service delivered it to the royal offices for King Morgan. We're checking now to see who paid for the delivery.

"We're taking care of everything," he assured the older woman, wishing the younger one would leave. "But we'll have to speak later about what remains to be done regarding the alliance." He paused, a muscle in his jaw jerking, as it tended to do when inner frustration leaked out. It would have been so much simpler to take care of all his business with the queen right now. But, right now, because of the petite blonde staring icicles at him, he couldn't. "It's no longer safe to speak by telephone. There's too much risk of conversations being intercepted," he explained, ignoring the chill. "It will be best if we meet to talk."

The queen said nothing. She simply stared at him long enough for him to get the feeling that the alliance was the last thing on her mind before giving him a rather numb nod.

"Please keep me informed," she murmured.

"I will."

"About my son," she clarified.

"Of course, Your Majesty," he replied, and watched her give her lady-in-waiting a look of pure distress before she walked regally across the antique Aubusson carpet to the tall double doors.

Harrison could have sworn the temperature in the room dropped another ten degrees in the time it took her to step into her salon and close the door with a dignified click.

"I'll let myself out," he muttered, and turned on his heel.

Gwen would have been more than happy to let him leave on his own. As shaken as Marissa had looked to her, she would much rather have gone after her friend, but duty demanded that she escort the queen's guest from the room.

"Her Majesty wouldn't hear of it," she returned politely, and turned ahead of him. "I'll see you to the door."

She was fairly certain he'd expected her to stay put. He was, after all, the sort of man who ordered and expected people to obey.

She tended to bridle around any man, other than the king, who automatically expected such total deference. There were many like him in the circles in which she moved. Her own father being one of them. Yet, even her father wasn't as hard or ruthless as the admiral was rumored to be.

To be fair, ruthless or not, she knew that if anyone could be counted on to find the prince it would be the man following her across the room and the men he commanded on the Royal Elite Team. The RET consisted of the best of the best, the cream the king himself had skimmed from his Royal Intelligence Institute with its top scientists, doctors, military and economists. All were at the admiral's disposal.

"May I ask something of you, Admiral?" Feeling as protective as a sister of the woman she had served for the past ten years, she reached for the gilded handle of the door. "For Her Majesty?"

"Put that way, I can hardly refuse."

"Then, please," she requested, overlooking the flatness, or maybe it was the fatigue, in his tone, "don't burden Her Majesty with details of the trade alliance."

His eyebrows knit into a single slash. "Excuse me?"

"The alliance," she repeated, wishing he wouldn't frown at her with such displeasure. "It's the king's project. All the queen needs right now is information about her son. You should speak with His Majesty about anything else."

Her tone was faintly disapproving, her manner utterly calm and certain. At that moment, with her cool guard firmly in place and the soft vulnerability he'd glimpsed nowhere in sight, she looked very much like the very proper matron of a school for incorrigible young boys.

He was in no mood for a reprimand. Or to be told what he should or shouldn't do, something that seldom happened to him, anyway. Taking her hand from the latch, surprised to find her slender fingers so warm, he replaced it with his own and turned to face her.

Despite the way she clasped her hands in a knot, the way she looked up at him made her seem every bit as regal and poised as their queen.

"Lady Corbin," he began, his tone a shade shy of patient, "I realize it's your job to protect Her Majesty from whatever she doesn't wish to deal with around here. You screen her visitors and answer her mail and do whatever is required of you to insulate her from what takes place beyond the scope of her duties and these walls. But there are forces at work here about which you haven't a clue.''

Most people would have backed down. The faint-hearted would even have backed away. Remarkably, admirably, she did neither—though he did catch a telltale hint of color rising beneath her maddeningly calm facade.

''And those forces would be?''

''Nothing you're cleared to know about.''

''The alliance with Majorco is hardly top secret, Admiral.'' Years of training kept her tone even, her manner unfailingly polite. He wouldn't have any idea that she was practically gritting her teeth. ''The queen and I have been planning the state dinner to celebrate its signing for the past two months. Everyone from the royal printers to the kitchen staff knows about it.''

''I'm not talking about the alliance.''

''Then what are we talking about? The alliance is what I asked you not to bother Her Majesty with.''

He caught a hint of her perfume again. The scent was subtle, warm. Like the air on a tropical island when flowers scented the sensuous breeze.

Distracted, annoyed because he wasn't a man who distracted easily, he took a step closer—for no reason other than to prove she had no real effect on him at all.

''We're talking about matters to which even the king's council isn't privy,'' he informed her, ignoring the unwanted tingle of heat low in his gut. ''But just so you'll have some idea of what is going on, a special team will be arriving any minute to tap in to Her Majesty's telephone lines. It's possible that Prince Owen's captors have her personal phone number and will try to make contact that way. It's no secret how close she is to her children.''

His voice dropped like a rock over Penwyck's sheer

cliffs. "They will also be tapping the telephone in your apartment," he informed her, failing to mention that telephone communications of all staff with access to the royal residence would be monitored. "Where are your rooms?"

A flicker of hesitation passed through her eyes. "Directly upstairs."

"Then, I imagine they'll do yours right after they're finished here. One never truly knows who one can trust."

He was baiting her. Deliberately. Gwen caught the odd glint in Harrison's eyes as he waited for her reaction. Refusing to give him the satisfaction, she bit her tongue, swearing she almost perforated it in the moments before he released his visual hold and pulled open the door.

An instant later he was striding out down the long, wide hall, guards jerking to attention as he passed.

The guard near Gwen remained stiffly still, his eyes straight ahead, his rifle at his side. Not until she started to close the door did he reshoulder the weapon in three motions as quick as they were precise.

As he did, Gwen noticed the black holster resting against the red wool of his jacket. He was also wearing a side arm.

It had been ten years since she'd seen armed guards inside the private residence. Normally they kept posts only at exterior doors.

An old sense of loss, of anger, rose inside her. Uneasily, she pushed it right back down. She didn't want to think about the events that had last required such tight security. Even though there never had been a sense of closure about them for her—or for her daughter—they were over and done with. They also had no part at all in what was going on now.

Reminding herself of that, she let the latch click quietly

into place and pressed her hand to her stomach. She would think only of the present. Of this moment. And at that moment, she could still feel an odd, lingering heat where Harrison's fingers had gripped hers when he'd so abruptly moved her hand. Preferring to ignore the sensation, she drew a breath of air that still smelled faintly of citrus and something distinctly, boldly male.

His aftershave.

Even when he was no longer physically present, the man had the power to unnerve.

Not wanting to think about him, either, Gwen headed for the desk, thinking about him, anyway.

She'd had little occasion over the years to directly encounter the admiral, but she could swear that, on the rare occasions they did meet, he made a point of provoking her. She had no idea why that was. Nor was she going to waste energy trying to figure out his warped power-hungry psyche. She knew only that he was reputed to be frighteningly intelligent, obsessed with his job and position and impossible for any woman to land.

Not that one would want him, she thought, heading for Mrs. Ferth's painfully neat desk. The man possessed the sensitivity of stone.

There had been no blood. At least none that was immediately visible, he'd said, oblivious to the mental pictures such doubt would put in a mother's mind.

She couldn't believe the blunt way he'd responded to the queen's request for information about her son. She couldn't believe, either, that he would burden the queen about the alliance. Not that the queen wouldn't be able to handle matters of state. The woman was enormously bright, well-read and far more politically astute than His Majesty tended to realize, or admit. It was just that King Morgan, though an eminently kind and wise monarch, wasn't the most liberated ruler in the western hemisphere. To his royal mind, politics was man's work. His queen was to tend their children and the plethora of women's duties that kept Penwyckian arts, charities and hospitality the envy of the civilized world.

She had the feeling the admiral was just as narrow.

Frowning at how he invaded her thoughts, she automatically picked up a stack of lists near the queen's personal calendar.

She had planned to check the silver services for the state dinner with the chef's captain that morning, and to meet with the royal sommelier about the wine, provided that she had been able to get a decision out of the queen. The chef had made his recommendations, but he needed Her Majesty's approval to serve the Margaux with the fois gras, rather than hold it for the main course of filet with truffles. Aside from the queen's uncharacteristic indecision, there was the matter of champagne. It was nonexistent.

The cellar had been depleted of champagne last month due to Princess Meredith's hastily planned and executed nuptials, and the order of Dom Perignon had yet to be received. Monsieur Pomier, the sommelier, lost sleep each night those dark-green bottles were being agitated by drivers and deliverymen and not resting properly in his cellar.

Returning the lists to the desk, Gwen stepped back. Because many of the elements for the dinner had been borrowed for the wedding, she had scrambled to redesign seating arrangements, floral displays, the menu, the music. But she felt none of the energy, or the urgency, that had sustained her for the past weeks.

What she felt was concern. Even before the horrible, unbelievable news of the prince's kidnapping, the queen's manner had seemed oddly withdrawn. Over the past week she had also become totally apathetic about the preparations for the dinner. It wasn't like her to not care about such an important function. Her fingerprints were usually all over everything, from the choice of silver to be used to the color of ink on the place cards. But lately Marissa couldn't have cared less about such details.

The queen had dismissed her own lack of enthusiasm as postwedding letdown following the frantic preparations for the royal wedding. Gwen wanted to believe that was all that was wrong, but she'd known the queen too many years not to feel that something more was going on.

When she'd asked, Marissa had insisted there wasn't— and spent most of the past several days avoiding her by going for long walks. Alone.

Knowing that the woman didn't need to be alone just then, she headed for the door of the salon. It didn't matter at the moment why the queen had been acting so strangely. The dinner didn't matter, either. With the prince missing, it would undoubtedly be postponed, anyway. All she really cared about was Prince Owen.

For his sake and the sake of his mother, she hoped desperately that he hadn't been harmed.

She also hoped that Admiral Arrogant and his men could find him.

The same thought was on Harrison's mind when he was awakened by the telephone before the sun rose the next morning. But with that call, concern about the prince was replaced with a more pressing problem.

Chapter Two

The kidnapping of Prince Owen was not the Royal Elite Team's first priority. Under most other circumstances, it certainly would have been. But the RET was presently perpetrating a royal hoax they were duty-bound to continue. That was why the complexities of locating the missing heir simply blended into the mix of duties and dilemmas Harrison took to bed with him a little before midnight.

Ordinarily he slept like the dead. Some would have claimed that was because he had no conscience. But his conscience was just as keen as the rest of his mind, and if he slept well, it was because an exhausted body had no choice. Sleep tonight was fitful, though. He still felt a niggling dread every time his subconscious stirred with thoughts of who was actually wearing the king's robes.

What the public didn't know was that their beloved King Morgan was at that very moment locked away in the bowels of the palace, deep in a coma. He was being cared for in secret by an elite medical team with access to the most brilliant minds in modern medicine, but that didn't change the fact that the monarchy was not precisely what the RET was honor bound to make it appear on the surface.

The situation, as Harrison had come to think of it, began over six weeks ago when King Morgan had unexpectedly fallen ill and slipped into unconsciousness. Viral encephalitis had been the diagnosis. A rare form from Africa that the king's body might be able to fight off—if it didn't kill him first.

No one had any idea how he had contracted it. But once the diagnosis had been made, there had been no real question about what needed to be done. Because Penwyck had been—and still was—involved in its history's most critical treaties and alliances, the RET had been forced to implement a plan the king himself had devised years ago in the event of his incapacitation.

His Majesty wanted his estranged identical twin, Prince Broderick, to impersonate him. Plan B, he had called it. *B* for Broderick.

The RET had collectively cringed at the idea. All any of them really knew of the prince was that his relationship with his brother had been as volatile as it was strained while they'd grown up, and that Broderick had been estranged from his family ever since the boating accident that killed both their parents when the elder royal twins were in their early twenties.

It had been known for some time prior to that, that the reigning king and queen had favored Morgan over his ineffective, unproductive sibling. When it was discovered upon their parents' deaths that Morgan had been named heir-apparent and was crowned king, Broderick had bought himself a surprisingly modest estate on Majorco and quietly gone into seclusion.

No one knew if he'd been grieving for his parents or merely licking his wounds. It was as if the man had dropped off the planet. For years Broderick ignored all of King Morgan's attempts to draw him back into the fold. When Broderick finally did respond to the overtures, he'd returned long enough to cause grief by impersonating his brother to embezzle funds, and King Morgan had sent him packing. After that, the king had heard from him only once—the evening Broderick called to warn him of an assassination attempt that was about to be made on his life and that of Queen Marissa and their children.

That call had saved their lives, but Broderick had promptly withdrawn once more to the reclusive life he'd chosen to lead. By then he'd already been little more than an afterthought to the public. Because so few knew of the assassination attempt that had taken place those ten long years ago, he had now all but disappeared from the public's memory. His heroic act, however, had made the men of the RET look at him with less skepticism, but not one of them was totally comfortable with the man presently playing king.

Broderick could run as hot as lava or as cold as the earth's poles. He could be cooperative or demanding. But so far he had proven worthy of the confidence his brother had placed in him and been a model king in public.

King Morgan himself had told Harrison that Broderick would be convincing in the position. He had said that, if worst came to worse, his brother could take over quite ably in the role because, even though Broderick hated him, Broderick had always loved power and would work to foster the image of a great monarch.

Harrison would never disobey the king's command.

Yet, as much as Harrison respected His Majesty's opinions, he couldn't shake the thought that nothing about Broderick was what it appeared to be.

That was the thought preying through his fitful sleep when the telephone beside his bed jerked him awake at four o'clock the next morning.

Within seconds of groping for the receiver and grumbling, "Monteque," he learned that Plan B had been blown wide open.

Even as his feet hit the floor, the muffle-voiced reporter on the other end of the line was saying that he couldn't reveal his source, but that the headline would explain everything. Before Harrison could try to demand that source, anyway, his caller told him that he'd just left a copy of the morning paper outside the admiralty's office. The rest of the copies would be hitting the streets in a little over an hour.

The RET didn't have a headquarters with a plaque or signage to identify it as such. Since it consisted only of four men whose daily duties kept them in the palace or elsewhere in the capital city of Marlestone, and who met solely when an emergency situation threatened the royal family or its government, the RET met wherever it was expeditious and secure.

Security was a definite priority with Harrison.

Half an hour after the call, showered, shaved and still bleeding from the nick on his chin where he'd been a little too aggressive with his razor, he opened a steel door deep beneath the palace's grounds and stepped into a brightly lit and austere gray hallway. There were few places on earth more secure than the rooms he was about enter.

Few people knew of the tunnel beneath the palace that

the royal family used to avoid walking through the palace's public areas. Even fewer knew of the tunnel intersecting it through a boiler room that connected to the Royal Intelligence Institute a mile away.

It was the second tunnel Harrison had just entered.

The doors here were unmarked and the same pale gray as the walls. The floor was industrial tile. Overhead lights were long, fluorescent tubes. Cameras followed the movements of whoever stepped inside. Many of the unseen rooms were soundproofed and lined with lead so no communication inside could be overheard or intercepted by equipment from the outside world.

A Star Wars array of the most sophisticated surveillance equipment known to man occupied a cavernous space behind the unobtrusive door a couple hundred yards down. A door beyond that led to a suite, complete with kitchens and a year's worth of supplies for the royal family and necessary staff in the event of an attack. Another on the other side led to a medical clinic with a surgical suite and hospital beds.

One of those beds was occupied now—by King Morgan.

A soldier in the khaki uniform and black cap of the Royal Army appeared from behind the only glass door.

Shoving the newspaper he carried under his left arm, Harrison returned his salute.

"Sir," the young man began, still at attention, "the men you asked your secretary to summon are waiting in the conference room. Except for Colonel Prescott. He's on his way," he explained, his words as clipped as the bristle of brown hair covering his head. "Your secretary also asked you be told that the minister of foreign relations has requested your presence at a meeting in his office as soon as possible. She said it was urgent."

It appeared that no one had slept much that night. That meeting would be about Majorco, Harrison thought. And there wasn't anything that wasn't urgent at the moment. "I need coffee. Black."

"It's already waiting for you, sir."

He had his secretary to thank for that. He was sure of it. If the woman wasn't already married, he'd consider marrying her himself. "What's the holdup with Colonel Prescott?"

"I wasn't informed, sir."

Harrison gave the young man a nod. "As you were," he muttered, and pressed a code into the pad by the unmarked conference room door.

In one salute, Harrison returned those of the two highly trained men rising to their feet around a gleaming mahogany conference table. The walls here were richly paneled wood, the carpet beneath his feet a deep burgundy.

"Sorry to call you out so early," he said to men who had to be every bit as tired as he felt. "I know neither of you got to bed before midnight."

"I'm not sure the colonel got to bed at all," said Carson Logan, referring to Colonel Pierceson Prescott, Duke of Aronleigh. Logan, the king's loyal and powerful bodyguard, was a duke himself. "I think he's on to something."

Harrison stopped halfway between the table and the coffee tray on the matching sideboard. Pierce Prescott was also head of Royal Intelligence.

"On to what?"

"He didn't say. He called half an hour after you did and said he'd meet us here. You'd probably already left or he'd have called you, too."

Harrison headed for the caffeine.

Sir Selwyn Estabon, the king's personal secretary and

secret member of Royal Intelligence, settled back into one of the burgundy leather chairs. "Before we get into why you called," he said, over the sound of coffee being poured into a white ceramic mug, "I just spoke with the king's nurse. He had an uneventful night."

Cup in hand, Harrison eyed the tall, rather elegant-looking man through the steam rising over the rim. "His condition is the same, then?"

"Still critical but stable," the king's secretary confirmed. "And he's still quite comatose."

Logan leaned his big frame forward in his chair. The king's bodyguard was a man of action who'd proven his loyalty time and again protecting the king. He was clearly frustrated by his inability to protect him now. "I thought once they'd discovered that Princess Meredith had the same thing, they'd be able to come up with something to help him. I don't understand why her case was so mild and his is so severe."

"It's as Doctor Waltham told us before," Selwyn reminded him. "He feels it a matter of exposure. Somehow Her Highness was less exposed than His Majesty."

"But how was either exposed in the first place?" Logan demanded of his compatriots. "Everything we hear is that the disease is contracted through a mosquito bite. Neither had a bite anywhere on their bodies. It makes no sense that he contracted a form of encephalitis found only in Africa when he hasn't set foot on the continent in forty years. Her Highness has never been there at all."

He wasn't voicing anything they hadn't all puzzled over for weeks.

Harrison, tired of having no answers himself, simply let his friend vent.

Selwyn, ever the diplomat, sought to soothe.

"Perhaps they'll find an answer now that they've dis-

covered the virus can be grown. A sucrose medium is
what I believe the doctor said the lab found worked
best.''

"I sure as hell hope they come up with something
soon,'' Logan muttered over the click of the electronic
lock on the door. "None of this is making any sense.''

Even as everyone murmured their agreement, all eyes
swung toward the handsome young officer in uniform.
Colonel Pierce Prescott acknowledged them with a nod
as the door clicked shut behind him.

His gray-green eyes looked bleary as he tossed his beret on the table. "The bad news is that the courier service
was paid in cash to deliver the envelope,'' he began, not
bothering to waste breath on formalities. "It was dropped
off at their largest downtown office location which takes
in anywhere from three to four thousand business enve-
lopes a day. But,'' he stressed, sinking into the nearest
chair, "one of the clerks remembers it because it was the
first package she checked in that day. It was brought in
by an old woman with curly gray hair, big hands and a
bad case of laryngitis.''

"Great,'' Harrison muttered. "A guy in drag.''

"You got it. We found a wig and a housedress in the
trash bin behind the building. We're going through the
netting in the wig for human hair.

"The good news,'' he continued, pushing his fingers
through his own, "is that we've identified the paper the
ransom note was written on. It was run on a laser printer
on the king's personal stationery. The letterhead was cut
off.''

Sir Selwyn's dark eyebrows formed a single heavy
slash. "The king's personal stationery? The beige paper
with the royal crest and banner on the side? Not the
white?''

"What we have is beige," Pierce informed him, "with remnants of a thin red line down the left side. Microscopic analysis discovered a micrometer of crimson ink that hadn't been trimmed away."

"But that is kept only in the royal residence."

Harrison's eyes narrowed at the trusted secretary's certainty. "There is none in the royal office?"

"It's never kept there," Selwyn insisted. The royal offices were inside the main gates of the palace grounds. That was where the daily affairs of running the kingdom were handled by the king, his ministers and dozens of assistants, secretaries and clerks. Correspondence flowed through his staff like rainwater, all manner of memoranda and letters issued on the standard white stationery bearing the small tasteful seal of Penwyck above its letterhead. "The king's personal stationery is used only for his most personal correspondence," he continued. "It is always addressed from his office in his private apartments."

Harrison took his coffee and offered it to Pierce. The younger man looked even more desperate for caffeine than he felt himself.

"Have a seat," he muttered, and poured himself another cup as the importance of something that ordinarily wouldn't seem significant at all turned all four men silent.

Whoever had kidnapped Prince Owen had also been in the king's private apartments.

The conclusion was so obvious that not one of them felt compelled to mention it.

"Not to add insult to injury," Harrison prefaced, "but was the printer used the one in the king's residence office, too?"

Pierce had taken a grateful sip of what his colleague had offered him. Preparing to take another, he muttered, "It appears so."

Harrison's grip on his own mug tightened. "How do you want to handle General Vancor?" he asked, speaking of the head of the royal guard.

"I think it's best that whatever evidence we have remain among us," Logan asserted.

"I agree," Harrison concluded, his voice going hard as he wondered how many other ways security might have been compromised that night. "Just tell him we have reason to believe Prince Owen's kidnappers were also in the king's apartments and find out how security was breached. If he doesn't have answers from his men by this afternoon, I'll pay him a visit myself."

Having delegated that task, he picked up the newspaper he'd dropped onto a side chair and slid it faceup to the center of the table. "We also have another security problem." His tone was matter-of-fact, his manner amazingly calm considering how furious he was at whoever had broken their confidence. The situation before had been delicate, to say the least. It now held the potential for disaster. "I received a call from a reporter of the *Penwyck Herald* about forty-five minutes ago. This is already hitting the streets."

The bold, black headline screamed up at them all: *King Morgan in Coma; Prince Broderick in Power*

The other three men rose to their feet, each turning the paper so he could better see, the sounds muffled by their expletives.

Having already uttered a few oaths himself, Harrison glanced from one to another. These were the men the king had chosen to trust with his kingdom. There wasn't one Harrison didn't trust himself.

"We need to find whoever leaked this information."

"What did the reporter say?" Logan demanded darkly.

"Only that he thought the palace should know before

the public found out. He hung up before I could ask anything else.'' To Harrison, Logan looked as if he could cheerfully choke someone. He could sympathize. Refusing to cave in to fatigue or frustration, he shoved his hand into his pocket instead. ''My secretary is tracking him and his editor down now.''

''Aside from us,'' Logan growled, ''the only people who knew were the doctor and the three nurses tending His Majesty. They all have top security clearance and wouldn't have anything to gain by leaking this.''

''The queen knows,'' Pierce reminded him.

''Well, we know she wouldn't do anything to jeopardize the Crown,'' the bodyguard conceded. ''What about someone in a lab somewhere? The king's bloodwork is still being handled under an alias, isn't it?''

''I'll check with the doctor,'' Pierce replied, fully sharing his peer's frustration. ''But questions raise questions and we need to tread lightly there. I think our best source right now is the reporter and the editor.''

''I'll stay on it,'' Harrison promised. ''But who leaked this isn't our biggest problem at the moment.'' He was unable himself to imagine where the leak had occurred, though he did agree with Pierce about Her Majesty. If the queen were to confide in anyone, it would be Lady Gwendolyn, and he had already eliminated her as a suspect. Had she known, she would have immediately understood why he had to consult with the queen about the alliance. But she hadn't betrayed so much as a hint of such knowledge. All he remembered seeing in her intriguing blue eyes was the unexpected and beguiling plea with which she'd greeted him, and the quick, damnably annoying way that sapphire blue had frosted over before she'd come to her queen's defense.

With a swift frown, he shook off the thoughts. He

didn't need to be thinking about the ice maiden—especially while three of the most intelligent, wealthiest and most powerful men in the country were waiting for him to continue.

"The entire kingdom is waking up to these headlines," he pointed out, determined to stave off disaster. "Press from all over the world is going to descend like locusts in less than an hour…if the pressroom phone isn't ringing already." The thought had him starting to pace. "The good news is that the reporter apparently hadn't been told how long the king has been ill. As far as anyone will know from that article, King Morgan took ill last evening rather than weeks ago.

"However," he continued, pacing behind the men, "now that the public does know the king's condition, it is imperative that Prince Broderick cease the masquerade as the real king and make a statement to the people that he will be taking his brother's place in a ceremonial capacity. With those headlines," he muttered, dismissing the offending wording with the wave of his hand, "we also need to make it very clear to the public and the world that Prince Broderick is a figurehead only. In the absence of an appointed heir, Penwyckian tradition passes power to the queen."

Selwyn was inevitably the voice of reason. "I for one am relieved to have this out in the open. Prince Broderick has proven far more amenable than I would have expected, but I don't know how much longer we could have kept up the charade."

Pierce nodded. "I never liked this. I've always felt he was too much of a wild card."

"We all share that feeling," Harrison assured them both, "but we had no choice but to play the card we were handed. Our concern now is the effect this news will have on pending negotiations. Nothing must happen to jeopardize either the alliance with Majorco or the alliance with the U.S."

"No question," muttered Logan.

Sir Selwyn smoothed his tie. "Absolutely."

"Pierce." Harrison paced the length of the table again, his mind totally focused on a new battle plan. "I think it would be most expeditious if you met with Broderick to advise him of his change in status while Selwyn heads off the press. Are you all right with that?"

A sharp nod confirmed that he was.

"Selwyn," he said to the Royal Secretary, "we need to arrange for the king's press secretary and staff to meet with Prince Broderick."

"Consider it done. Do we want cameras? All the trappings?"

The king's twin would love that.

"Whatever it takes to make it look as if everything is totally under control. As to official statements," Harrison continued, pacing back the other way, "Prince Broderick needs to assure the kingdom that official business will be conducted as usual. That message needs to be strong enough to assure the citizens of Penwyck that their government is and will remain stable but nonspecific enough to allow us time to track down Prince Owen before his abductors realize the alliance will be signed as planned." He stopped at the head of the table and turned to face them. "Agreed?"

"Agreed," they replied in unison.

"Good. In the meantime, I will ask the appropriate ministers to meet with the ambassadors of the United States and Majorco, and assure them that nothing will stand in the way of their alliances."

"Is that where you're headed now?" Logan asked.

"No." A muscle in Harrison's jaw jerked. "Right now I'm going to see the queen."

It was barely six in the morning when the guard at the entrance to the royal residence rang Gwen's apartment on the second floor overlooking Castle Cove. Her three rooms, once a nanny's quarters, were appointed modestly and were quite small, considering the size of the rooms below her. Still, decorated with the comfortable provincial furniture and personal treasures Gwen had brought with her ten years ago, they had proved more than adequate for a young widow with a small child to raise.

That child was now a twenty-year-old woman, who was presently on holiday with a friend and her family in the Scottish highlands—which was why the telephone rang five times before Gwen snatched it up.

Amira would have jumped on it by the second ring. With the blow dryer running, Gwen had barely heard it at all.

"He's on his way up now?" she asked, tucking the receiver under her chin to snatch up her beige suit skirt. "Where exactly is he?"

The formal male voice on the other end of the line informed her that Admiral Monteque had just passed through the vestibule and turned into the queen's hallway. He would be at the doors of the queen's apartments in less than a minute.

Gwen's heart felt as if it were beating out of her chest as she hurried to her wardrobe and stuffed her feet into a pair of taupe leather pumps. The only reason she could imagine him needing to see the queen—and at such an hour—was because something had happened with Prince Owen.

In her years of service to the queen, Gwen had always preferred two-piece suits because they were neat, comfortable and layers could be added or dispensed with beneath the jacket, depending on the season. There would be no layers today. Grabbing the beige silk jacket that matched her skirt, she shoved her arms into the sleeves, pushed back her freshly dried hair and rushed through the doorway beside her small Italian marble fireplace, zipping her skirt as she hurried down the narrow staircase that led directly to the queen's drawing room.

Stepping through the narrow door by Mrs. Ferth's desk, she closed it behind her and hurried soundlessly across the pale butters and creams of the carpet.

She was buttoning her jacket over her bra when she reached for the long gold handle and opened the carved door.

The red-jacketed guard beside it was already at attention. But it was the tall, powerfully built man in the navy uniform who commanded her attention as she stepped back.

Feeling totally thrown together, she watched the admiral close the door, her anxious eyes seeking his.

"Is it news of the prince?"

Harrison opened his mouth and felt his breath snag halfway to his lungs. Her usually restrained hair tumbled around her face and shoulders in a shimmering fall of platinum and honey. The thick, dark lashes of her sapphire eyes were as unadorned as her flawless skin. She smelled of soap, shampoo and fresh powder.

The combination sent something sharp and hot straight to his groin.

"I'm afraid not," he murmured, the tightness gripping his body slipping into his voice.

An odd sense of regret licked through him as he watched the light of hope slip from her eyes.

Before he could question it, before he could stand there

staring at her any longer, he pulled the newspaper he carried from beneath his arm. "It's about the morning paper. Has Her Majesty seen it?"

Aware of the edge in his voice, Gwen took a step back and blinked at the shaving nick in his chin. "The paper?" she repeated, thinking that little wound terribly human for someone who seemed to have a rock for a heart. "She was up most of the night. Worried about Prince Owen," she explained, in case that might not have occurred to him. The queen had called her at midnight to come sit with her. Gwen hadn't gone to bed herself until after two. "I wasn't even going to order up her tea for at least another hour."

He took her response as a no and tried to ignore how soft her mouth looked without the pale-peach lipstick she'd worn yesterday. He'd obviously caught her dressing. Something she hadn't quite managed to fully accomplish. She was without makeup, which made her look temptingly touchable. She hadn't had time to restrain her hair, which made her look even more so. She wore no necklace, no earrings—and she'd missed the top button of her jacket.

Trying to ignore the latter, he held out the paper.

She took it from him, looking faintly puzzled at its importance.

When she read the headline, her flawless skin lost a hint of the natural peach that blushed her cheeks.

Utter disbelief washed her delicate features as she looked back up. "Is this true? It can't be," she concluded, before he could respond. "How is this possible?"

"The part about Prince Broderick isn't true," he assured her, wishing she weren't standing so close. Standing in front of her as he was, towering over her, he could see a small strip of her champagne-colored bra. The scalloped lace lay taut against the firm swell of her breast. A small bow centered with what looked like a tiny pearl rested at the base of her cleavage. "He isn't in power. The queen is. As for the rest of it, it's quite accurate."

Incredulity and concern turned her voice to nearly a whisper. "The king is in a coma? From what? And why wasn't Her Majesty notified last night?"

He could practically see the wheels spinning in her mind. But whatever else she was about to say seemed to vanish like woodsmoke in a coastal wind, when he reached over and slipped his fingers beneath the lapel of her jacket to fasten the button himself.

The glimpse of her breast was entirely too tantalizing. But the feel of that soft swell beneath his knuckles nearly made his mind go blank.

His glance jerked to hers, their eyes colliding, his fingers still brushing her skin. In the space of a heartbeat, the air turned as heavy as the atmosphere on the island when clouds rolled in from the sea with a blast of wind, thunder and jagged bolts of lightning. Electricity snapped. Her breath stalled.

"It was distracting," he muttered, and finished what he'd started by sliding the oyster-colored disk into place.

He could swear he felt her heart slam against her breastbone. He knew his own wasn't beating too steadily. But as he slowly pulled back and let his hand fall, his only thought was that he couldn't believe what he'd done. He never took liberties with a woman who hadn't made it clear that she wanted his touch. And this woman, the queen's best friend and lady-in-waiting, had never given him reason to think anything other than how glad she would be to see him leave.

He had no idea what she was thinking at the moment, however. Or what she was about to do. She took a step back, her hair draping forward to hide the hint of heat in her cheeks as she glanced at the paper she still held.

"It says he has encephalitis," she murmured, focusing on the one word that jumped out as her lungs began to function again. The headlines had shaken her, but she felt rattled beyond belief by his touch. It felt as if he'd branded her. The feel of his knuckles still burned her flesh. More disconcerting still had been the way that initial jolt of heat had shot straight to her toes.

Duty demanded her concentration. Latching on to it, she did her best to ignore her scrambled senses and the rather uncertain way Harrison was watching her. "I must tell Her Majesty about the king."

"She already knows. She was told days ago," he said, confusing her further still.

"But I saw him in the garden just yesterday."

"We had tried to keep the king's condition from the public," he said, thinking the queen could explain later, "but Her Majesty needs to be informed that the public now knows. There will be a press conference within the next couple of hours."

The queen had known? Gwen thought—only to suddenly realize why Her Majesty had seemed so ambivalent about her duties of late.

"Of course," she murmured, wishing her friend had confided in her, wishing she knew why she hadn't. Wishing the air in the room were easier to breathe.

She could practically feel the tension radiating from the admiral's big body. It snaked around her, through her, as tangible as the warmth still lingering on her skin.

"If you will wake her and break the news of this to her yourself, I'll come back to talk with her after I've met with the minister of foreign affairs." He glanced at his watch, his other obligations clearly pulling at him. "There is much she and I must discuss."

Gwen gave him a nod, took a step back. As she did, his edgy glance fell to where her hand protectively covered the vee of her jacket.

Silence echoed off the ornate walls. In the taut moments before his eyes lifted to hers, his jaw had hardened enough to shatter his back teeth.

The silence was disturbing enough. But the banked heat in his gaze was knitting her nerves into a knot when one of the double doors behind her opened.

She turned to see Queen Marissa cautiously watching them both.

Chapter Three

Queen Marissa stepped into the room. Her shawl-collared dressing robe of white Egyptian cotton was tied snugly at the waist and flowed in loose folds to the floor. Like Gwen, she hadn't taken time with her usual chignon. She'd simply brushed her straight dark hair back from her striking and strained features. Faint shadows bruised the skin beneath her eyes, attesting to her lack of rest.

Clearly worried by their presence in her receiving room, she glanced between the mountain of tension in navy and gold braid and her surprisingly unfinished lady-in-waiting. The sight of Gwen looking less than her polished self seemed to alarm her even more than the early hour.

"Gwen," she insisted of her friend. "What's going on?"

"There's been…"

"A development," Harrison supplied. "Your Majesty,'' he added, because it would have been unpardonable not to.

''A...development? Of what sort?''

Relieved to have his attention off her, Gwen immediately handed him the newspaper. Seeming relieved by the reprieve himself, he deliberately avoided her glance as he took it and moved across the room. With his broad back to her, he dominated the feminine space as he handed the paper to the statuesque royal, who warily regarded its print.

''We've had a security leak,'' Harrison said, dutifully overlooking the fact that his queen was in her bathrobe as she stared at the morning headlines. The woman was unquestioningly beautiful and quite formidable in her own right. But unlike Gwen there was nothing about her that provoked him in anyway. She was simply his queen. The woman behind him was...temptation.

''The public now knows that His Majesty is ill,'' he continued, too focused on his task to question the admission. ''There has been no change in his condition overnight. He rested comfortably,'' he advised her, since the king's condition was of paramount importance to them all, ''and his status remains the same.''

With a nod of his dark head, he indicated the paper that held the queen transfixed. ''As to what we must do about that,'' he proceeded, ''Colonel Prescott is with Prince Broderick advising him now of the change in his...role...shall we say.'' He wasn't about to go into the bit of shuffle and switch they'd been playing. Not with Lady Gwendolyn listening. ''Sir Selwyn will oversee his carefully worded statement about how he is here to represent the Crown in a ceremonial capacity.

''The public will need a statement from you, too,'' he went on to advise her, taking her silence for consideration. "The royal press secretary will issue a statement within the half hour, confirming the king's condition. He will also clarify that due to the king's incapacitation, without an appointed heir, the power of the monarchy passes to you."

To Harrison's way of thinking, that was how matters should have been handled all along. It was how they had been handled ever since they'd had to involve her directly...days ago. The queen hadn't been terribly pleased to know that the RET had kept news of her husband's condition from her, or to know that they had been acting on her behalf when the power should have come to her to begin with. But she knew her husband well, and she knew his men had had no choice but to acquiesce to his plan.

Penwyck was not a democracy.

"Your Majesty." He paused, wanting to make sure he had her full attention as he reached the most important point of all. "It is imperative that you assure everyone that the business of the Crown will be conducted as usual. You need to offer that assurance as soon as possible."

The queen drew a deep breath, her slender shoulders rising beneath her robe. He felt sure she was about to agree. Time was of the essence. Everyone needed to act, and quickly.

Instead she pinned him with a look of sheer incomprehension.

"You've said nothing about my son." The paper rustled as she dropped it to the beautifully painted occasional table between her and a dainty Queen Anne chair. "Do you know where he is? Do you know if he's all right?"

A tug of impatience tightened the muscles in Harrison's broad shoulders.

"We haven't located him yet," he was forced to admit. "But we have no reason to believe he's been harmed," he hurried to assure her, thinking that might help. "Intelligence is still working on it."

His impatience made its way to his jaw as his queen sank into the chair beside her. He needed her to get dressed, to meet with Selwyn, to address the kingdom. Sitting wouldn't get any of that done. "Your Majesty," he prodded, hoping to nudge her on.

Incomprehension turned to sheer pain when she looked up at him. "You have no reason to believe he's been harmed? How can you say that? There was a struggle in his room," she reminded him, her voice suddenly, precariously close to cracking. "Of course there's reason to believe he's hurt. And all you can tell me is that they're 'working on it'?"

There was moisture in her eyes, a thin ribbon of it that lay just above her lower lashes. The tears were sudden and totally unexpected, but they were definitely there. So was the telltale hint of pink on her nose that made him fear those tears might spill at any moment.

A swift and certain unease had him at an unfamiliar loss for words. He had never seen the queen behave in any manner that couldn't be described as stoic, reserved or regal. At the moment she looked frighteningly close to crying.

He had been through battle with the allies in the Gulf War. He'd led covert missions as a young soldier. He knew the threat of nuclear war and the delicate game certain countries played with armed detente. But the combination of a woman and tears was the only thing he could think of that struck true fear in his heart. He'd been trained for those other circumstances. He knew the measures and countermeasures to mitigate loss and damage.

He hadn't a clue what to do with a distraught woman. His only defense was to pretend he didn't notice.

"I'm afraid it is, Your Majesty. As soon as there is anything else to report, I'll be sure to let you know. In the meantime," he continued, determined not to sound as anxious as he felt to turn her over to the woman he could feel staring at his back, "it would be best if you could meet with the king's speechwriters as soon as possible to work on your statement."

The queen felt utterly betrayed. Gwen could see that, in the bow of her shoulders, the bend of her neck. Someone had kidnapped her son. Now someone close to the Crown had broken its confidence by conveying privileged information to the press. She looked the way Gwen imagined she had to feel—sick and completely overwhelmed.

That was how she sounded, too, as she slowly rose and rested her hand on the back of the chair. "If you'd kindly arrange it, I'll meet with the speechwriters in an hour," she said to her.

Gwen could barely get through some of those greeting-card commercials without choking up. Seeing her friend's distress, her throat began to feel suspiciously tight. "Here or in the royal office?"

"Here. Please. You might also have Mrs. Ferth start canceling preparations for the state dinner," she added, turning to her rooms. "And I could use some tea and headache tablets."

Fully prepared to do as she'd been asked, Gwen gave an automatic little curtsy. But the door had no sooner closed behind the queen than Harrison blocked her path to the telephone.

"That dinner can't be canceled."

The burning in her throat gave way to a choke of disbelief as Gwen blinked at his very solid-looking chest.

Certain she had misunderstood, she looked up at him as if he'd spoken in an utterly alien dialect.

"I beg your pardon?"

"You can't cancel, it," he repeated, his tone as unyielding as his stance. "It's too important."

"Considering everything else that's going on, a dinner is too important?" Incredulous, she stared up at him, crossing her arms beneath her breasts. Thinking better of the position when his glance immediately dropped between her lapels, she settled for clasping her hands in front of her.

"Calling these preparations off is the very first thing we should do, if for no other reason than to make Prince Owen's captors think Penwyck isn't going to sign the treaty. That would keep the prince safe. At least for a little while," she amended, having no idea how his safety could be ensured after that.

"It can't be canceled," he repeated flatly. "Just continue with your plans for the celebration."

At his stubborn insistence, or maybe it was the order, the delicate arches of her eyebrows drew toward center. "I don't believe the queen or anyone else cares to think about celebrating with the king ill, one of her sons off climbing mountains heaven-only-knows where, another son missing and an estranged member of the royal family standing in for the Crown. In case you didn't notice, Her Majesty is upset."

She was upset, too—with the inconceivable turns of events, the uncertainty of their outcomes and with him. Especially with him. He'd shown no compassion whatsoever for their queen.

He betrayed no sympathy for her now, either. "None of this is about people having a good time at a party," he informed her, the frustration he'd held back finally taking hold. "It's about perception and power and Penwyck's credibility as a nation with the United States, Majorco and some two-bit subversives who don't have the guts to play by the rules. The alliance will take place. It will be celebrated as planned. It's what the king wanted, and it's what he'll get."

"At the cost of his son?" she demanded, still torn by the pain she'd seen in her friend's face.

For a moment Harrison didn't say a word. With her eyes locked on his, he realized how easily she would be able to push him to reveal more than was wise to defend his decisions. Feeling a certain sympathy for the men who'd come up against Mata Hari, his irritated glance moved from the blue fire flashing in her eyes to the challenging tilt of her chin. When he realized he was staring at her incredibly tempting mouth, he jerked his glance back to hers.

"You do your job," he growled. "I'll do mine."

"I take my orders from the queen."

Silence fell like a rock.

In that echoing stillness, Gwen suddenly realized she was shaking…inside, where the man looming over her couldn't possibly notice. But the nerves in her stomach were quivering all the same.

She was normally utterly correct in protocol, and never would she have dreamed of challenging the man regarded by many as being nearly as powerful as the king himself. But as far as she was concerned, protocol had taken a royal hike about the time she had allowed him to button her jacket instead of pulling back to do it herself.

Her only excuse for not having done just that was because he'd caught her so completely off guard.

Her only excuse for not letting him know, even subtly, that she didn't appreciate his boldness was that she didn't want him to know she was still thinking about it. She didn't even want to consider how he'd react if he knew he'd caused her to feel sensations she hadn't felt in so long she'd forgotten they existed.

His eyes darkened as he took a step closer, causing the quiver to catch.

"If you won't take orders from anyone but the queen," he murmured, his voice deceptively, dangerously civil, "then it is up to you to convince her that the show must go on. If you don't," he warned softly, "the prince's life will be worth less than this island's dead coal mines."

He was close enough that she could see the individual spikes of his dark eyelashes. Close enough that she could see the small white scar just under the hard line of his jaw and the carved lines of his sinfully sensual mouth.

He had just placed the prince's life squarely in her hands.

Realizing that, she swallowed a hint of alarm.

"You're not going to put that sort of responsibility on me."

He leaned farther into her space, turning alarm to panic. "I just did," he told her, and reached for the handle of the door. "Make sure she's ready in an hour."

Gwen wasn't sure if it was fury or fear pumping through her veins as he walked out and left her staring at a carved medallion on the door. All she knew for certain was that she felt totally disconcerted by the events of the last twenty minutes—and that the man responsible for most of that unease possessed all the finesse of a tank.

Make that a battleship, she mentally amended, making herself breathe deeply. Or a destroyer, or whatever those big hulking masses of steel were that left the sea so turbulent in their wake.

She needed air.

She needed an hour in the palace gym.

She needed tea.

The thought that the queen needed tea, too, had her moving immediately toward the phone. Gwen had always known her priorities, and those priorities took precedence over her own needs now.

After ordering tea and toast from the cook, she placed three more quick calls, took a small bottle of analgesic from Mrs. Ferth's desk and quietly opened the door to the queen's salon. The anteroom was decorated much as the receiving room, only there were more family pictures here, and the desk was the queen's.

Passing the damask-draped windows overlooking the cove with its sheer rock cliffs and sweeping view of the city and sea, she knocked on the door on the other side and nudged it open.

Queen Marissa sat on the edge of her huge powder-blue-draped canopy bed.

"Please tell me this is all simply a nightmare, Gwen. Tell me I'm going to wake up now and the only thing I need to do is have breakfast with my children before their nanny comes to take them to school."

She wanted her children to be babies again. She wanted to be able to control the influences around them, to ensure their safety, to protect them from the very real and adult world they all lived in now.

With a daughter she'd cherished and protected all her life, Gwen understood that desire completely.

"I wish I could." Opening the bottle, she shook two tablets into the queen's palm and handed her a glass of water she poured from a crystal carafe.

As the older woman murmured her thanks, Gwen smoothed the edge of the watered-silk comforter and sat down beside her friend. The queen was ten years older than she, and at fifty-three Her Majesty had certainly suffered and seen more. But Gwen knew heartache, too. The loss of her husband was why she was there now. The handsome young officer she had been married to for eleven wonderful years had died during an assassination attempt on King Morgan ten years ago.

"They'll find him," she murmured, touching the queen's sleeve. "We both have to believe that."

Marissa's hand covered hers, her touch as desperate as her voice. "It doesn't sound as if they're even concerned about him, Gwen. I doubt the admiral would have even mentioned him if I hadn't asked myself."

Gwen doubted it, too. "That has to be because of everything else that is happening right now. You know yourself how focused these men are." She wasn't defending the admiral. She couldn't. "But he did say that Intelligence is still on it," she reminded her. "That means hundreds of men are working to find him even now."

Troubled eyes lifted to hers. "Thank you," the queen whispered. "I know somewhere in my mind I realize that they're working around the clock. It just didn't seem so when the admiral was here. I'd been waiting all night for news." With her free hand she pinched the bridge of her nose to ease the pain above it. "It's just so difficult not being able to do anything myself and having to rely on everyone else for information."

"I wish you'd told me about the king."

Marissa's hand fell, the gesture weary, her tone apologetic. "I wish I could have. But it was made very clear to me that it was too sensitive for anyone but those who had to know. I wasn't told myself until recently that this had been going on for weeks."

"Weeks? But I've seen His Majesty. Just yesterday, in

fact. He was speaking with Old Pierre in the kitchen garden.''

"That was Broderick." Fatigue and stress merged in her deeply exhaled breath. Her glance turned pleading. "But no one is to know that, Gwen. The only reason I'm telling you is because of what you've heard already. I know it will go no further."

"I heard nothing," Gwen assured, her mind reeling with the intrigue someone—the RET undoubtedly—had been engaged in. "But His Majesty. King Morgan," she emphasized, thinking of how incredibly the king's twin had played him. "How is he?"

"He's as the admiral said. They're calling his condition critical but stable. Dr. Waltham seems to feel he could come out of the coma, but if he does, there is a possibility that certain symptoms will linger for a very long time."

"You've seen him?"

"Twice a day since they told me. I've gone after you've retired for the night and instead of going for my morning walk with the hounds."

Sympathy tugged hard. "It's no wonder your mind hasn't been on your schedule," Gwen murmured, only to find herself reminded of Harrison's decidedly imperious command.

Catching the sudden displeasure in Gwen's expression, the queen frowned. "What is it?"

"Another problem, I'm afraid." Giving her friend a cautious look, she squeezed her hand in a show of support and slipped from the edge of the bed. The thought of Harrison filled her with a sudden need to pace. "Monteque said the dinner couldn't be canceled."

"Of course it can."

"That's what I told him. But he said it's too important.

I even pointed out that it would benefit Prince Owen because his captors will think we're doing what they want and not signing the alliance.''

Reaching the small white and gilt chest holding a large Waterford crystal lamp, she turned to pace toward the Louis XVI armoire. "He said that if we don't proceed with the preparations, the prince could be in more danger.''

That wasn't exactly a direct quote. But it was close enough to get his message across. She wasn't about to be as blunt as he had been and tell a woman whose husband was in a coma and whose son was being held heaven-only-knew-where that her son's life wouldn't be worth squat if the party didn't go on.

"That makes no sense,'' the queen replied flatly. She rubbed an aching spot on her forehead, "Unless,'' she murmured, "he feels they will then demand more.''

Or that the prince will have served his purpose, Gwen thought grimly.

"I have no idea how his mind is working. I've never understood men like him.'' Men like her own father, for that matter, she thought. Men who seemed to thrive on tactics, maneuverings and rules that seldom allowed for any shade of gray. Political and military struggle had always seemed such a waste of time and resources to her. It was people who should come first. Not power.

"That's because you're an idealist,'' the distressed woman murmured. "Which is what I wish we all could be. But I'm afraid I do understand them. And I'm not going to do anything that will jeopardize my son. I just can't help but feel that not canceling that dinner will be a mistake.''

"He seemed quite certain it would be.''

"Then, find out why.''

There was no time now to consider what that particular instruction would entail. Gwen gave her a nod, then glanced at her wrist—only to discover that she hadn't put on her watch.

"It's six-thirty," the queen told her, reading the ornate clock on her fireplace mantel that had been a gift from the king and queen of Spain. "I suppose we'd better get on with it." She threaded her shaking fingers through her dark hair. "What suit should I wear?"

It was a true sign of her distress that she even asked such a question. Queen Marissa had a celebrated sense of style and never failed to know which ensemble would be absolutely correct for any given occasion.

"The maroon St. John would be good. Or the purple Chanel. Either color would be somber enough without being bleak."

After a deep, bracing breath, the queen nodded. "The purple."

"There will be cameras," Gwen said as a knock on the salon door sounded. There was no time to waste. "I sent for everyone," she explained, and pulled the cord on the heavy drapes.

Early-morning light slashed across the pale-blue and rose carpets, flooding the room, making gold shimmer, white marble shine. "That will be your tea and Cynthia," she continued, on her way across the room. "Roberto will be here in half an hour."

Mrs. Cynthia Westerbrook had been in charge of the queen's wardrobe since Marissa had come to the palace as a young bride. Roberto Deluca owned the most exclusive salon in the city, an establishment that had developed an international clientele since his appointment as the queen's hairdresser years ago. He would also do her makeup.

Having arranged for what the queen would need, Gwen now needed desperately to steal a few minutes for herself. She had attended Her Majesty at every imaginable sort of function, and learned long ago to never set foot in public without being prepared to be caught by a camera. It was usually the people in the background who fared the worst when it came to newspaper and magazine photographs.

"I'll be upstairs trying to perform a miracle," she said, scraping her hair back from her unadorned face. "I'll be back as soon as I can."

"Grab Roberto for yourself first. He can do you while I bathe." Untying her robe, Marissa straightened her shoulders and headed for her spacious marble bathroom. Duty called. Worried or not, tired or not, she would do what needed to be done. "You've barely had time to shower and cover your body. We could both use a miracle this morning. If any mortal can pull one off, we know he can."

The exhaustingly energetic middle-aged hairdresser with the long black ponytail and goatee was a genius.

Gwen had no idea how Roberto had done it, but he managed to whip her hair into a simple but elegant French roll and pat, powder and gloss the long night from her face in a matter of minutes. Upstairs in her own room, she clipped on gold button earrings and tucked a pleated apricot scarf under her jacket. She had to turn back at the door when she remembered that she'd forgotten her watch again, but moments later she was on her way down to the reception room to receive the very dignified Sir Selwyn and two male speech writers who arrived with laptop computers and a decided sense of urgency. Mrs. Ferth arrived right behind them, her gray bob bobbing and her pleasant features pinched with annoyance and concern behind her silver-rimmed half glasses. The men had already taken over her desk.

As for the queen, by the time Her Majesty was armed with her speech and escorted into the king's office next to the grand council chamber where the members of the king's council and the media had gathered, the shadows beneath her eyes were gone, color pinked her cheeks, and she appeared every inch the calm, confident regent the men who'd counseled her needed her to be. The only bit of magic Roberto hadn't been able to pull off was to remove the strain from her dutiful smile.

Gwen knew that the queen was doing her best to mask that strain herself, however, as she and Sir Selwyn accompanied Marissa inside the king's richly appointed office and stopped before a bank of built-in television monitors. All were tuned to coverage of the press conference. From six different angles, Gwen watched the royal press secretary end his statement and introduce Prince Broderick.

The queen, stately in purple, gave no visible reaction as she watched Prince Broderick step behind the podium. Gwen, however, couldn't help the quick, quiet breath she drew.

She remembered once hearing that the king had an identical twin. She realized now that he was identical right down to manner, bearing and the cut of his gray-streaked wavy brown hair. Even his voice sounded eerily familiar as he addressed the ministers, the country and the foreign nations represented by the cameras in the balcony.

"I have come to assist Her Majesty with her duties in any way I can. I am completely at her disposal," he continued, somehow managing to exude modesty and authority at the same time. "I realize that this is a difficult time for her and for our country with our beloved King Morgan so ill, and I will serve in whatever capacity I am needed.''

He went on to say how proud he was to be Penwyckian and how he had missed his homeland. He spoke of the strength of tradition and the need to keep traditions strong, and as he concluded his brief remarks, there was no way anyone could have convinced her that the tall, dignified and dynamic gentleman in the Armani suit and ascot was not the king himself.

Only when he took a seat beyond the small throne-like chair next to the larger empty one on the dais, did she accept that he wasn't.

The king's chair remained empty.

''Well,'' Sir Selwyn said, sounding a hint relieved. ''That went well.'' From beside the queen, he motioned her toward the door leading into the chamber. ''If you will, Your Majesty. Your people await.''

Judging from the applause coming over the monitor, the prince's statement had been well received. That applause, however, was short-lived. Total silence fell the instant the king's door to the mahogany paneled chamber opened and the uniformed herald beside it blew the four note announcement of the royal presence.

Lightbulbs flashed from the press gallery above as the queen and her small entourage entered. Tradition dictated that Sir Selwyn take his place at the small writing desk near the podium, his duties as royal secretary now more symbolic than practical in chambers than his predecessors of past centuries.

As her own predecessors had done, Gwen slipped behind a small privacy screen near the door, invisible to nearly all but Her Majesty, ready to attend her at the slightest signal. At that same moment the Lords and Dukes seated behind the podium rose with the muffled rustle of fabric. Ministers and privileged heads from the Royal Intelligence Institute rose in the semicircle of tiered seats in front of it.

The queen ascended the three steps to the dais with its flags of Penwyck and all its shires and took her place behind the podium. Again the rustle sounded as everyone sat back down.

Because everyone else was seated when Gwen glanced across the huge room with its tiny coats of arms woven into the carpet, she couldn't help but notice Harrison standing by the guards' door opposite her. Colonel Prescott and Duke Logan, the king's bodyguard, flanked him. But it was Harrison's powerful, commanding presence that seemed to dominate the room full of men and a smattering of women who wielded enormous power of their own.

A small chair had been placed behind her screen. Suddenly too agitated to sit, blaming it on nerves for the queen, Gwen folded her hands in front of her and tried to concentrate on the well-modulated tones of Her Majesty's voice. Having rehearsed the speech with her, Gwen knew exactly what she was to say. She just didn't hear much of it as Harrison's steady gaze urged her glance back to him with the pull of a homing beacon.

She couldn't believe that he'd caused her to do what she didn't want to do from a hundred yards away. Out of sheer sense of self-preservation, she deliberately pulled her glance from his and forced her focus to the poised woman behind the microphone.

''…and I wish to thank Prince Broderick for so kindly answering our request that he represent the Crown on those occasions I cannot attend myself,'' Queen Marissa continued, making it sound as if calling on a man who'd virtually disappeared years ago had been nothing at all extraordinary. ''I trust everyone will understand that I

wish to be at my husband's side and at the palace awaiting news of Prince Owen. Even thus occupied, I assure
this country and our esteemed allies that I am in full
communication with the lords and ministers of this realm,
and that the business of the monarchy will proceed as
King Morgan has intended.''

The queen went on to say how she and her family
appreciated the support they had been offered, and how
grateful she was for their prayers, but it was what she
didn't say that caught Gwen's attention. She knew how
difficult it had been for Marissa to mention her son. She
had deliberately downplayed mention of Owen, giving
the press and the kidnappers nothing to go on as far as
official reaction to his kidnapping. But she had also pur-
posely omitted specific mention of the alliance with Majorco. Something Harrison and Sir Selwyn had made
clear she needed to do.

Across the crowded chamber, Gwen saw Harrison's
accusing glance arrow straight to her. It seemed he'd noticed the omission, too—which didn't surprise her at all
given that he'd made it as clear as the crystals in the
overhead chandeliers that it was up to her to convince
the queen she needed to play along.

The queen concluded her brief address and stepped
away from the podium.

By the time Gwen glanced back again, Harrison was
gone.

Given the way the day had gone so far, Gwen would
have bet her favorite flannel nightshirt—the one embroi-
dered with So Much Chocolate, So Little Time—that he
was headed for the king's office. Since that was where
she was forced to go herself when the royal press secretary took the podium to answer the clamor of questions
and Sir Selwyn escorted the queen back through the door,

she braced herself for a confrontation the moment she stepped inside.

The Fates must have decided she needed a break. Within moments Sir Selwyn and the queen's bodyguards were sweeping them back to the royal residence by way of the secret tunnel the royal family used to avoid the public, protecting Her Majesty from any member of the press who may have slipped past security that was now as tight as her Great Aunt Gwendolyn's whale-bone corset.

The relief she felt over avoiding an immediate encounter was painfully short-lived. Within five minutes of the queen retiring to her room, Sir Selwyn departing and Mrs. Ferth leaving for lunch now that the worst of the frenetic activity was over, Gwen remembered the request the queen had made of her earlier that morning.

If she was going to find out why the dinner couldn't be canceled, she was going to have to speak to Harrison whether she liked the idea or not.

Looking at the phone on Mrs. Ferth's desk as if it were about to turn into a snake, she tried to think of something—anything—else she needed to do at that particular moment that might possibly be more important. Since the prince's welfare might well be directly affected by the ultimate decision, other than donating an organ, nothing came close.

She inched toward the desk, reminding herself as she did that she was accustomed to obtaining information for her queen. Because of the various connections she had made in the diplomatic circles she'd grown up in and friends she'd made at the Royal Intelligence Institute, she was actually very good at getting information, too.

She just really didn't want to talk to Harrison Monteque. She couldn't remember any man who disturbed her as much as he did. There was no man in recent memory, either, who had caused her nerves to knot when he touched her. Granted, that touch had been incredibly intimate, but that only troubled her more. Not because of the embarrassment she'd felt. Because of the disturbing jolt of desire.

She could only imagine one reason she would react like that to a man she didn't really like.

Years of abstinence.

Telling herself she was going to get out more when this was all over, she took a determined breath and reached for the phone. With any luck she wouldn't be able to reach him now, anyway.

"He's expecting your call," the incredibly efficient-sounding woman announced the moment Gwen identified herself. "Please hold while I put you through."

So much for leaving a message, Gwen thought, and heard Harrison's rich voice rumble through her within a second of the connecting click on the line.

From the hollow noise in the background it sounded as if she'd been connected to a cell phone.

"What happened?"

She met his demand with utter calm. "Nothing happened," she replied, undoubtedly annoying him by stating the obvious. "Her Majesty needs more information."

She could swear the beat of silence sounded impatient. But she understood that there wasn't much they could say over the phone without risk of their call being intercepted.

"Meet me in the east rose garden in half an hour."

She told him she would. What she really had wanted to say was that he could have at least said please.

Chapter Four

The abundance of gardens within the palace walls were a testament to the skills of the architect who had designed them over four hundred years ago and Old Pierre. Old Pierre was the royal gardener. He had been for as long as anyone could remember, and was about as old as the dirt he lovingly fertilized, weeded and raked. Gwen wasn't even sure what the old Frenchman's last name was. He was simply Old Pierre, and the gardens he tended with the care of a lover bore every imaginable shade of flower.

It was a fair indication of her preoccupation that Gwen barely noticed the profusion of geraniums lining the wide travertine walk leading to a huge, five-tiered fountain. A sliver of sun peeked from the heavy gray clouds, teasing everyone with hints of its golden rays and a faint glimpse of blue sky. A morning shower had left leaves glistening.

Dew-like droplets made the yew maze to her right glow like emeralds.

She was hardly aware of any of it. Wanting only to get her meeting with Harrison over with, she simply put one foot in front of the other, promising herself with each step that she wouldn't let the man get to her, and followed the path to the myriad blooms of stark-white, shell-pink and blood-red roses.

This was where Harrison had said to meet him. Ordered, actually. But he wasn't there. In the vast open space, she saw no one other than a guard near a wall of the queen's residence and another beyond the circle of the bubbling fountain. The path there split to lead to the government offices where the press conference had been held, or to the formal gardens.

It struck her as odd that Harrison would have chosen the gently curving pathways of the rose garden. The formal one with its tortured topiaries, sharp triangular beds and geometric precision would have suited his personality so much better.

The damp sea breeze pushed the clouds closer together. Through the light wool of her suit jacket, she rubbed her upper arms against the chill and stopped near a cement bench with gargoyles for feet to glance at her watch. He had said half an hour. That had been precisely thirty-one minutes ago.

She should have thrown on a coat, she thought. Would have had she thought she'd be outside for long. If it started to rain, she was leaving. He would just have to meet her somewhere inside.

Bolstered by that decision, she glanced back toward the distant royal offices, wondering from which direction he would come. When a minute passed, then five more, and he hadn't come from any direction at all, she began to wonder if she'd heard him correctly, if, perhaps, he'd said the west rose garden, instead.

She hated to admit how much the man rattled her. It wasn't like her to get such a detail confused. Details were what she did for a living. But even as that small doubt surfaced, she heard the purposeful thud of heavy footsteps behind her.

She didn't want to be impressed when she turned to see him approach. She didn't want his shoulders to look so wide beneath the epaulets and gold stars on his jacket, or his stride to be so commanding. It would have helped, too, she thought watching his piercing eyes pin hers from beneath his navy beret, if he'd seemed a little less sure of himself as he stopped in front of her and took her arm.

"I'm sorry I kept you waiting," he murmured, his manner edgy, his tone amazingly civil. "It will be better if we walk while we talk." The pressure of his fingers increased ever so slightly as he turned her toward the rose garden paths. With a glance toward the guards in the distance, to the roof lines, the gardens surrounding them, he deliberately slowed his pace to a stroll. "I'm not sure that the bugs around here are friendly."

Her first thought was that Old Pierre wouldn't allow any bugs that weren't. Her second was that Harrison wasn't talking about insects.

"Now," he continued, crushed shells crunching beneath their feet as he guided her between long islands of crimson Damask roses, "you said Her Majesty needs more information. What sort of information does she want?"

Harrison glanced toward the woman walking quietly beside him. Gwen looked infinitely different from when he'd first encountered her a few short hours ago, far more polished, far more restrained. He remembered thinking how composed she had looked at the conference, her cool blond beauty as exquisite as cameo, but cool nonetheless.

With her hair tumbling to her shoulders that morning and her eyes filled with confusion at his touch, he'd found her nearly irresistible.

Quite deliberately he released his hold and dropped his hand. He didn't want to think of how soft her skin had felt to him—or to wonder why he'd felt so compelled to touch her again just now. He just wanted to get through this meeting without doing anything that would make her go cold on him again. The RET needed her right now.

Her soft voice matched his confidential tone. "It is her opinion that canceling the dinner will send a message to whoever has the prince that their demand is being met, and that will keep him safe until your men can find him. She needs to know why you believe the prince will be in more danger if the dinner is canceled."

"I thought that was your opinion."

It is, Gwen thought. "Her Majesty shares it."

He expected a touch of defense. He heard none. With her focus on the ground as they walked, he could see none in her profile, either.

She had crossed her arms over her jacket. The position looked vaguely protective to him, though he supposed she could simply be warding off the damp chill. Feeling guarded himself, determined not to show it, he pulled his glance from the button he'd buttoned himself and the scarf hiding her silken skin and clasped his hands behind his back.

"Then, please tell Her Majesty we need that dinner to proceed in order to gain information. We need to figure out who is trying to sabotage our alliances," he explained, beginning to suspect that she had more influence than he'd realized with the queen. "If the captors think their demands are being met…which is possible if the dinner is canceled," he agreed, "then, they will have no reason to communicate with us.

"If we present a front of business as usual…especially by making it a point to mention our alliance with Majorco," he emphasized, since that was the one thing the queen had not done, "it will appear that Penwyck isn't taking the threat seriously. If they believe that, they'll be forced to warn us again of their intentions. Every contact gives us more clues as to who and where they are. It's six days until the signing," he concluded over their rhythmic footsteps. "Since the prince is all they have to bargain with, he should be safe until then."

From beyond the distant palace wall, Gwen could hear the surf pounding the sheer cliff face. All around them, birds chirped and flitted from dew-drenched flower to damp shrub. The brisk sea air was scented with every imaginable nuance of rose.

She should have felt utterly peaceful here. Usually she did. But nothing was as usual at the moment. Not even remotely close.

Should wasn't a very strong assurance to take back to a worried mother. "Do you have any idea who has the prince?"

He hesitated. "I can't tell you that."

"I'm asking for the queen."

"I realize that," he replied with remarkable patience. "But your security clearance isn't high enough for me to give you that information."

"It's high enough to have access to the royal family and their residence," she pointed out, certain he'd choke if he had any idea of the things she'd overhead over the years.

"But not high enough to be included in a military investigation."

"So you're saying you don't know?"

"I'm not admitting or denying anything."

When it came to rules and regulations, he played by the book. She didn't doubt that for a moment.

Not that it mattered. The hint of rebellion her parents had dutifully suppressed in her as a child tended to reassert itself whenever she was faced with a person who dealt in absolutes. With one glaring exception in her youth, her rebellions tended to be subtle, though, and inevitably designed to find a way around a rule.

"Have you called my father? Ambassador Worthington," she reminded him when he frowned. "Our ambassador to the United States?"

"I know who he is." He even knew the distinguished diplomat was her father, now that she'd reminded him of it, anyway. "Why would I call him?"

"To help you negotiate with whoever has the prince."

"I never said I knew who had him," he reminded her right back.

"Well, if you did know," she countered, wondering what other approach to take, "he might be able to get him back for you more quickly."

Harrison came to a halt. The sun drifted behind a cloud as he did, snapping off the glints of silver and gold in her untouchably restrained hair. Even as the clouds closed, a few drops of rain leaked out. One clung like a tiny diamond between two strands near her crown. Another darkened a spot on her shoulder. Intent as she seemed on her mission, she didn't seem to notice that it had begun to sprinkle.

His eyes narrowed. "I can't decide if you're being naive, desperate or devious."

"I am not naive," she assured him, calmly meeting his glance. "And, yes, I'm feeling a little desperate right now because there is a young man out there who is caught up in something that is none of his own doing. He's in danger and I fear for him for that. As for devious," she concluded, her voice still low, "I am no more so than you."

Something faintly dangerous flashed in his eyes. "I'm doing my job."

"So am I."

"Then keep in mind as part of your job that Penwyck does not negotiate with subversives. Ever. When you do, you give them power."

"They already have power. They have the prince."

She had a point. He wasn't about to concede it, however. "They have power," he said grimly, "only if we concede that their collateral has value."

Disbelief lowered her voice to an appalled rush of air. "Of course it has value. Their 'collateral' is a human life."

"It's a royal human life," he emphasized, "which makes it worth even more. But only if we let them know we perceive them as a threat."

"You don't think that Prince Owen perceives them as one?"

Droplets spotted her jacket, landed on his cheek. He stepped closer, too caught up in her failure to comprehend logistics to care that the rain was falling faster. She clearly couldn't separate her sympathies from strategy. But then, she was an ambassador's daughter, the sort of woman who'd been schooled in manners, diplomacy and social grace. Now she lived her life tucked away in the palace, working for a woman who was protected and coddled and undoubtedly as blissfully unaware as her lady-in-waiting of the delicate maneuverings that went on in their government nearly every single day.

"We don't yet know who we're dealing with," he admitted, refusing to waste any more time playing games with her. He didn't care, either, that he had her back up again. There was something he needed to make sure she—and the queen—understood. "Even if we did, this is a military operation. Not a diplomatic one. You're not to talk to your father about this. Neither he nor anyone else is to know what these people are demanding." He kept his tone deliberately even. The warning was only in his eyes. "Is that clear?"

Her chin edged up. "It was clear when you mentioned it yesterday morning."

He had no idea why her cool poise never failed to push his buttons. "As for talking it out nicely," he continued, determined to make that coolness crack, "that isn't even an option. I'm sure it must seem to a woman like you that there is a more civilized way to handle people who refuse to play nice, but I assure you, tea and diplomacy have no place in this scenario. Orders will be given to do whatever is necessary to protect the integrity of the Crown."

It was as obvious as the hard edge sharpening his voice that he thought her utterly clueless about what went on in his world.

Despite the knot his chauvinistic attitude put in her stomach, her tone remained deceptively, impressively calm.

"Admiral Monteque," she said, using the distance of formality like a shield. She felt safer behind it, far less vulnerable. She always had. "I would appreciate it if you would stop talking to me as if I am the leak your men can't seem to find. I have no intention of saying anything to my father or anyone else about what is going on.

"You also don't need to remind me of the lengths to which the military will go to get its job done," she continued, the knot growing tighter. "I was an officer's wife for eleven years. My husband did whatever was necessary to protect the Crown. He gave his life doing it."

For a moment the only sound to be heard was the faint tick of raindrops on leaves. Even the birds had quieted, taking refuge under eaves and passageways.

Gwen barely noticed.

"I never did understand what happened that night," she admitted, thinking of how little men like him had told her of the events that had led to her husband's death. "But I don't believe for a single moment that 'tea and diplomacy' had been an option then, either. I'm sure it all came down to training, instincts and adrenaline. Just as it has on any number of other occasions. So please don't speak to me as if I have no idea what goes on when men grapple for power."

A rumble of thunder sounded in the distance.

"Your husband?" Harrison asked, hesitating.

"Major Alexander Corbin." Alex, she mentally amended, remembering how she had repeatedly asked for more information that first year. She'd inquired politely, through channels, by the rules. Then she'd demanded when her requests had been ignored. They'd paid attention to her then, but they'd sought only to placate her. The official account she'd been given had been miserably inadequate. "He was royal guard."

The name seemed familiar to Harrison. At least Gwen thought recognition was why his firm mouth thinned in the moments before droplets turned to a deluge. In the space of a blink, the sky opened. Rain hammered the ancient travertine at their feet, bent the heads of the roses and had Gwen whipping the scarf from her neck.

Harrison swore. Gwen heard him as she turned to see which way was best to run. She'd just lifted her scarf over her head when she spun back toward him and felt herself go still.

His hand was slipping down the double row of brass buttons on his jacket. It seemed he'd scarcely flicked open the last one when the lapels parted and he shrugged it off.

She barely caught the impression of a massive chest, a crisp white shirt and precisely knotted black tie before she felt the weight of that jacket around her shoulders.

His body heat still clung to the lining. That warmth enveloped her an instant before she pulled the finely woven wool over her head and his hand splayed at the small of her back.

"The colonnade," he muttered. "It's closest."

The cloudburst blurred the landscape around them, making the distant palace walls appear even farther away and bouncing rain back up to her ankles. As absorbed as she'd been in their discussion, she hadn't realized how far around the curve they had walked.

Her slim skirt and heels weren't conducive to running, but by hiking up her hem Gwen managed to match his long strides as they jogged toward the enclosed walkway with its marble columns, arched windows and vaulted ceiling. By the time he pulled open the nearest door and pushed her inside, her stockings and feet were soaked.

So was his shirt. She noticed it the instant she lowered his jacket to her shoulders and turned to face him. The fine white cotton clung to his broad shoulders and muscular arms as he lifted his hand, pulled off his beret and slapped it, water flying, against his thigh.

The heavy beat of boots doing double-time on marble spun them both around. Two guards, their lethal rifles braced and ready, suddenly slammed to a halt.

"Sir," they said in unison. Rifle butts hit the floor as they jerked to attention. Both snapped a salute. "Sorry, sir," the stockier of the two immediately said. "We didn't…I mean, from back there you did look…without your jacket— We didn't recognize you, sir," he finally admitted.

Security remained at its highest level. Considering that she and Harrison had just burst through a doorway into an area used by the royal family to enter their private quarters, the young men's response was exactly what it should have been.

"No apology necessary, Corporal."

The soldier's glance darted to Gwen, then to his superior's wet shirt.

"Ma'am," he said, by way of acknowledgment, but clearly didn't know if he should address his superior's…dress.

"May we do anything for you, sir?" he decided to ask.

Harrison had followed the guard's glance. To Gwen's quiet surprise, he seemed totally unfazed to be all but dripping on the floor.

"You can call my driver at the main guard gate. I'll be leaving for the Admiralty in five minutes."

The young man hesitated. "Will that be all, sir?"

"That will be all," he confirmed, and dismissed them both.

The even cadence of their retreat was echoing through the wide corridor when she saw him staring at her hands. Suddenly realizing that she was strangling his lapels, thinking he wouldn't appreciate the wrinkles, she smoothed the fabric, slipped off the heavy jacket and held it out to him.

"Thank you," she murmured, totally disarmed by what he'd done. Never would she have anticipated that bit of chivalry. He couldn't have thought about his actions. There had been no time.

Caution crept through her. His first instinct had been to shelter and protect.

"You're soaked," she murmured.

"So it would seem."

His easy command with the soldiers gave way to distance as he folded his jacket over his arm, then stuffed his hands in the pockets of his trousers.

That distance increased with each passing second. Moments before the rain had damped their discussion, she'd been busy letting him know that she didn't appreciate his lack of trust—and that she fully comprehended his methods. At the moment she didn't much care if he'd grasped her message or not. She felt more dismayed with the way she'd gone off about the man she'd married. She hadn't intended to share anything so personal.

"Admiral—"

"Lady Gwendolyn—"

He watched her eyes meet his as they both spoke. Mercifully, the sadness that had slipped into them as she'd spoken of her husband was no longer there. Neither was the bewilderment. Or the defense. But it was clear from the uneasy way her glance fell to the scarf she threaded through her fingers that their interrupted discussion remained on both of their minds.

The topic of that discussion had his defenses locked firmly into place.

There were things he knew about her husband that she couldn't. Whether she realized that or not, he didn't know. He just knew he didn't trust the tug of empathy he'd felt for her. He wasn't accustomed to feeling empathy with any woman.

A peculiar sense of self-protection had him seeking more familiar ground.

"Is there anything else I can answer for Her Majesty?"

Willing herself to stick to their task, she quickly shook her head. "I believe you've covered everything," she replied, looking from his shirt. "I'll tell her what you said…about how you need the captors to contact you again." Sounding as distracted as she suddenly looked, a faint frown pinched her brow.

"What?" he prompted, recognizing disagreement when he saw it.

Thinking he did, anyway.

The frown deepened as if she were considering whether or not to reply. "You're going to catch pneumonia as wet as you are," she finally said. Her glance skimmed his shoulders and chest, then promptly jerked back up when it slipped to his thighs. "Duke Logan is about your size. Would you like me to send someone to borrow a shirt from him?"

She looked a little damp herself. Not bedraggled, the way she could have. She had suffered most from her shapely calves down. But she didn't seem to care at all that she was standing in wet shoes and stockings. She actually seemed more concerned about him.

That she would feel concern for him at all threw him completely. Not wanting it to matter, he drew a breath—and felt it stall in his chest. Her delicate scent drifted from his jacket.

"It's only five minutes to the Admiralty," he finally said, unwillingly touched, anyway. "I have another in my office."

Gwen gave a restrained little nod. The Admiralty was the navy's headquarters at the base of the hill. His car would be heated. He could take his shirt off in it, she supposed, only to call her thoughts to a halt before they could go any further.

He was a big boy. He could take care of himself. Aside from that, thinking of him without a shirt didn't seem terribly wise with him staring at her mouth.

The thought remained, anyway. "Good," she murmured, repeating her vow to get out more when this was over. The last she'd heard, Sir Michael Tynley was still available. She'd served with him on the queen's library restoration council and they'd gotten along quite well.

He also had a clammy handshake, she remembered, and stifled a shiver at the thought of him touching her as Harrison had.

"I'll...ah...I'll let you know what she says."

Refusing to meet his glance again, on the off chance that he could read her thoughts, she turned away.

She'd taken a single step when his deep voice stopped her cold.

"Make sure she says yes, Gwen. That dinner is the best thing we have going for us right now."

With her back still to him, she turned her head, looking at him over her shoulder. He'd never called her by her first name before. Aware of the odd way her heart had skipped at the deep sound of it, she murmured, "I understand."

Harrison watched her turn away from him then, her bearing unconsciously graceful, her smile ready when she passed the guards who had intercepted them a while ago.

For a moment he simply stared after her.

He'd forgotten about her husband. Rather, he hadn't connected the loss of that unsung hero to the woman he'd thought of only as an attendant to the queen. He knew of Major Corbin. Everyone on the RET did. As he recalled, Pierce Prescott had even served with him on that fateful night.

Neither he nor Pierce had been members of the RET at the time. It hadn't even existed then. The group had been formed afterward by the king as a direct result of the event. But the major's sacrifice was well-known to a privileged few. And those few knew that the major had stopped the last man anyone would have suspected from assassinating the entire royal family.

Harrison had compartmentalized the incident. Just as he'd done with countless other sensitive situations and nightmarishly close calls he'd been told about, or had to deal with himself over the years. He'd analyzed those events, learned from them as commanders throughout history had done. But he never dwelled on them. He couldn't, and still survive himself. Contrary to what Gwen obviously thought, he constantly weighed the human factor in his actions. Everything he did was about people and protecting their rights, their freedoms. It was just that emotion clouded issues best handled by cool logic. Aside from that, the sense of idealism that had carried him through the first promotions of his career had died long ago. Without it, he wondered why he'd ever wanted that career at all.

His jaw locked at his last thought. He knew exactly why he did what he did. It was only because of the way Gwen seemed to constantly challenge him that he was even thinking about this.

Ignoring the cold seeping into his skin, he headed opposite the direction she had gone. He was an analytical man. A practical, pragmatic man. He knew how to deal with men like himself who understood duty, strategy and acceptable risk…not with cultured and stubborn females. Especially one particularly stubborn female who wasn't proving nearly as unexposed to his realities as he'd thought her to be. A woman who had the disturbing habit of reminding him every time he was with her of just how long it had been since he'd had a woman in bed.

"Oh, Lady Gwendolyn, I'm so glad you're here. The main switchboard has been absolutely jammed with calls about the king's health. And Princess Anne and the archbishop got disconnected while I was talking with them because every call is being monitored and there aren't enough tapes or whatever it is they're monitoring calls with to get them all and I don't know what to tell anyone about the dinner."

Mrs. Anne Ferth ran out of air. Wringing her hands, which wasn't like her at all, she peered at Gwen over the top of her half-rimmed glasses, took a deep breath and started to plunge in again.

Gwen beat her to it. "Princess Anne and His Eminence called Her Majesty?"

Mrs. Ferth's gray bob bounced as she nodded. "And both were disconnected while I was telling them that she was resting. I pray they'll realize things are a bit confused here at the moment," she hurried on, her ruddy complexion even more so in her distress, "but I'm truly at a loss as to what to say about the dinner. Five hundred guests have been invited and everyone from secretaries of dignitaries to the royal pastry chef wants to know if it's being postponed because of the king's illness. The queen has given me no instruction. All she has said is that the only calls she'll take are those regarding her husband and her children and that she wants to see you as soon as you return."

"Do you know if she actually is resting right now?"

"I doubt it. Mrs. McDougal was in a bit ago to make up her room and said she was sitting on the settee in her salon staring out her window."

"Did she say anything else?" Gwen asked, speaking of the middle-aged chambermaid.

"No," Mrs. Ferth murmured. The woman favored cardigan sets and tweeds. Always with a silver chain and a single pearl. Today's set was mud brown. "But I took it upon myself to cancel her appearance at the Children's Hospital this afternoon. Oh, and she refused lunch."

The older woman's pale-blue eyes suddenly narrowed on Gwen's somewhat flattened French roll. "You got caught without an umbrella."

"I did," Gwen murmured, not bothering to share how that had come to be. Before she'd come into the drawing room, she had hurried upstairs, changed her stockings and shoes and retucked her scarf. There had been little to do with Roberto's handiwork other than smooth the slightly damp strands back into place.

Had it not been for Harrison, she might well have been soaked to the skin.

"I'll be back in a few minutes," she said, grateful when the quiet ring of the telephone drew Mrs. Ferth's attention. "I'll try to get some answers for you."

The queen's private secretary gave her a relieved nod as she headed for her desk.

The beleaguered woman was still there, explaining to whomever she was speaking with that she would have to get back to them, when Gwen returned from the queen's salon five minutes later.

Expectation lit Mrs. Ferth's face as she hung up and added the phone memo she'd written to the three-inch high stack of pink slips piled on her desk.

"The dinner will be held. That means we need to continue with the preparations," Gwen told her, as concerned about the queen as she was the decision she had finally, reluctantly made. "Rather than have Lady Brigham and Lady Galbraith answering Her Majesty's mail today," which was the usual task of those particular ladies-in-waiting, "you might ask them to assist you in returning calls. With so many guests, it might also be a good idea to have the press secretary mention to the media that the preparations are continuing. That should cut down on inquiries from those who haven't called yet."

Mrs. Ferth never questioned her instructions, never hesitated to follow through. She simply, efficiently, did what the queen needed to be done.

Sitting as straight as a pillar, she pulled her note pad toward her. "How does Her Majesty wish the statement handled? Will she be drafting it herself or does she wish to have it drafted by someone else for her approval?"

"I believe it will be best to let the RET handle it. I'll speak with Admiral Monteque."

The impact of the morning's news about the king appeared to finally hit the sixty-something grandmother of four as she blinked down at her pad. Despite the assurances made to the world that morning that it was business as usual at the palace, it most definitely was not. "Yes. Of course," she murmured. "And what of Her Majesty's schedule?"

"That will have to be changed. I think all she had today was the luncheon at the Children's Hospital. There was nothing this evening." Mentally envisioning her photocopy of Mrs. Ferth's calendar, Gwen paced toward the window. "Tomorrow morning is the opening of the new Queen Marissa Library in Sterling. We could ask Princess Meredith to represent her mother, but she is as distressed about her father and brother as the queen. It might be best to ask Lady Colwood if she will represent Her Majesty. The speech is already written. All she has to do is read it.''

''What about the tour of the gardens she was to give afterward?''

''If this weather continues, I doubt anyone will mind if it's canceled.''

Pushing back one of the filmy curtains, Gwen toyed with the top button of her jacket as she looked out at the gray. Rain still fell, merging sky and sea in shades of pewter and slate.

''What does she have the day after?'' she asked, wondering how much time Harrison had spent out on those turbulent waters. He commanded the navy. To reach that position, he could well have spent an accumulation of years out there, riding the waves, fighting the elements.

''A meeting with the royal chef to confirm the menu for the dinner Saturday evening. An appointment with her couturier for the final fitting of her gown. The symphony, followed by a reception for the guest violinist.''

''I'll take the meeting with the chef. The rest we'll take as it comes.'' She let the curtain fall. Her idea of adventure was a short sail around the harbor. The only time she'd been beyond the breakwater of the cove was to fly over it. ''Hopefully, by then they will have found the prince and the king will be showing some improvement.''

''Do you really think that will be?''

Tightening her hold on the button, she faced the concern in the dedicated secretary's angular face. ''I can't honestly say I know what to think,'' she murmured, wishing she possessed the bold confidence of the man she'd left a little over half an hour ago. She doubted he ever questioned himself, ever felt uncertainty or fear.

"I just know we have a lot to do in the next several days," she concluded with a sigh.

"Where would Her Majesty like me to begin?"

"By calling Admiral Monteque." Her hand fell. "Her Majesty wishes to see him here at his earliest convenience."

Chapter Five

Gwen was a worrier. She always had been. She stewed over details. Fretted over decisions. As a child, she'd feared constantly that she wouldn't do well enough in school, that she wouldn't be ladylike enough to suit her parents, that she might break one of her father's rules about decorum or her mother's about appearances. She'd lived her life in embassies and cut her teeth on protocol. Appearance was everything.

She had also spent much of her youth wishing she had the guts to go wading in the Trevi Fountain or climb onto the memorial in Trafalgar Square.

Had she done that, however, her mother would have had apoplexy. And her father would probably have sent her off to live with Tibetan nuns. Having no desire to ruin her mother's health or live in seclusion, she'd remained the dutiful daughter—until she'd met and married a man who'd made her realize that she didn't have to be perfect for someone to care about her. Not that she had ever even come close. But Alex Corbin had, among so many other things, given her the courage to break the familial chains.

She was still working on getting up the nerve to climb a statue.

And she still worried. Only, now she worried about her friends and her family. At the moment her concern was for the queen and the queen's daughters. The three princesses had arrived nearly an hour ago, and promptly disappeared into their mother's salon.

From the chair behind Mrs. Ferth's desk, she hung up the phone and fished around with her foot for her shoe. She had just canceled her own appointment with the Marlestone Library Restoration Committee that afternoon and rescheduled a meeting with the cellarmaster.

The afternoon had passed in a blur of telephone calls and more interviews with security personnel about who had been where in the palace when the prince had been kidnapped. In between, she had helped the queen's secretary prioritize the earlier inquiries about the state dinner. Mrs. Ferth was now in the ladies' office downstairs where she had enlisted the aid of Ladies Brigham and Galbraith in the effort of returning the 116 calls regarding the status of that event. As of half an hour ago, the switchboard was taking all other messages. Only internal calls were coming straight through.

"Gwen. I'm glad you're still here." Princess Meredith stepped through the salon door, stylish in a sage-green Armani pantsuit and with her lovely brown hair caught low at her nape. At twenty-eight, she was the oldest of the king and queen's children, and considered by many to be one of the most intelligent women in Europe. To Gwen, her charming and outgoing personality also suited her perfectly for her work as a liaison between the royal family and the Royal Intelligence Institute. "When was the last time you saw Owen?"

Having found her shoe, Gwen slipped on the low pump and rose, smoothing her skirt. "I saw him the night before last. A little before seven." The security team who'd interviewed her—twice, now—had asked the same question. "I was taking the main staircase up to my room and passed him on his way down. He said he was on his way to dinner with all of you."

"But you didn't see him after that? Or hear him go back up?"

"I was in my room. As I told the gentlemen from security, as far as Amira's and my rooms are from everyone else, all I could ever hear from there would be you and your sisters giggling when a night was warm enough to leave a window open."

It had been years since she'd had that experience. Those young girls were young women now. Lovely young women, Gwen thought as Princess Anastasia slipped past her sister and gave her halfhearted smile. The willowy Princess Ana, dressed in her riding clothes, possessed her father's great love of the outdoors. She could also be every inch as opinionated as he was, but her fair coloring and striking blues eyes were definitely inherited from her mother.

"The security people keep asking questions, but no one is giving us any answers. We're just trying to figure out the sequence of events ourselves," Ana explained, looking less weary but just as strained as her mother—who walked in behind her. "Meredith and Pierce left first, and Mum and Meg and I left a bit after. Owen was finishing a brandy and said he'd be up shortly.

"When he didn't come down to breakfast yesterday,"

Ana continued, pacing restlessly toward the marble fire-place, "we all thought he'd decided to go out and do a little partying of his own with his friends. To celebrate Meredith's engagement to Pierce," she explained, since the dinner the night before had turned into an impromptu engagement party of sorts. "I thought maybe he'd gotten himself stewed and was sleeping in."

"His bed apparently wasn't even slept in," Meredith expanded. "And there were signs of a struggle. A door to his bureau was open, and the things atop it had fallen over or onto the floor. It was as if someone had been thrown against it." She pulled in a deep breath, remaining stoic for her mother. "That is absolutely all we know. The only reason we know that much is because Owen's valet told my chambermaid."

Distressed that they could obtain more information from the royal grapevine than from their own security people, trying to mask it, the oldest princess turned to her mother. "Did you say it was about eleven o'clock when the three of you left?"

Standing by the damask divan, Marissa gave a shallow nod and slowly sank to a cushion.

Gwen thought the queen had made it beautifully through the circus of the press conference and second round of security interviews, but she had refused break-fast and lunch, and her lack of rest last night was becoming more visible by the hour. Even Roberto's artfully applied makeup could no longer hide the worst of the stress.

"It seems so," Marissa said to Meredith, "but we've been over it so many times I'm beginning to question even what I thought I knew. I simply can't believe that someone was inside our home and that no one...not even a guard...saw or heard a thing."

Princess Megan, the shy new bride of Jean-Paul Augustuve, the Earl of Silvershire, sat down quietly next to her mother. Meg had come from a walk on the beach with her new husband and her bodyguard. A few grains of sand clung to the hem of the designer jeans she wore with a baggy white sweater.

Her shoulder-length brown hair gleamed with auburn highlights, but her green eyes betrayed little of the joy that had brightened them only days ago when she'd returned from her honeymoon.

"None of us can believe any of this." Her wedding ring flashed brightly as she placed her hand on her mother's. "Not about Father. Not about Owen…"

Marissa folded her free hand over Meg's. "At least we know you and the baby are all right. I don't know what I'd do if we had to worry about you, too." New concern deepened the lines of worry, anyway. "You're certain Dr. Waltham said everything was all right?"

"Positive. He said all the test results look great. It was the same strain of encephalitis as Father's, but my case was so mild that the baby wasn't affected. Your first grandchild is just fine."

Anastasia had been studying a small silver-framed picture of her and her siblings as she stood by the fireplace. Placing it back on the marble mantel, she arched an eyebrow at her middle sister. "Do you know what it is, yet?"

A hint of animation slipped into Meg's pretty face as she placed a protective hand over the tiny bulge of her stomach. The child she carried had precipitated one of the hastier royal weddings on record. "We don't want to know. We want it to be a surprise." Animation faded. "And we want Father to be well. And for Owen to be found safe."

"It doesn't help that they're leaving us in the dark," Meredith murmured. "I can't get anything out of Pierce. I haven't even seen him today."

The young woman's frustration was completely understandable to Gwen. Meredith had been engaged to Colonel Prescott less than twelve hours when the rug had been pulled out from under her family's world.

"It's possible that we know all they know," Gwen offered, suspecting that the colonel was as swamped as Harrison appeared to be with all that was going on.

Meredith gave her a thin, uneasy smile. "That's what I'm afraid of." Her restlessness growing, she turned from the window. "I'm going to the office. At least there I can find out what rumors are going around. Here there's nothing to do but wait until someone decides to tell us something."

As protective of the princesses as she was of her own daughter, Gwen turned to the door. "I'll call your bodyguard and your escort."

"Is the escort really necessary?" Meredith asked.

All it took was the thought of a threat to another of her children to return certainty to the queen's voice. "Absolutely," Marissa insisted before Gwen could say a word. "We are all under full security. You girls have all known since you were children what that means. If you leave the residence, you have a full guard."

Ana spun from the mantel, distress marring her refined features. "Even to go for a ride?"

Apprehension slipped into Marissa's eyes. Seeing it, Gwen interceded.

"That probably wouldn't be a good idea, Ana." Whenever the headstrong princess had been troubled as a child, she could inevitably be found in the stables. The horses seemed to be her refuge. "Anyone could be in the woods."

"Rory would be with me," she insisted, speaking of the bodyguard she'd had for years. "He's always protected me. I don't need other guards."

What she meant was that she didn't want those men around. She was seeking solitude—something she definitely wouldn't find flanked by soldiers bearing arms.

"You're best off staying in the palace," Gwen gently insisted. "Or going to work."

"I'd rather go for a ride. I can't concentrate on work. And I can't stand just sitting waiting to hear something."

"None of us can," Megan offered, her tone conciliatory. But whatever else she was about to say was abruptly silenced by the sharp rap on the outer door.

"That will be the admiral," Gwen murmured. Caught a bit off guard by the way her heart bumped her breastbone, she glanced toward the queen. "What do you want me to do?"

The look in Marissa's eyes seemed to say, Ask him to go away.

"Marissa?" she quietly prodded.

The breath the woman drew momentarily straightened her shoulders. "I sent for him. Since the man is practically running the country at the moment, I supposed we'd best let him in."

Harrison had run from one meeting to another that afternoon, all with the minister of foreign relations, the RET and the royal press secretary. Or some combination thereof. He would meet again with the press secretary the moment he left there. Hopefully, to give him the statement the queen had omitted from her speech that morning.

He needed a definitive response from Her Majesty about the state dinner.

He needed a firm commitment from her about a laundry list of details he had yet to address with her because he could never get her alone.

When the door of the queen's drawing room was opened to him, he decided that more than anything else, he needed a break.

The last thing he'd expected was to be greeted by a roomful of women. Beautiful women, he had to concede, nodding to the royal females clustered around the divan. Consciously keeping his glance from drifting to the particularly disturbing lady who'd opened the door, he stepped inside.

The Princesses Meredith and Anastasia moved back to reveal their mother. Princess Megan remained where she was on the cushion beside her.

"Your Majesty," he said, covering his quick dismay with a deep bow. He had exactly thirty minutes before the United States ambassador arrived from Washington. Meeting with the press secretary first no longer looked like a possibility. "I came as soon as I could get away. I didn't realize I would have the pleasure of seeing Your Highnesses."

Princess Anastasia immediately demanded his attention.

"Admiral Monteque," she said, frowning. "Since you're here, you can answer something for us."

Moving into the room behind Harrison, Gwen watched Ana's glance slide nonchalantly over the impressive rows of medal ribbons on his equally impressive chest as she tipped back her head. In the rarefied atmosphere the girls had been raised in, they had become as accustomed to men of rank as they were other royalty and celebrities.

"We understand an escort is necessary if we wish to leave the residence."

The crystal chandelier above them caught the threads of silver in his dark hair as he nodded. "That is correct, Your Highness."

"Do you have reason to think something is going to happen to us?"

"I have reason to think we should be cautious," he replied, the deep tones of his voice utterly certain. "Security was breached here. I believe Sir Selwyn explained that until the situation with your brother is resolved, we can't be too careful with any of you."

"I want to go for a horseback ride."

"The woods are the last place you should go. We have no way to secure them."

"Gwen...Lady Gwendolyn," the queen quickly corrected, "already told you that."

"I just don't understand why," Ana insisted. "No one will tell us anything."

It wasn't petulance in her tone. It was frustration.

Feeling as if he could pace out of his skin himself, Harrison couldn't help but think there was a lot of that going around.

"It's because whoever took your brother could easily decide they need another hostage," he told her. "If something were to happen to him, they would have backup. Historically, female hostages don't fare as well."

Princess Meredith's astute glance pinned him. "I'm sure you don't mean they fare worse because women are considered weaker, Admiral Monteque."

Being a gentleman, he hesitated. Colonel Prescott's fiancée was normally not the sort to challenge. Apparently she was feeling that same frustration, too. "No, Your

Highness. The reason they don't fare as well is because of the temptations they present to their captors."

As his meaning sank in, the girls' glances faltered.

Gwen apparently noticed that, too.

"Do you want me to call for an escort?" she asked Meredith.

"Please," came the princess's complying reply.

"I think I'll just go to my room," Princess Anastasia murmured.

Princess Megan rose and brushed a kiss against her mother's cheek. "I'll come with you," she said to her sibling. "I've already canceled my day at the foundling home. You can help me write thank-you notes for wedding gifts."

"We'll see you for dinner, Mum." Meredith kissed her mother, too.

So did Anastasia.

"We'll see," was the queen's only reply.

Harrison suddenly felt like the proverbial bull in the china shop as he stood to the side waiting for the princesses to depart. There was none of the formality here that he'd always seen among the royal family. Even with the undercurrent of anxiety about their brother, a sense of casualness permeated the very feminine room. But it was the way they treated Gwen that he found most interesting. Seeming mindless of his presence, the princesses each walked up to her on their way out, stopping to give her a hug as if she were family herself. Gwen murmured something to each of them, words of encouragement, a reminder to call if she could be of help.

Meredith was last.

"Make her join us," she muttered to Gwen. "She needs to eat."

"I know," Gwen murmured back. "I'll work on it.

And, Meredith, I'm sorry this all had to happen the night of your engagement. This should be such a wonderful time for you." A smile lit the depths of her eyes. "Your Pierce is a very lucky young man."

Stepping back, Gwen released her. "You girls be careful."

"We will be," the princess assured her on a whisper and, after giving her another quick hug, followed her sisters past the guards in the hall.

Harrison found himself staring at her back as she finally closed the door. He'd already suspected that she was far more influential with the queen that he'd first thought. Considering what he'd just witnessed, he realized she was also the anchor here, the person they were all looking toward to get them through a rough stretch of stormy sea.

He hadn't expected that. Nor had he expected the very real affection between her and the queen's children. Watching her with them, he'd seen none of her reserve. Just genuine interest and a gentleness that put another crack in the ice maiden image he'd once had of her.

Had it not been for the other affairs on his mind, he might have wondered at how easily she'd been sabotaging his concentration all afternoon. She was doing it at that very moment. Having fewer moments by the second to spare, the only other thought he allowed himself about her was that she didn't need to be there now.

As if she'd just read his mind, she turned to where Queen Marissa remained seated on the divan. From the moment he'd come in, he'd been aware of her. He was aware now of the way she deliberately avoided his eyes.

"Do you wish me to stay or leave?" she asked the queen.

"Stay." Her Majesty's ringed fingers were clasped in

her lap, her knuckles nearly white against her sapphire skirt. "Please.

"Admiral," the queen continued, oblivious to the quick disapproval shadowing his rugged face. "Would you like to be seated?"

With his hands clasped behind him, he glanced at the groupings of dainty chairs. The queen was sitting on the only piece of furniture he wasn't afraid he'd break. Gwen stood next to the only chair he might have considered next.

"I'm fine standing," he decided, impatient to get through the civilities and on to the point of their meeting. "But thank you."

"Well, then." Though her posture was erect as always, there was a weariness about the queen that washed the color from her skin. Beneath the slashes of pink on her cheeks, she looked as pale as milk. "I have considered the information you provided me through Lady Corbin. She explained your rationale regarding the dinner, and convinced me it would be in the best interests of my son to do as you are insisting. But I need you to understand that I'm only doing this because of him. He is my first concern."

"I do understand," he quickly assured her, more relieved than he cared to admit that he wouldn't have to argue his point yet again. "You have made the right decision."

"I truly hope so." The strain in her features entered her voice. "I also hope you will understand that I meant what I said this morning. Preparations will continue for the dinner, but we have canceled my other engagements for the next several days.

"I can't convincingly present the unruffled front you say you need," she informed him, suddenly looking beyond tired. Now she simply looked drained. "I don't understand why it would be necessary, anyway. Lady Gwendolyn and I have discussed the matter at length and we feel the public will expect me to be at my husband's side and here awaiting news of my son. I said as much in my address, so my absence from the public eye during this time should cause no undue alarm. Especially with Prince Broderick being so...visible."

With the exception of her last statement, Harrison could find no fault at all in her logic. Broderick was still an unknown entity as far as he was concerned. The rogue wolf of the royal pack, as it were. But his interest now was in finishing his business with the aristocratic and decidedly pale woman rubbing the middle of her forehead. It was she who held the power to make or break the alliances the RET was struggling to keep intact.

"You obviously understand how important appearances are just now," he told her, carefully considering the logic behind her conclusions. "And your rationale is good. Prince Owen's captors shouldn't have any problem buying it, either."

His brow furrowed in concentration, he paced toward the fireplace. "Your lack of visibility could serve another purpose, too," he murmured, his mind racing with each deliberate step. "We've been concerned that your sudden presence in the political arena will make the people even more aware of the king's absence. They're accustomed to seeing you in your usual venues. Education. Charities. The arts," he enumerated, mentally perusing the lengthy list of her normal activities. "If you are suddenly seen with heads of state in chambers or are associated with the alliances, it would just cause people to remember our present situation. Your absence from the press will be the easiest way not to constantly remind them that the king is ill.''

Gwen had remained as still as an alabaster statue beside the exceptionally ornate chair. Despite her disagreements with him, she had clearly understood what the RET needed. Because of that, he would have thought she understood his rationale now, too—which was why he had no idea why she was regarding him with obvious disapproval.

''Thank you, Your Majesty,'' he said, intent on ignoring Gwen's frown. ''This will truly assure our allies that we are committed to our agreements.'' He hesitated, having to think of Gwen, anyway. ''Which brings me to the other matters I must discuss with you.''

The small clock on the mantel struck six o'clock with genteel pings. The ache in the queen's head seemed to throb with each note.

''I told you, Admiral, I don't care about the other matters. I've agreed to what you wanted.''

''There is still more to be decided.''

''Not now.''

''It has to be now,'' he insisted, politely. ''The next twenty-four hours are critical.''

Looking numb, the queen simply shook her head and started to rise.

''Your Majesty—''

Gwen had resisted as long as she could. ''Her Majesty is tired.'' She stepped forward, inserting herself between him and the woman he didn't appear to hear. He'd actually seemed to think that the queen was talking strategy moments ago. ''Please leave her alone,'' she quietly asked.

Giving her a look that clearly said he would go when he was through, he deliberately stepped around her.

"There is too much at stake to delay," he insisted, utterly determined to do his duty. "You know our trade agreement with the U.S. is contingent on signing the alliance with Majorco. We have only five days left to negotiate certain points. You need to hear your advisors."

"Anything I need to hear can come through Lady Gwendolyn."

A muscle in his jaw jerked. "With all due respect," he said, doing a commendable job of keeping his frustration from his voice, "that won't work. The lady's security clearance isn't high enough to be privy to such matters."

"Then see that she gets whatever clearance she needs." Fabric rustled as the weary regent moved between the divan and a footstool. "Thank you for coming, Admiral," she murmured and, without another word, turned to her room.

Because Harrison was there, Gwen stuck to formalities and dropped a quick curtsy as their queen departed.

Because he had no choice, Harrison kept his mouth shut.

He had a knack for never quite overstepping the line with the king or the queen. Not that he'd dealt that much personally with the latter before. But so far, his experience had served its purpose. He could suggest, recommend or advise, but he knew that to question a direct order would have definitely put him over it.

That didn't stop him from silently questioning what the queen wanted as the door to the salon closed with a decisive click. Feeling shackled, hating it, he bit back an oath and turned to meet the displeasure shadowing Gwen's eyes.

His eyebrows merged. "What?" he asked, practically biting off the word.

"I didn't say anything."

"No," he agreed, frustration fairly leaking from his pores. "But I can tell that you want to. Go ahead and say it."

She didn't much care for the fact that he could read her so easily. It seemed to put her at an even greater disadvantage than she already felt whenever she was around him.

Wanting badly to avoid another disagreement, she sought to explain rather than accuse.

"I was just thinking that you somehow missed Her Majesty's point." She could see his agitation. That she could actually feel it tugging the nerves in her stomach was even more disconcerting. "She couldn't care less about that alliance right now."

"Well, she needs to care." Aware that his voice had just risen, he glanced to the closed doors behind him. When he turned back to her, his voice dropped like a rock in a well. "Dozens of people are waiting for her decisions so documents can be finalized. The longer they have to wait for those decisions, the more easily our position could deteriorate. There is nothing more important—"

"There is nothing more important to her than her child," she quickly concluded for him. She rarely interrupted anyone. But he simply wasn't getting it. The man was a brilliant tactician, intelligent to a fault, but this one simple fact refused to gel. "She is scared to death for her son. Imagining him in all sorts of horrible scenarios. I imagine she's even bargaining with God, asking Him to take her in Owen's place if that is somehow possible. A blind man could see how distressed she is, but you just keep pushing."

For a moment he said nothing. He simply moved to stand in front of her, slowly, like a panther approaching cornered prey. His body blocked hers, surrounding her with the tension radiating from his large form. That tension prickled the hairs on her neck, her arms. The nerves in her stomach jumped.

His voice dropped to a furious whisper. "I push because these agreements are critical to the future of this country. There hasn't been a time in the last hundred years that we have been in the position to accomplish what the king has spent the past three years putting together. There isn't time for her to indulge emotion now."

"Indulge emotion?" The phrase stiffened her spine, pulled up her chin. The way he crowded into her space, taunting her with his heat, totally destroyed decorum.

"Haven't you ever loved anyone?" she demanded, her voice matching his so they couldn't be overhead. "Haven't you ever been sick at the thought of what that person might be going through? What they might be suffering, or needing or feeling? Haven't you ever cared about someone so much that it makes you ill at the thought of what your life would be like without them in it?"

She was practically toe to boot with him. With her head tipped back, Harrison could see the flashes of blue fire in her eyes, the flush of indignation on her flawless skin. Her impossibly erotic scent filled his lungs, urging him closer, making him more aware by the second of how close her curvy little body was to his.

All he'd have to do was slip his hands around her waist and he could pull her to him. Twelve inches. One foot. A lousy point-three-oh meters and he could taste her incredibly stubborn, incredibly seductive mouth.

Realizing what he was tempted to do, wanting badly to do it, he ruthlessly reined in his libido.

"I've done my best to avoid that particular complication."

The low growl of his words doused the heat in her eyes. "That probably explains a lot about you."

"It explains nothing. It's just a fact."

"Then, I really do feel sorry for you."

"Don't. From what you just said, it sounds as if I've saved myself a lot of grief."

He wasn't feeling anywhere near as callous as he sounded. What he was feeling at that moment was defensive and angry, and he wasn't exactly sure why. Maybe it was because she seemed to believe he enjoyed badgering a woman who carried an unbelievable burden on her shoulders. Maybe it was because he hated pushing the queen, but he had no choice because of all that was as stake. Or maybe it was simply because something about the lady warily watching him constantly reached past his armor and yanked at parts of him he hadn't even realized were there—parts he'd had to shut down simply to do his job.

The thought caught him totally unprepared as he watched caution enter the luminous depths of her eyes.

"Do you honestly believe that?"

The disbelief in her delicate features was echoed in her voice.

Her question also stopped him cold.

He couldn't believe how transparent she was. The way she'd met his challenge moments ago had made it clear how deeply she cared about Queen Marissa and her children. In her irritation with him, he suspected she'd also revealed a great deal of how she'd felt about her own husband. He never would have believed it, but she was woman who cared intensely and with passion. What she felt, she felt to her soul.

He'd never in his life known that kind of caring. Certainly, no woman had ever felt it toward him.

Not his ex-wife.

Not his own mother.

The thought brought an involuntary wince.

Lifting his hand, he dragged it over his face, covering his reaction, hiding the thought. Fatigue. It had to be fatigue making him think such things. Weeks of stress and little sleep were bound to affect a man's brain.

"It's been a long day," he muttered, avoiding the question he truly didn't know how to answer. He didn't want to spar with her anymore. Not if he was going to have to work with her. Most especially not with her looking at him with what he could swear was real concern. "This isn't getting us anywhere."

"No," Gwen quietly agreed. "It's not." She backed down even further. "I hope the queen's decision about the dinner will give you enough to work with tonight."

It would go a long way. Certainly, it would appease the delegation from Majorco, he conceded to himself, but he wasn't about to take her into his confidence with more details now. Not when what he really wanted to do was take her to bed and forget everything he'd been forced to deal with in the past two days. The past two months, for that matter. Sex was a great escape. The entanglements afterward were what he had no intention of dealing with. "It would probably be best if we talk in the morning."

"Probably," she echoed. She had no idea what to make of the grim set of his jaw, or the sudden bleakness she'd caught in his eyes moments ago. All she knew for certain was that he seemed cautious, too, as he moved to the door.

His hand was on the latch when he glanced back to

her. "Did you know she was going to ask that you be her liaison?"

"Not until you did."

"It wasn't something you encouraged?"

"It wasn't anything we'd even discussed."

His jaw tightened again. But his only reply was a tense nod before he opened the latch and was gone.

Chapter Six

The sun streaked the gray clouds with hints of pale mauve as it rose over the ocean the next morning. From where Harrison sat at his wide mahogany desk in his office at the Admiralty Building, he was aware of that color turning more intense by the moment. It turned the air in his office pink. Even the papers he was reading became tinted with that faint pastel glow.

A red sky in the morning, he thought, recalling the old sailors' adage. It would be a rough day at sea.

Still, that was where he wished he were.

Life was simple at sea. There was order. Discipline. Everyone knew their job. When to rest. When to work. He'd always found a certain comfort in the routine.

He had always found a certain loneliness in it, too.

Leather squeaked as he leaned forward in his chair. He'd managed six hours of sleep. Two more than usual lately. But apparently it hadn't been enough, he thought, reaching for his coffee. Not if his mind was still wandering off in such foreign directions.

Coffee would definitely help. Shaking off thoughts of the loneliness he had never considered before, anyway, he lifted the heavy Penwyck Soccer League mug and took a sip of the stout brew. It wasn't as bad as some of the liquid sludge he'd used to kick-start his brain in the past, but it was always better when his assistant, Lieutenant Sotheby, made it. He'd called her in early two days in a row, but he couldn't justify doing it again. It hadn't been as if he needed her to get what he'd wanted, anyway. He'd simply called Pierce, who'd undoubtedly pulled rank himself by calling in an off-duty clerk in Royal Intelligence to get the file he'd requested.

Intelligence maintained files and ran checks on all palace personnel—and anyone else who had access to the Crown.

It was Gwen's file he was reading now. Just because the queen wanted him to give Lady Gwendolyn Elizabeth Worthington Corbin top security clearance, didn't mean he would do it without checking out the woman first. More than curiosity fed that need, though he was honest enough with himself to admit that curiosity was there. He had taken an oath to protect and defend the Crown and all who came under it. It wasn't an obligation he took lightly.

From what he'd read, it didn't appear that Gwen took her responsibilities lightly, either. With one small, rather interesting exception, she appeared to be an absolute model of loyalty and discretion.

Because of her father's position, the chronology in her file began shortly after her birth. According to the dry words on the neatly printed sheets, she was the daughter of Ambassador Charles and Lady Patience Worthington, which he'd already known—and that she had been at the top of her classes through school and university, which he hadn't.

She had also once been an administrative assistant in the Office of Tourism. Among her duties there, she had acted as a guide for foreign diplomats and their families for tours of Penwyck's monuments, memorials and major attractions. She'd held that position throughout her eleven-year marriage to Corporal—who ultimately became Major—Alexander Corbin of the Royal Guard.

Because of the circumstances surrounding it, there was nothing in the file about the major's death, other than that he had died in service to the king. Following that notation was mention that the queen had invited Gwen and her then-ten-year-old daughter to live at the palace and join her personal staff—and that a check for the appropriate level security clearance had been run. That level allowed access to the royal family's living quarters and had immediately been granted.

According to notes after that, Lady Corbin's duties had always dealt with the daily lives and responsibilities of the royal family. The queen's in particular.

There was no evidence anywhere that she had a life beyond that.

Nowhere did he find mention of a single suitor or romantic relationship—something some industrious reporter would have undoubtedly picked up somewhere for the society pages or local tabloids, because anything remotely royal seemed to be fodder for their press. Personal relationships were also something Intelligence would have learned of and checked into because of Gwen's easy access to the royal family. It wouldn't be unheard of for someone to use a person with such access for less than honorable purposes.

Gwen, however, appeared to be either impossibly discreet or truly was the ice maiden he'd suspected she was. She had no man. No life beyond her job. The only places her name appeared in the press or in the file notes were in connection with various charity committees as representative of the queen.

There was one item in the file, however, that didn't fit at all with the image of the otherwise proper and dutiful woman.

Her marriage to Alex Corbin.

According to a newspaper clipping from a twenty-one-year-old society page, that marriage had been something of a scandal. Her parents had even refused to comment, a dead giveaway that they had not been pleased. He figured he could understand why. She'd been engaged to one man when she'd eloped with another.

He was holding the yellowed article, studying the picture of Gwen as a breathtakingly beautiful young woman of twenty-two, when a uniformed woman with short black hair, red lips and the square build of a fireplug stopped ramrod straight in the middle of the open door. She also had a don't-mess-with-me air that tended to give pause to anyone under the rank of commodore.

"I've put on fresh coffee. You didn't add enough water again."

So that was the problem. "Thank you, Lieutenant." Paper rustled as he slipped the article into the file and place it all back into a manila enveloped marked confidential. Her husband's and her daughter's file went in, too. "Why are you here so early?"

"You have a meeting with your fleet commanders in an hour. I wanted to make sure we touched base before you leave so I can make any changes you need in your schedule." The sharp wedge of her hair didn't budge as she nodded significantly toward the large leather-bound day planner on his desk. "You've been behind lately."

The command meeting, he remembered with a groan, thinking she had a true gift for understatement. In the craziness of the past couple of days, he'd almost forgotten he still had a navy to run.

That meeting was too important to the daily operations of his bases to cancel. But everything else would have to wait.

"Lieutenant," he muttered, pushing his cup toward her for a refill. The woman looked as hard as the rivets in a submarine, but she did her job and did it well. She didn't know the half of what was going on. It wasn't her job to know. But she protected his backside and covered for him without question, which made her a damn fine officer, as far as he was concerned.

Gwen, on the other hand, questioned nearly everything he said.

At the thought, a scowl lowered his brow.

"How far away are you from a promotion?" he asked.

There wasn't much that caught Carol Sotheby off guard. As far as Harrison knew, the only thing that had ever flustered her was the day her husband—who had then only been her boyfriend—had balloons delivered to her office, then candy, then flowers and finally showed up himself with a ring. The big construction worker had had her in tears.

The question Harrison had just asked now had her frozen to the industrial gray carpet.

"Promotion, sir?" Focused on his disgruntled expression, confusion pinched her angular features. "Ah…about three months, I think."

"Remind me to put a commendation in your file. You've gone above and beyond the past few weeks. And call Lady Corbin at the palace for me,'' he asked, ignoring the surprise he could see in her eyes. ''She's the queen's lady-in-waiting. I should be finished here by noon. Find out what time after that she can meet me and Colonel Prescott.''

Gwen hurried along the narrow underground corridor that ran from the public buildings and staff offices to the royal residence. As she understood it, the passage had originally been part of an escape route for the royal family. Now the royals and certain members of their staff took it simply to avoid unplanned encounters with those who'd come to do business at the palace.

She wasn't using it to avoid anyone herself. It was just an easy way to stay out of the rain. Aside from that, the route was quicker than winding her way along halls and the colonnade.

Her meeting with the cellarmaster had taken far longer than she'd expected. The shipment of premium Beaujolais they had eagerly awaited had apparently become overheated while sitting on a tarmac somewhere and was, according to the agitated Monsieur Pomier, undrinkable. That meant the Margaux would be served with the fois gras.

The royal chef would not be pleased to have his choices made for him, but she would have to deal with the equally temperamental culinary genius later. She was more concerned about the champagne. It still hadn't arrived. According to Monsieur Pomier—who just knew it was being mishandled wherever it was and that he was going to be fired because of it—no one could seem to trace the shipment.

Hating to see anyone so upset, she had spent twenty minutes assuring him that he was not going to lose his position if another label had to be served. There were many lovely champagnes, and she was certain he could procure the needed cases over the next four days. She had then suggested that he forget dealing directly with the vintner and call local merchants. Surely, on all of Penwyck there were enough decent bottles of champagne to fill five hundred glasses.

After puzzling over the idea for a moment, he'd declared her brilliant, kissed her hand and grabbed the telephone book. When she'd left, he was looking up wine distributors. She truly hoped he could pull together 110 cases of an appropriate bubbly somewhere. As soon as he did, she could stop worrying about it herself.

As it was, that worry had already given way to another. Because her meeting had taken so long, she now wouldn't have time to see if the queen had returned from sitting at her husband's bedside and learn if there were any changes in his health. She barely had time to make her meeting with Harrison.

She wasn't at all anxious to see him again. He pushed buttons she didn't even know she had, and had made her restless night even more so. Still, she refused to be late. After his parting remarks last night, and those he'd made before, it was clear enough that he didn't really trust her. If they were going to work together, it was time he learned there probably wasn't anyone he could trust more.

Her footsteps echoed on the flat stones as she moved past walls stained with torch soot from past centuries. In the light of the electric lamps, strung sometime in the early forties, she passed a metal door that had also been added a few decades ago—when a boiler room had been built for central heat—and opened the heavy wooden door at the end of the long corridor. Checking her watch, she hurried up a flight of narrow stairs and opened yet a heavier door that led to a small alcove. From that secluded space, she slipped through the false front of a massive pillar and moved into the foyer.

She was to meet Harrison that very minute in the reception area leading to the royal residence. Yet when she entered the spacious foyer separating the east wing from the west, only the usual pair of red-jacketed guards were there—and a square-jawed soldier in army khaki and a black beret who bore down on her the moment she stepped in view.

"Lady Corbin." With the practiced eye of man who checked out everyone he met, he managed a deferential nod while skimming an impersonal glance from the sleek twist of her hair to the hem of her slim caramel-colored pantsuit. "Admiral Harrison asked that I bring you to him. If you'll come with me, please?"

"Where?' she asked, since the direction he motioned toward led only to the passage through which she'd just come.

"Behind you," was all he said and preceded her through the secluded alcove to hold open the hidden wood-and-iron door.

He obviously knew where he was going. Assuming they were heading back to the royal offices, wishing she'd known that so she could have just stayed there, she headed down the stairs and stepped once more into the cool, rather damp limestone-lined passage.

The corridor was barely three feet wide. Begging her pardon when he stepped past her, her escort took a dozen echoing steps and came to a halt in front of the metal door.

Opening the door with a key, he murmured, "Follow me, please."

She stayed right where she was. "Into the boiler room?"

"I realize it appears unusual, my lady."

That was all he said before he moved inside and held the door so she could pass.

It wasn't wading in a fountain. And it certainly lacked the charm of sitting atop a bronze horse, but as she eased inside and heard the door slam with a solid clank, she had to admit that she'd just stepped beyond her normal, sedate and admittedly nonadventurous routine.

She'd never been in the boiler room before. Carefully avoiding a rather oily-looking pipe running waist high beside her, she admitted that she wasn't all that thrilled to be there now. Above her head, steel grating formed walkways that ran between two enormous furnaces. Black pipe formed a giant maze that poked from the furnaces and disappeared dozens of yards away through the walls and the ceiling. She figured that some of those pipes brought in fuel. The rest carried out steam and hot water.

As interesting as it was to know how the radiators were heated, she couldn't help thinking that Harrison was taking his need for security a little too far. A walk in the garden so they couldn't be overheard was one thing. A tête-à-tête in the dim, oily-smelling bowels of the palace grounds was another matter entirely. "We're meeting in here?"

"No, my lady," the soldier replied, then pointed to the floor as he stepped onto the thick industrial matting. "You're wearing high heels," he said, obviously having noted even more than she'd thought in his split-second perusal. "Please, watch your step."

"Can you tell me where we *are* going?"

"We're almost there, my lady," he replied, which apparently meant he could not.

It was because she was watching her step, and uneasily wondering where she was being led, that she didn't notice the other door they approached until she nearly ran into her guide's square back.

He stopped between two stacks of large metal drums. Ahead of them was nothing but wall. Or so she thought before he pressed his palm to a flat pad and a slab of slate-gray metal slid to the side with a quiet whoosh.

All she could see ahead of her was another wall of slate gray.

"If you'll step forward, Admiral Harrison and Colonel Prescott are just through here."

"Here" seemed to be another solid wall. Following him into an elevator-like area, the wall behind them closed the moment she stepped over the threshold.

The pitch-black lasted only long enough for her heart to skip a beat before the soldier said, "Look down." An instant later the wall ahead of her opened and she faced a wide expanse of white light.

He had known the light would be blinding. But she hadn't done as he'd instructed. Squinting, and with her hand to her forehead to cut the glare, she felt him touch his fingers to her elbow and nudge her onto a floor of gray tile.

For years she'd heard rumors of another secret tunnel beneath the palace grounds. As her eyes adjusted, she saw her escort salute another soldier behind a large glass wall and realized those rumors were actually true. Except this wasn't just a tunnel to get from one point to the next. For as far as she could see, unmarked doors randomly appeared along its length. And its length was incredible.

The pale-gray walls, the floor, the ceiling itself disappeared into a single pinpoint somewhere in the distance.

The thought that the corridor might well run all the way to the RII in the Penleigh Hills above the palace was interrupted the moment she heard a male voice call her name from behind her.

"Lady Corbin. We're glad you could meet with us." Colonel Pierce Prescott, Princess Meredith's handsome fiancé, offered her a reserved smile. It wasn't often that their paths crossed, but when they did, he was always enormously polite, his manners impeccable.

There was also always a certain reticence that he displayed toward her. One that she shared with him herself.

Colonel Prescott was the man who had been with her husband the night Alex had died. He was also the one soldier his superiors had refused to let her talk with when she'd gone looking for answers. Other than to approach her after the funeral and say he was sorry for her loss, he had never spoken to her about that night himself, either. Even when she'd asked if he could at least tell her what her husband's last words had been, his only reply was that Alex had said nothing.

She hadn't believed him. He'd looked away from her too quickly before he replied for his words to have been the truth. But she'd eventually come to realize that it hadn't been a lack of empathy on his part. It had been duty that prevented him from saying more.

She was certain of that. She didn't like it. But she understood it. She also didn't doubt for a moment that he remembered that night every time he saw her.

"Thank you, Colonel. I'm glad to be here, too. I think." Wishing as much for his sake as hers that that night could somehow be put to rest, unable to imagine how it ever could be, she offered a game little smile of her own. There was always the future to think of. "Before I forget," she murmured, thinking of that future, "congratulations on your engagement."

Incredibly, the reserve vanished from his gray-green eyes. "Thank you, ma'am. I don't think I've actually had time to get used to the idea that she said yes."

"Circumstances have been such that I don't think she quite believes you asked," she confided. "I'm just sorry the timing is so unfortunate."

His sharp glance slid down the hall. Someone had stepped into it a city block away, his red uniform marking him as Royal Guard. "Me, too," he murmured, his attention clearly compromised by the dark-haired man's approach.

Duke Carson Logan nodded to them both.

"We're all here now." His mind totally on duty once more, Pierce motioned her forward. "We should go in."

She had no idea where "in" was until she saw the duke open the blank gray door ahead of them and waited for her to proceed. The king's charming and powerfully built personal bodyguard didn't seem at all surprised to see her there.

When she stepped into the conference room, neither did Sir Selwyn. Seeing the king's private secretary, it was actually she who paused. She'd had no idea that he was one of the king's chosen few.

There was no doubt in her mind that she was meeting the entire Royal Elite Team.

She'd known there were four.

She'd never before known who they all were.

Sir Selwyn, every inch the distinguished gentleman in his impeccably tailored slate-gray suit, rose from one of the red leather chairs lining the mahogany conference table and told her he was glad she could join them. But even as she acknowledged him, it was the dark-haired mountain of muscle in the navy uniform who commanded her attention.

Harrison stood at the side of the oval table, latent tension crackling around him as his glance skimmed the length of her body. No one but her seemed to notice how the muscles in his jaw tightened before he pulled out the chair to his immediate left.

"If you'll sit here, Lady Gwendolyn, we'll get started."

The men, all commanding, all powerful in their own rights, settled into chairs as if it didn't matter where they sat. There was no jockeying for position. No order of importance. With Harrison, the head, at a place that wasn't even centered, there appeared to be no rank among them at all. Their opinions were equal here.

Surrounded by all that power and testosterone, she felt like the proverbial fish out of water as she took the chair Harrison held for her and slowly sank into the soft leather. His manners weren't unexpected. With the exception of Sir Selwyn, they were all officers. All were titled. With a couple of notable exceptions on Harrison's part, they were all gentlemen.

"The first thing you need to convey to Her Majesty," Harrison said to her, making no attempt whatsoever to ease her into the deep end of the ocean as he sat down himself, "is that our negotiators haven't reached an agreement about the size of the military base to be located on Majorco. They want full naval presence. We feel our proximity to that island doesn't require that large an investment of capital and personnel."

"Unless their government is willing to pay for the infrastructure," Sir Selwyn interjected.

Sounding very much as if they'd agreed to indoctrinate

her by total submersion, the king's private secretary leaned forward, his hands clasped on the polished wood, his expression earnest. "That is what is on the table now. We can't see the need for a large base there, but what we really want is the trade agreement with the United States. Because of that, we're willing to bend, but not be abused. Our economy has suffered greatly since our coal mines played out years ago, and the agreement with the U.S. is critically important. The U.S. won't sign the trade agreement unless we agree to protect Majorco by signing a military alliance with it.''

Duke Logan absently toyed with his gold pen. "The admiral said he mentioned that in your presence with Her Majesty the other day."

''He did,'' she replied, but she really hadn't given the magnitude of the matter any thought. Her concern had been for the prince.

"What he didn't mention," the duke continued, "is that these agreements are so important we've had to take rather...extraordinary measures to see that the negotiations were not interrupted. As close as we are now, we can't afford for anything to go wrong."

Gwen's careful glance moved from one man to the next.

"What?" Harrison asked, clearly seeing the question forming in her mind.

Those extraordinary measures had to be Broderick. But no one offered to confirm that, and she couldn't ask. After the queen had told her that he had actually been there for weeks impersonating the king, she had asked that she speak to no one about it.

"Nothing," she murmured. "I was just listening."

He didn't believe her. She didn't doubt that for a moment as his piercing eyes held hers and he reached for a letter-size envelope.

"The size of our military presence is our largest unresolved issue. We feel a fair offer would be to refuse their insistence on a full presence and counter with an offer to train their soldiers on Penwyck with our own. There is a list in here of the other points we need to deal with," he said, but stopped short of handing it over when the telephone on the credenza interrupted with a low electronic ring.

Reaching behind him, he snatched it up. "Monteque."

Listening, he pressed the button for the speaker phone.

"...about two minutes ago," came the disembodied male voice. "The call went to Prince Broderick in the office we set up for him yesterday."

"Is it on tape?"

"Yes, sir. Just confirmed that."

"What's the prince doing?"

"He's...pacing, sir. And issuing orders to disburse troops to 'find that boy.'"

"His orders are to be ignored."

"Yes, sir."

"Is that all?" Harrison asked.

As the voice echoed its last statement, Colonel Prescott pushed back his chair. "I'll check next door," he said, and left the room as Harrison hung up.

"It appears we got the reaction we hoped for from whoever has Prince Owen," he murmured to everyone remaining, and picked up the envelope again. "As I was saying," he continued to Gwen, looking as indifferent as he sounded to what had just happened, "this list contains several more points the queen will need to decide."

He then proceeded to enumerate them, explaining what

the other side wanted and what the team recommended. His tone was even, his manner amazingly unaffected.

She couldn't begin to imagine how he could shut himself off the way he had so obviously done. Whoever had taken the prince had just made contact with the palace. It was the break they'd been waiting for. Yet he didn't show a trace of concern for what he'd just heard. He'd even ordered whoever had called to ignore Prince Broderick's demand that Prince Owen be found. His only interest was in the agreements and in what it would take to get them signed.

She was trying to reconcile his dispassionate sense of purpose with the unexpected dejection she'd sensed in him last night and failing miserably, when she noticed that the other two men kept glancing toward the door. Even they were showing more reaction than he had. More interest, anyway.

"Do you understand?" he asked, speaking of the matters he'd just explained.

No, she thought. She didn't. She didn't understand him at all. "Yes," she murmured, and repeated what he'd last said. "Penwyck needs two years to complete the building of a runway and docks. Not one."

"And you understand that nothing you hear or see here is to be discussed with anyone but Her Majesty?"

She wanted badly to tell him that he didn't need to continually remind her to keep her mouth shut. But with others present, the best she could do was give him a look that held remarkable patience, before the door opened and the colonel walked back in.

All eyes settled on Pierce as he took his place at the table and pushed the small sheet of paper he'd brought with him toward the duke. "We got it," he said to them all. "The voice was electronically filtered. Definitely male. Possibly British or Penwyckian."

"'You don't believe how serious we are,'" the duke read. "'To prove our point, look at what happened to the king. If the alliance with Majorco goes through, Prince Owen will be dead by midnight the day it is signed. His demise will give you something to think about while you celebrate.'"

The big bodyguard's mouth thinned as he pushed the paper back to Pierce.

Sir Selwyn frowned and rubbed his chin.

Only Harrison remained impassive. "Did we get a trace?"

Pierce gave a nod. "The call was traced to Majorco before it disconnected."

"Majorco." Harrison repeated the word slowly, as if searching each short syllable for whatever clue it might yield. "The only enemy we know we have there is—"

"The Black Knights," the other three said simultaneously.

"Exactly." An unholy light suddenly entered Harrison's eyes, gold glinting in their amber darkness. "We've suspected that island to be their headquarters for years. Of course they wouldn't want the alliance."

"It would put our military right on their turf," Pierce concluded, clearly on the same track.

"Which is absolutely the last thing they would want."

"It would help if we had some idea who their leadership is," Sir Selwyn interjected.

"It would help if we knew who *any* of them are. They've been a thorn in the side of the Crown for years." The duke, pondering, pocketed his pen. "What was that about 'look at what happened to the king'? Are they claiming responsibility for his illness, too?"

Pierce muttered, "Sounds like it."

Gwen's glance bounced from one man to the next. Their deep, masculine voices ebbed and flowed with speculation about how they could have accomplished such a thing, who would speak with the doctor about possibilities, what the anarchical group might do next. Each man clearly fed off of the others' intellects. Each clearly respected the others' responses, ideas, advice. Each also pretty much seemed to have forgotten she was sitting there, taking in their every word.

The name Black Knights was familiar to Gwen. Evidence had pointed to them in a thwarted robbery of the crown jewels years ago. They had also claimed responsibility for the deaths of Morgan and Broderick's parents. What she remembered most about them was that they were purported to dress in black and that they always left their mark at or near the scene—the symbol of a black sword.

Her husband had been killed by a black-garbed intruder. But she'd never heard any mention of the symbol being found.

So far that symbol didn't appear to have shown up in the investigation of Prince Owen's kidnappers, either.

"Perhaps you should consider calling in Gage Weston."

At her quiet suggestion, the room suddenly fell as silent as Tut's tomb.

Four pair of eyes turned to where she still sat.

It was Harrison who had her attention, though. From the way his eyebrows jammed together, she had the feeling he was going to react the same way he had when she'd suggested he call in her father.

"What do you know of Gage Weston?"

Not wanting a lecture, which she swore she could see

brewing, she simply shrugged. "Enough to know he could be of help, if you'd let him."

"How do you know he could be of help?"

That was none of his business. "I know a lot of things about a lot of people, Admiral," she replied, refusing to bristle outwardly at his accusing tone. "Some of which you might find rather surprising. I'm just not in the habit of divulging privileged information. To anyone. Ever."

Pierce made a small choking sound. Immediately he covered it with a polite cough.

Sir Selwyn's thin eyebrows arched halfway up his forehead.

For a moment Harrison said nothing. He just sat watching her watch him, not fooled for a moment by the lack of heat in her tone and knowing without a doubt that she was now biting her tongue.

He'd caught the look she'd given him when he'd made it clear that she was to repeat nothing she heard here. It was the same veiled irritation he'd seen when he'd informed her that she was to say nothing to her father. And when he'd deliberately taunted her with his comment about not knowing who a person could trust on his way out of the queen's drawing room yesterday morning.

Obviously, that comment still rankled.

"Lady Gwendolyn," he began, admitting it probably would have eaten at him, too, "you wouldn't be here if I thought for a moment that you couldn't be trusted." He truly had never doubted her loyalty. No one had. Her Majesty had even wanted to tell her of the king's condition before the team had talked her out of it. "For the record, the four of us can be trusted, too."

"I doubt I can tell you anything about the king's nephew that you don't already know. I just suggested you consider calling him."

Carson Logan leaned forward, speculation in his glance as it moved cautiously to his peers. It seemed that he, like the others, caught the faint crackle of tension in the air.

"You are undoubtedly aware of the duke's connections, my lady. And your suggestion is a good one. It will certainly be considered."

"Thank you, Your Grace." She knew that, aside from being the king's nephew, Duke Gage Weston was an international spy, an operative in which the Crown had the utmost confidence. Since the king's bodyguard was kind enough to acknowledge that she must be aware of that, she kept his more sympathetic ear.

"I realize that everything here is privileged. Even this location," she surmised, saving the man frowning at the side of her head the bother of pointing that out, too. "But may I tell Her Majesty what I have heard about the contact you just received?"

"We have no desire to keep information from the Crown. Our duty is to serve." He nodded toward the man she was ignoring. "That is why the admiral wanted you to meet with us all."

"No one of us has any more influence here than the other," Harrison said from beside her. "We wanted you to be able to honestly tell the queen that the recommendations you offer are what we all agree to be in the kingdom's best interest."

In other words, she thought, he didn't want her thinking the decisions were his and disputing them the way she usually did.

"Unless you have any questions," he concluded, pushing back his chair, "I think that should take care of everything."

He'd say one thing for her. She knew how to take a

hint. Clutching the envelope he'd given her, she immediately assured him she didn't and turned a gracious smile to Pierce when he rose to pull out her chair.

He didn't mind her sass and her spirit when they were alone. If he were to be honest with himself, he would have to admit he was drawn to it, in fact. Yet, as she said goodbye to his counterparts, his only thought was that he wanted her out of there. Now. He didn't want any sparring matches with her in front of the other men, no matter how subtle they were.

This just wasn't the time or the place for him to suggest a cease-fire.

But he had the perfect time and place in mind.

Chapter Seven

There were only a handful of people Harrison's assistant immediately put through to him when they called: any member of the royal family, any member of the RET and any ship's commander. To that list, he had recently added Lady Gwendolyn Corbin.

Lieutenant Sotheby patched her call through to his cell phone as he was leaving a meeting with the Majorcan delegation and heading for—and dreading—the meeting he now had with the ambassador of the United States, Mr. Anthony Fielding. Under any other circumstances he would have liked the man enormously. They shared a love of sailing, sports and an occasional good cigar. At the moment he didn't care for him much at all. He was insisting on seeing the queen.

"Gwen," he said, using her first name without thinking about how intimate it sounded, "what's the matter?"

The cell phone connection wasn't as good as it could

have been. "Nothing is the matter," came bits and pieces of her soft voice. "I just wanted to tell you that the queen has agreed."

"I told you I'd arrange tonight to talk with you. This line isn't secure."

"It doesn't need to be secure. She agreed. That's all."

"To everything?"

"Everything," she repeated.

"I still need to talk to you. What time are you free this evening?"

"Not until nine."

"I'll send an escort for you then."

The pause definitely wasn't a break in the signal. It was hers. She wanted to ask why it was so necessary that they speak this evening. He would have bet his commission on it.

All she said was, "Will this involve the boiler room?"

He had no idea why her skeptical tone made him chuckle. Maybe it was the deadpan way she posed the question. Maybe it was the thought of her gamely working her way through the industrial maze of that forbidding space in heels and the slim tailored suit that had made her legs look a mile long. Maybe he was just relieved to know Her Majesty had okayed the RET's recommendations.

"No," he promised, wondering how long it had been since he'd felt himself smile. "It won't."

The Admiralty Building was a half a mile from the palace at the base of the hill. The sprawling, multistoried structure with its marble columns and the royal crest above the soaring glass entry doors stood like a sentinel above Castle Cove and Marlestone Harbor. Moored in the calm waters of the city's huge port were part of Penwyck's carrier and battleship fleets. The rest, as well as its submarines and basic training facilities, were based on the north end of the island.

Gwen knew that because, years ago, she'd taken some of Penwyck's more important visitors there as part of their tour of the kingdom.

In the dark of the evening, the uniformed chauffeur pulled the limousine in which she rode around to a side entrance of the building. The long black vehicle had barely come to a stop when a navy guard stepped forward, opened her door and led her inside to a private elevator.

She had honestly thought the phone call to Harrison that afternoon would end her dealings with him for the day. He had what he wanted—which was everything he'd asked for. She couldn't imagine what he needed now. Especially at this hour.

As she smoothed the simply tailored jacket she'd worn all day and touched her earrings to make sure they were still in place, she also couldn't imagine, either, why he'd had her brought here.

The guard put her in the elevator, pushed the button for the top floor and wished her a good-evening. After her foray through the boiler room earlier, she felt a bit like Alice, wary, curious and not sure at all what she'd find on the other side of the rabbit hole when the brass doors slid open again.

When they did, she found herself in a small and sparsely furnished foyer, facing Harrison, who filled the threshold of the entryway's only door.

Her first thought was that he was out of uniform. Parts of it, anyway. His jacket and tie were gone, his collar open. His white shirt stretched across his broad shoulders and was tucked neatly into the trim waist of his navy-blue slacks. She'd seen him without his jacket before. Yesterday in the garden, when he'd given it to her. But there was a casualness about him now that gave her definite pause.

When she glanced back up, he was watching her unabashedly checking him out.

"Thank you for coming," he said, as if he'd actually given her a choice.

Feeling hesitant, not sure why, she ventured as far as the doorway. The moment she reached it, he stepped back to let her in.

Across the room from her, a wall of night-blackened glass revealed a sparkling view of the lights of the harbor. Black leather furniture and chrome-and-glass tables were grouped on plush carpeting of pearl gray.

"I hope you don't mind coming to my quarters."

His quarters, he'd said. Not his home.

"Why did you have me brought here?"

"Because I wanted a place where we could be comfortable while we talk."

Comfortable? "Why?"

He turned to a built-in wet bar, leaving her to decide whether she wanted to stay or go.

"I want to call a truce."

"With whom?"

The look he gave her was as dry as dust. "With us."

Feeling a little like Alice again, she hesitated. "We're not at war."

"You could have fooled me," he muttered. "I can't think of a single time we've been together in the past few days that we haven't struck sparks off each other." His dark eyebrow arched, his dark eyes piercing hers. "Can you?"

She easily held his visual challenge. Several seconds passed, however, before she finally murmured, "No."

"Maybe someday we'll figure out why that is," he suggested, his glance drifting from her mouth to the indentation between her collarbones, "but right now I need your influence with the queen."

Heat tingled along the path his glance had taken. Doing her best to ignore it, she watched him take a heavy tumbler from a sparkling glass shelf and set it on the black marble bar counter. Between the overhead light and the table lamps, hard surfaces gleamed everywhere.

"I know she doesn't want to deal with anyone but you right now," he admitted, making it clear that his interest at the moment was in her mind and not in her body. "I need you to change her mind about that. I figured we can work better together if we take off the gloves." He raised one eyebrow. "You don't drink scotch, do you?"

"No."

"Wine?"

"Sometimes."

"Would one of those times be now?"

The man was being totally up front with her. He didn't want to argue anymore. He didn't want to worry about why it was that they inevitably did. He just wanted them to cooperate. Willingly. He would do whatever it took to get her cooperation, too, including, apparently, the civility of offering her a drink.

She didn't want him to be so impressively honest. It made him seem far less formidable and rather... charming, in a reluctant sort of way.

She closed the door with a soft click. She definitely didn't want to be charmed, but considering that they did have to work together, for a while anyway, a truce was probably a good idea.

In that spirit she murmured, "Please."

Preoccupation etched his handsome face as he took a bottle from a glass-fronted wine grotto and deftly removed its cork. Moments later, he'd poured her a goblet of ruby-red wine, himself a scotch and held the goblet out to her.

"To a cease-fire." Thin crystal rang against heavier as he touched the rim of his glass to hers.

Quietly, dutifully, she echoed him and watched him take a sip. A breath later she jerked her glance from the strong cords in his neck to take a sip of her own.

She was thinking he'd be much easier to take if he were built more along the lines of an oar when she closed her eyes in pure bliss.

Liquid heaven, she thought with a sigh. The man was not only trying to get along, he knew good wine.

When she opened her eyes a moment later, she found that his had narrowed in interest at her silent approval.

Aware of warmth in her belly, knowing it wasn't the wine, she headed for his incredible view. He'd brought her here for business. Not to seduce her.

"As long as I'm here," she said, quickly pushing past the heart-stopping thought, "would you answer something for me? About the Black Knights?"

In the reflection of the window, she watched him come up behind her. "What about them?"

"Do you think it's possible they infected the king with the virus?"

"Anything is possible," he admitted.

The certainty in his tone had her facing him again.

"If you were to ask if I thought they did do it," he continued, studying her as he spoke, "I'd have to say that I do. We're still trying to figure out what they used as

An Important Message from the Editors

Dear Reader,

Because you've chosen to read one of our fine romance novels, we'd like to say "thank you!" And, as a special way to thank you, we've selected two more of the books you love so well, plus an exciting Mystery Gift, to send you absolutely FREE!

Please enjoy them with our compliments...

Pam Powers

P.S. And because we value our customers, we've attached something extra inside...

Peel off seal and place inside...

EDITOR'S
FREE GIFT
SEAL
THANK YOU

How to validate your Editor's
FREE GIFT
"Thank You"

1. Peel off gift seal from front cover. Place it in space provided at right. This automatically entitles you to receive 2 FREE BOOKS and a fabulous mystery gift.

2. Send back this card and you'll get 2 brand-new Silhouette Special Edition® novels. These books have a cover price of $4.50 each in the U.S. and $5.25 each in Canada, but they are yours to keep absolutely free.

3. There's no catch. You're under no obligation to buy anything. We charge nothing—ZERO—for your first shipment. And you don't have to make any minimum number of purchases—not even one!

4. The fact is, thousands of readers enjoy receiving their book by mail from the Silhouette Reader Service™. They enjoy the convenience of home delivery...they like getting the best new novels at discount prices BEFORE they're available in stores...and they love their *Heart to Heart* subscriber newsletter featuring author news, horoscopes, recipes, book reviews and much more!

5. We hope that after receiving your free books you'll want to remain a subscriber. But the choice is yours— to continue or cancel, any time at all! So why not take us up on our invitation, with no risk of any kind. You'll be glad you did!

6. Don't forget to detach your FREE BOOKMARK. And remember...just for validating your Editor's Free Gift Offer, we'll send you THREE gifts, *ABSOLUTELY FREE!*

GET A
FREE MYSTERY GIFT...

SURPRISE MYSTERY GIFT COULD BE YOURS _FREE_ AS A SPECIAL "THANK YOU" FROM THE EDITORS OF SILHOUETTE

Visit us online at
www.eHarlequin.com

The Editor's " Thank You" Free Gifts Include:

- Two BRAND-NEW romance novels!
- An exciting mystery gift!

PLACE
FREE GIFT
SEAL
HERE

YES! I have placed my Editor's "Thank You" seal in the space provided above. Please send me 2 free books and a fabulous mystery gift. I understand I am under no obligation to purchase any books, as explained on the back and on the opposite page.

335 SDL DNTT

235 SDL DNTN
(S-SE-06/02)

FIRST NAME	LAST NAME

ADDRESS

APT.#	CITY

STATE/PROV.	ZIP/POSTAL CODE

Thank You!

Offer limited to one per household and not valid to current
Silhouette Special Edition® subscribers. All orders subject to approval.

DETACH AND MAIL CARD TODAY!

the medium to get it into him, but there's no doubt in my mind that they're responsible.''

''How can you be so sure?''

It wasn't challenge in her question. It was curiosity.

He must have realized that. His tone remained as casual as his shrug. ''Because it all fits. They don't want that alliance, so they tried to kill him to keep him from signing it. When it looked as if they'd failed to even make him ill…because we'd brought in Prince Broderick to impersonate him,'' he told her, sounding as if he suspected she might now already know that, ''they needed another way to stop the signing. That's when they kidnapped Prince Owen.''

But the alliance would be signed anyway, Gwen thought and would have started to worry about the repercussions beyond that when Harrison tipped his head to study her.

''Now you can answer something for me.''

Ice clinked against the sides of his glass as he slowly swirled the amber liquid.

''What?'' she murmured, oddly transfixed by what he was doing. It was such a simple thing, that motion. So normal. So relaxed. There was less of an edge to him here in his own surroundings, more of a sense of ease.

Or maybe, she thought, it was simply seeing him without his uniform. Without it, she wasn't seeing the commander. She was simply seeing the man.

''I ran across something in your file this morning. I had to pull it to screen you for a higher security clearance,'' he explained, focused on his glass himself. ''I checked your daughter's, too.''

Confusion colored her tone. ''You checked Amira?''

''It's standard procedure to investigate anyone close to a candidate for higher clearance.'' He lifted his glass toward her, the motion a congratulatory toast. "She sounds like a very accomplished young lady."

"Thank you," she murmured. "She is."

"And a very protected one. It seems you've always kept her quite close to home."

Gwen's confusion compounded itself. She could understand the need to check her background. What she couldn't understand was his interest in how she'd chosen to raise her daughter. "I'll admit I've always been protective of her, but I don't understand why that's a problem."

"I didn't say it was a problem," he said mildly, pointedly overlooking her hint of defense. "It was just something I noticed. There was something else, though, that has me a little curious."

"In my file? Or, in Amira's?"

"Yours."

"And that is…?"

"Why you dumped your fiancé to elope with a man you'd only known for a month. It seemed a little out of character to me."

What she'd done had seemed more than out of character to him. It had smacked of outright defiance, but he didn't want to color whatever response she chose to give him by mentioning that. It also had seemed terribly impulsive, which didn't fit at all with the background of someone so well-bred and refined. He hadn't been born into those circles himself. His roots were far more common. But he'd worked his way up and been around enough to know by now that elopements simply weren't "done" in society. Weddings in the circle where she'd been raised were always huge, frequently ostentatious and more often than not, between parties of equal prominence.

Before he'd seen her file, he would have bet his biggest boat that she would have settled for nothing less than an utterly proper celebration and a properly titled mate—had he given the matter any thought at all.

"If it makes you uncomfortable to talk about it…"

"No," Gwen murmured, caught completely off guard by what had caught his curiosity. "No," she repeated, "it doesn't."

Not the way he meant, anyway. She was uncomfortable, but not because of her past. She cherished what she had done. What she found disconcerting was Harrison's unexpected interest into her private life. But turnabout, she supposed, was fair play. After all, she'd pretty much insisted on knowing if there had ever been anyone he'd cared about. And when she'd asked, she'd practically been in his face.

She took a sip of the lovely wine, understanding completely why a truce was necessary. "I did it because I didn't want the same kind of duty-driven relationship my parents have."

"'Duty-driven'?"

"You know the kind," she prompted. "She's from the right family. He has the right connections and the right career. There's no warmth. No vitality. No…passion," she decided to say, because that was what had always been lacking in her parents union. They rarely laughed. On the other hand, they rarely argued. They simply…were. And were always very proper about it, too.

"No passion," he repeated flatly.

"None."

Beneath his dark eyebrows, his eyes grew more curious. "So who was this passionless fiancé of yours?"

"A young lord barrister my father was grooming for a position in the diplomatic corps." A soft frown formed at the memory. She hadn't thought of Allen Westerbrook in ages. "He'd been pressuring me into marrying him with my father's blessing. My father had always preached duty and station and rules," she confided, though anyone who knew the man would have guessed as much. "So, I finally said yes because everyone else seemed to think we were so perfect for each other."

The furrows deepened. "He didn't love me, though. And I couldn't marry him no matter how beneficial it would have been for everyone. I wanted love to be part of my marriage."

Her tone was utterly matter-of-fact.

Harrison's voice went flat with doubt.

"You found that with a man you'd known less than a month."

"I think I found it in about fifteen minutes. Maybe it was ten," she amended, wondering at the incomprehension in Harrison's carved features before she turned to the window. "I met Alex at an embassy ball. He was on guard duty there that night. Allen had been pressing to set the date and I'd gone out onto a balcony to get some air. Alex saw me leave and asked if I was all right.

"For some reason I wound up telling him everything," she confided, toying with the stem of her glass. "What he told me in return was that I deserved what I got if I let everyone else make my decisions for me." There were other things he'd said. Endearing things about how she was too young and too beautiful to be chained to a life she didn't want. No man had ever called her beautiful before. No one had ever listened when she'd voiced doubts. "Mostly I remember that he told me life was too short to settle for anything less than your own dream."

She felt strangely detached from that night over two decades ago. It was as if all that had happened, had happened to someone else. It had been another life. Another time. "It seems that Allen wouldn't believe the engagement was off until Alex and I eloped a month later." A faint smile curved her mouth. "He insisted that I had been seduced. I prefer to think it was love at first sight."

Catching Harrison's movement in the window, she watched his imposing reflection as he rubbed his brow and frowned at the back of her head. When it came to love and commitment and caring, he had no idea what she was talking about. She felt as certain of that as he had been about who had harmed the king. After all, he'd made it abundantly clear that he avoided anything that involved his heart.

"What I did was out of character," she conceded, because that was apparently what had raised his curiosity to begin with. "And it was naive and impulsive and it probably shouldn't have worked. But it did. Because I listened to him and my heart and didn't do what everyone expected, I can honestly say that I was far happier than either of my parents ever were."

Then, after eleven years, she thought, reaching the end of the memory, it was all over.

Those eleven years seemed to have passed in the blink of an eye. As she contemplated the dark window glass, she could no longer recall any image of her husband's face that hadn't been frozen in a picture. His voice, his scent, his smile, all were nearly lost to her now. In some ways it was almost as if he had only been a dream himself.

The way her glance dropped apparently belied her thoughts.

"You said you don't know much about what happened to him."

"I was told as little as they could get away with."

Harrison hesitated, watching her. There was a contemplative quality to his silence before he spoke again.

"What do you know about that night?"

"All his commanding officer told me was that there had been an assassination attempt," she quietly replied. "Colonel Prescott had been with Alex, but his commanding officer wouldn't let me talk to him. I was told only that Alex had died intercepting a black-garbed intruder beneath the king's bedroom window."

The major died honorably, my lady, she remembered the stone-faced officer telling her. *In service to the king.*

Behind her, she could feel the quality of Harrison's silence shift.

"You know," she murmured, not bothering to question how sensitive she was to him, "I can look back on it now and not feel all the anger and the pain. But I really wish someone had caught the man." Her voice dropped in profound disbelief. "From what I understand, no one even tried."

With the tip of one finger, she traced along the veins in the marble window ledge. Reflecting, contemplating, she took a deep breath and slowly shook her head.

"That's actually not quite true," she amended, her tone tightening. "I still feel anger. My little girl was ten when her father was taken from her. For years she had nightmares about that man in black coming to take her, too. She would wake at night crying and I'd hold her and tell her nothing was going to happen. I had to *lie* to her and promise that she was safe from the man who'd killed her daddy. But there were times when I was as afraid as she was because I knew he was still out there and I didn't know if I could really protect her or not."

Two veins intersected, then split off into different directions. That was what had happened to her life, she thought absently. She'd been at the point where everything had come together, then her life had split, shattered and taken off in a totally different direction.

"It didn't help that by then we were living at the palace, in the wing opposite the one where her father had died. But I don't remember having a lot of choice about where we lived, either. We couldn't stay in the house the military subsidized because I wasn't an officer's wife anymore, so that privilege was gone. And the queen had been kind enough to ask that I serve her."

Everything had happened so fast, she thought, remembering little but the numb haze in which the days and weeks had passed. She knew she had no enthusiasm at all for her job, no desire to look for another home. Living with her parents hadn't been an option in her mind even before they learned of the queen's offer—which her father declared the greatest compliment she could receive and informed her that she would be an ungrateful fool not to accept it.

"I'd had no idea how living in the palace would affect Amira," she confessed. "But Marissa helped me see that she would probably have had nightmares about losing her father no matter where we lived, and moved us to rooms as far from the king's wing as we could get."

"How is your daughter now?"

The unexpected concern in Harrison's voice drew her glance to his towering reflection. She thought it was concern, anyway. Remembering who he was, she supposed he might simply be fishing for information.

"She outgrew the nightmares years ago," she told him. "She's doing very well.

"I'm sorry." Forcing a smile, she turned, feeling awkward for allowing her thoughts to become so carried away. "I didn't mean to burden you with all of that. I don't usually even talk about it.'' Wishing she hadn't, wondering if what she'd just said would wind up in her file, she lifted her goblet. ''It must be the wine.''

Harrison glanced from the gentle curve of her mouth to the imported crystal she held in her slender hands. He couldn't believe how completely her guard had dropped. She hadn't even seemed to notice how distant her thoughts had become, or that she'd called the queen by her first name. ''You've barely touched it.''

''At least allow me the excuse.''

Her soft smile remained, touching him in ways he would have sworn he couldn't be touched. He hadn't expected her to be so open with him, to reveal so much. He hadn't expected, either, the odd disquiet he felt knowing what had been withheld from her.

For ten years she had believed that the man who'd killed her husband had escaped. For ten years she had believed that man was still out there and that none of her husband's men or superiors had even attempted to bring the murderer to justice. She'd spent that time frightened for her daughter and worrying about decisions she'd been forced to make because of someone who no longer even existed.

It was no wonder she'd always been so protective of her child.

Ice tinkled lightly as he set the tumbler on the dining table.

''They did try to catch him.''

A moment's hesitation passed through her eyes. An instant later her lovely smile faded.

''They did catch him, in fact.''

Framed by the twinkling lights from the harbor, she stared at him in pure incomprehension. She looked very fragile at that moment, he thought. Soft. Delicate. But there was nothing about her that would ever make him think her weak.

"They wouldn't have, if not for your husband," he continued, thinking of the cloak of coolness she often wore. He wondered now if it wasn't her protection, a way of keeping distance between her and potential harm. She'd had to be strong on her own for a long time now. "He wounded the intruder before he was shot himself. If the major hadn't disabled him, Colonel Prescott wouldn't have been able to make the capture."

She opened her mouth, closed it again. Trying to absorb what he'd just said, she set her goblet by his glass and crossed her arms. Her wide blue eyes were luminous with confusion.

"Who was he?" She slowly shook her head, strands of platinum and gold shimmering in her silken hair. "Why wasn't anything ever said?"

"Such attempts are always kept quiet if possible. It's standard security practice with any high-profile person. Once the media gets hold of it, they go nuts trying to poke into existing security measures and dredging up attempts in the past. Publicity breeds copycats, and exposes weaknesses. It was especially important that the palace be silent in this case."

"Why?"

"Partly because it wasn't just the king he was after. It was the entire royal family."

The queen. The princes. The princesses. No one would even have known what had been about to happen if not for the intervention of Prince Broderick. The call from the king's twin had been quick and frantic. He had heard of an assassination attempt to take place that night. He had refused to disclose his source, but he insisted that the entire royal family was about to be wiped out.

Had it not been for that call, it was possible that at least one or two of the royals would have died that night, too.

Had it not been for Major Corbin, the king would have died for certain.

At his thoughts, the distrustful sensation Harrison got every time he thought of Broderick kicked in. He wouldn't have believed the man cared about his brother at all, but his warning call to the guard house that night did seem to prove otherwise.

"The queen?" Gwen took a deep, disbelieving breath. "The children, too?"

"There was no need for anyone to know that. Not then. Not now. All right?"

The thin wool fabric of her jacket molded to her breasts as she tightened her arms. "Of course. But who...?"

"The assassin was the queen's brother," he told her, not sure if he was disappointed or grateful that the neckline of the jacket she wore was higher than the one she'd worn the day before. "We believe he was one of the early members of what we now know as the Black Knights."

For a moment she said nothing. He knew that the knowledge he had just given her was huge. It was also far more than he would ever have told her had she not had the proper security clearance.

At least, he wouldn't have told her about the scope of the attempt that night, he conceded to himself. Because of the odd need he'd felt to put her mind at ease, he wasn't so sure he wouldn't have told her the rest of it.

Not wanting to consider why he would have been willing to break rules for her, he simply waited for all he'd said to sink in.

"I thought Edwin was killed by some radical group," she finally said, speaking of Queen Marissa's only sibling. "Everyone thinks that."

His broad shoulders lifted in a shrug. "That's what the king wanted them to think. It was his desire to avoid the scandal that would have arisen had the public known the queen's brother had tried to murder them. He also wanted to protect her feelings toward her only sibling. Because that is the way he wanted it then, that's the way it must remain now."

Ordinarily Gwen would have agreed. Their sovereign's wishes were always obeyed. As kindly as King Morgan could be, he didn't suffer betrayal lightly. Yet it appeared that the blanket of silence His Majesty had thrown over the entire incident was slowly being tugged away. She knew that someone somewhere was talking.

"It might be a little late for that," she murmured cautiously. Even without the king's command, she couldn't possibly have told the queen of her brother's treason. With all Marissa was going through, it would kill her. But it seemed she might learn of it eventually, anyway. "The queen told me last week that Princess Meredith had been asking about her uncle. Apparently, the princess came across something that made her suspect Edwin hadn't been killed by radicals. She didn't seem to think that he'd even died on Penwyck."

Caution fell over Harrison's expression like a shadow over stone. "Where did she hear that?"

"I don't know." The queen hadn't said. "Maybe you could ask Colonel Prescott."

"What makes you think he'd know anything about this?"

"Because he's Meredith's fiancé," she replied, fairly certain from the quiet way he posed the question that the colonel had already mentioned it. "I don't imagine there's much of anything she hasn't talked to him about. And no," she continued, because she could swear she saw the query forming, "I haven't said anything about this to anyone else. Just as I won't say anything to anyone about what we've discussed here."

His glance held hers, resigned, certain. "I didn't think you would, Gwen." He was sorry he'd baited her as he had. Sorry, because it seemed to make it harder now for her to believe that he did trust her and for her to trust him. "I won't say anything, either," he promised. "Everything we've discussed so far is strictly between us. Everything." He needed to know she understood. "All right?"

The quiet intensity in his eyes said as much as his words to Gwen. He had given her information far beyond any official need to know. What he wanted her to know now was that what they'd discussed about her daughter and her husband was no one's business but theirs.

Grateful for the assurance, even more so for what he'd been willing to tell her, she complied with a quiet "All right" and broke his compelling gaze.

"As long as this is all staying between us," she murmured, hoping he would be willing to tell her even more, "would you answer one more question for me?"

"If I can."

"That night," she began, her glance falling to the row of buttons on his shirt. He had such a broad chest, she thought. So solid. So strong. Except for a platonic hug, she couldn't remember the last time she had been held in a man's arms. "I'd asked Colonel Prescott this before," she began again, thinking how unfair of him it was to remind her of that now, "but I didn't believe the answer I was given."

"About what?"

"About what Alex might have said. What his last words were," she quietly clarified.

Had Harrison not just read the account of the incident in her husband's file that morning, he would have no idea what Alex Corbin's last words had been. He wouldn't have known he'd said anything at all. But his last words had been typed in quotes on the incident report—and explained why Pierce hadn't aimed for the intruder's heart himself.

Thinking only of what she had asked, the sudden strain in her face didn't quite register.

"He said, 'It's Edwin,'" he replied, and watched her slender shoulders rise with her deeply drawn breath.

"Oh." That breath slithered out, her body seeming to shrink. "That was why he couldn't tell me."

A fist of guilt hit Harrison square in the gut. Until the light faded from her eyes it hadn't occurred to him that he might have somehow prefaced his response. He'd had the answer. He'd given it. But he could see that she'd been hoping for something more.

She had cared deeply about the man she'd married. More than that, she had loved him, though he couldn't honestly say he had any idea how the emotion made a person think or feel. He just knew that having ten years of wondering finally put to rest filled her with more disappointment than relief.

He wasn't responsible for any of what had happened. None of the actions or decisions that had changed the course of her life had been his to make. Still, he heard himself say, "I'm sorry."

He wasn't sure what he was apologizing for. The fact that she'd had to wait so many years for her answer. Or that the words hadn't been something more personal. He just knew that he was about to reach for her and remind her that those were her husband's last words, not necessarily his thoughts, when his sense of self-preservation pulled him back.

He'd never felt the need to offer comfort to a woman before. He wasn't sure he trusted the need now.

The sharp electronic ring of the telephone saved him from wondering if he even really knew how.

With a wary glance toward the woman deliberately straightening her shoulders, he crossed to the desk near the short hall that led to his bedroom and bath. Gwen had her back to him as he snatched the black instrument from its base.

As he did, he ran a glance from the gleaming knot of blond hair caught neatly at her nape and over her slender shoulders. The cut of her jacket and slim slacks was simple, tasteful, restrained. The woman inside was proving more complicating than he could have imagined.

"Monteque."

Gwen could practically feel Harrison's eyes on her back as his deep voice drifted toward her. There was no way to avoid overhearing. Not that he made any effort to keep his conversation discreet.

''Not yet,'' she heard him reply. ''I'm talking with her now. I'll get back with you as soon as we're through.'' He paused, checking his watch. ''The ambassador's assistant set the conference call for a half hour from now. I'll call you right after that.''

An odd ambivalence had filled her at finally knowing what had haunted her for years. The brisk no-nonsense tone of Harrison's conversation did wonders to help her shake it. It also shattered the dangerous ease she'd started to feel with the man who had allowed her to understand what she never had about that night so long ago.

Harrison had brought her here for a purpose, she reminded herself. And that purpose hadn't yet been served.

Chapter Eight

Gwen hadn't noticed how quiet Harrison's quarters were until she heard him hang up the telephone. With all the hard surfaces in the room—the marble, the black lacquered furniture, the glass—the sound of the receiver hitting the cradle seemed to echo through the decidedly masculine space.

The silence that followed turned tense as he walked back toward her.

"You told me about my husband to get me to cooperate, didn't you."

At the accusation in her voice, something like disappointment moved into his eyes. Feeling like a fool for having relaxed her guard around a man who's job routinely employed all manner of maneuvers, she didn't bother wondering why it was there.

"You've been cooperating all along," he informed her

flatly. "You haven't been happy about it, but you've been doing it."

That hardly made her feel better. "That doesn't answer my question."

"Then, the answer to your question is no. I didn't tell you about your husband to get something from you, Gwen. I told you because I thought it was something you deserved to know."

He told her because he sincerely felt she needed the information, that she had a right to it. Especially after these years of waiting.

He didn't need to tell her that. She could see it in the depths of his eyes.

The knowledge surprised her. It also struck her as totally unfair.

She didn't want him to be nice. She didn't want him to be understanding. It made it too hard to keep her defenses in place, and she truly needed those defenses with him. He made her aware of him in ways she had forgotten she could feel with a man, made her aware of herself in ways she'd long forgotten, too. Just meeting his eyes caused sensations she didn't realize she was still capable of feeling, and made her want things she'd begun to believe she no longer needed.

To be held.

To hold.

To be touched…the way he'd touched her when his knuckles had brushed her breast.

The memory pooled heat low in her stomach.

Disturbed by her thoughts, she reached toward her wine. Thinking better of it, she crossed her arms again instead.

"Who was that on the telephone?"

"Sir Cumberland," he replied, identifying the minister

of foreign relations. "I'd told him you and I were meeting tonight."

"And we're meeting because you want my influence with the queen," she reminded him, repeating what he'd said when she'd first arrived. She tipped up her chin, tightened her arms. "What do you need from her?"

Harrison watched her glance move from his chest to his mouth before falling away. The play of emotions on her face in the last few moments had been fascinating. In the space of seconds she'd gone from defense to confusion—and what he could have sworn was a hint of longing.

"For her to attend a meeting," he told her, wondering if she had any idea what it did to a man when a woman looked at him like that. "She can't maintain the seclusion she wants and expect everything to continue without her. The ambassador from the United States is concerned about the stability of the negotiations right now. Under the circumstances with the king, it's understandable that he would want to meet with the person in power to make sure the agreements will be honored. If she won't meet with him and offer that assurance, she's as good as telling him that the deals are off."

There wasn't a doubt in Gwen's mind that the queen would gladly tell them exactly that in order to save her son.

She was obviously becoming predictable. The thought had barely flashed in her head when Harrison's long, blunt fingers touched her mouth, and froze the words in her throat.

"I know the queen wants her son back," he insisted, needing her to understand something herself. "You don't need to remind me of that. But there's something the two of you aren't getting. You're hanging on to the idea that if this agreement isn't signed, the people who took the prince will simply let him go. We have no reason to believe the Black Knights won't kill him even if they do get what they want. We're not dealing with men of honor where they're concerned.''

Harrison wasn't so sure he was a man of honor himself. Not at the moment. He'd had no intention of touching her. He'd deliberately kept himself from it, in fact. Yet, he could feel the taunting fullness of her soft lips beneath his fingers. Her warm breath trembled against his skin.

Meeting the confusion clouding her eyes, he felt a distinct tug low in his groin.

She'd made no attempt to move from his touch.

The realization sharpened the desire already curling through him.

It would be so easy to slip his hand around the back of her neck, lower his mouth to hers and find out what it was about her that tested his control. But now wasn't the time to cave in to temptation. Not when her thoughts had been on her deceased husband only moments ago. When he tasted her, touched her, he wanted to be the only man on her mind.

''She needs to meet with them,'' he repeated, his fingers slipping reluctantly away. ''You're the only one she wants to see. The only person she'll listen to.''

She stepped back, looking very much as if she didn't know why she hadn't moved before now. He confused her. He was certain of that. But he figured that made them even. She was confusing the daylights out of him. He'd never had such a problem with concentration before.

''This is the very sort of thing she asked me to insulate her from.''

''I know that.''

"Then, I'm failing her faith and her friendship if—"

"This isn't about friendship. It's about—"

"It's about friendship to me," she insisted, having no interest at all in hearing him explain all over again. "She asked me to help her while she's going through the worst time of her life. I want to protect her, and you're making it impossible for me to do that."

"I'm just asking you to talk to her."

"Has it ever occurred to you that I might not have the influence you think I do?"

"Not lately," he admitted, and watched her glance drop like lead from his.

Tipping his head, he tried to catch her eye. "I thought we weren't going to do this."

"The truce was your idea."

"You agreed to it."

The glance she gave him held too much anxiety to be mutinous.

The responsibility being put on her was huge. He could tell by the distress she didn't even bother to cover that she fully realized just how enormous it was, too. But she was far stronger than she looked, he reminded himself, pushing his hands into his pockets to keep from reaching for her again. He needed to remember that.

The thought should have relieved him. She wasn't the sort of woman who buckled under pressure, the sort who had to be handled with the proverbial kid gloves. After all, she'd stood up to him time and again, and easily held her own. She also knew what it was to experience loss, to live with it, to move on. She was a survivor. Just like him.

The knowledge held no relief at all. Instead, he felt a tug of what he could swear was protectiveness himself.

"You might not believe it," he said, not wanting to

push, needing to, anyway, "but I don't want Her Majesty upset any more than you do. We've tried to respect her privacy, but staying in seclusion isn't going to help anyone. She needs to make this appearance."

Owen was as good as dead, no matter what they did. Unless the RET could find him first.

The thought totally drained her of spirit. She felt overwhelmed by things she didn't want to know, alone in ways she'd never felt before and totally unsettled by the man who could scramble her senses with nothing more than the touch of his fingertips.

"I'll relay your message," she murmured. She hated the position she was in. She wasn't totally sure how she felt about him, either. "It's not my right to withhold it."

It looked to her as if his hands had just formed fists in his pockets. "I'll let Sir Cumberland know you're speaking with Her Majesty. You might tell her that members of the Majorcan delegation will be there, too."

She nodded, bewildered by how rapidly she had gone from a lady-in-waiting to a liaison with the military. She had never been a woman of great ambition. She had never aspired to position. All she'd ever really wanted was a home, husband and family of her own. Yet there she was with the indomitable head of the RET and the men of three countries waiting for word from her—and no home of her own or a prospective husband in sight.

"I'll need a ride back," she murmured, when what she really wanted was for Harrison to touch her again. The hard strength in him, his nearness and the hooded way he was watching her made her crave the feel of his arms, the feel of his muscular body.

It wasn't a wise thing to want. She knew that. When this was all over, he would go his way, she would go hers and their paths would have no reason to cross until some official function six months or a year from now demanded their mutual presence. Still, with her view of everything else blocked by his solid chest, it was easy to wonder why that little detail even mattered.

"When will you talk with her?"

"Tonight, if she's awake. Not until morning, if she isn't."

He seemed to regard that as fair enough in the moments before he stepped back and turned to the telephone. He said nothing else to her, though, until he hung up and told her a guard was on his way.

She was at his door when she heard the ping of the elevator on the other side.

Harrison already had his hand on the knob, ready to get rid of her and get on to the next item on his agenda. Or so she thought before he hesitated.

"You're not failing her, Gwen."

He'd known what she was thinking. The realization gave her pause. So did the fact that he'd bothered to reassure her in the moments before he turned the knob and finally let her out.

The queen wasn't in her rooms. A guard in the residence told Gwen she was in the chapel.

Refusing to interrupt her at prayer, Gwen settled on the carved bench outside the arched door to the small room with its six pews and candlelit altar and waited for the queen's knees to grow tired.

When the ancient door finally creaked open, she was on her feet before the queen even noticed she'd been sitting there.

"I'm not here about Owen or the king," she said quickly, not wanting the woman to think she'd come with news. "There's been nothing since the call they recorded this morning. I was just waiting to walk back with you."

Looking even more pale than when Gwen had last seen her, Marissa lifted a trembling hand and pushed back a few strands of hair. It was unusual for her to look anything less than perfect when she ventured beyond her bedroom. Her complete lack of makeup and the wisps of hair straggling from her loose bun clearly attested to the toll the strain of waiting was taking on her.

"You didn't have to do that." Letting her hand fall, she offered a ghost of a smile. "But I'm glad you did."

"How long were you in there this time?"

"What time is it now?"

"After eleven."

"A few hours, then."

Concern narrowed Gwen's glance. "Did you have dinner?"

"I wasn't hungry. And please don't start," she begged, her tone lifeless. "My daughters are nagging me enough. The thought of solid food makes me nauseous."

"Is that what you told them?"

"No. I told them I had something to eat in my room. It was the truth," she defended when Gwen's eyebrow arched. "I did have something to eat in there. I never said I consumed it."

Gwen gave her a tolerant look. "I won't nag," she quietly promised. "I'll just go down to the kitchen and heat you some soup. You'll only make matters worse if you get sick yourself," she said ever so gently. "And don't worry, I won't tell your girls you lied to them."

Marissa opened her mouth, only to promptly give up when she saw the smile on her lady-in-waiting's face.

"You know, Gwen," she murmured, heading them both slowly down the dim limestone corridor, "I don't know what I would do without you right now. You know what it's like to have to be strong for your children. We're supposed to be the ones who make everything all right for them, and I have to bend the truth so my daughters can't see any more of my fear. They have enough on their minds with their father and their brother. I don't want them worried about me, too.''

She pushed her fingers through her hair, tugging loose another strand. ''I'm just so grateful to you for taking over the dealings with the RET. I can't imagine having to deal with all the political maneuverings right now. You are a true godsend.''

''Please don't say that.''

''It's true. Especially with the admiral. He can be so insistent.''

There wasn't much of anything the queen could have said that would have made Gwen feel worse than she already did about what she had to do. The woman thought she could count on her to keep the hounds at bay. Not open the gates to them.

''I know. I've bumped into that insistence myself,'' she admitted, though she wasn't about to burden her with that. ''And you may not think I'm so helpful after I tell you what he wants now.

''I truly hate to bother you with this,'' she said, hurrying on. ''If there were some way I could just carry a response back for you, you know I would do it. I've even tried to figure out some way to stand in for you, but it's you they want and I can't.''

Suddenly aware of the strain in her friend's tone, the queen drew to a halt.

''We stopped shooting the messenger a couple of reigns ago, Gwen. Stop hedging.''

''They need you for a meeting tomorrow.''

"They?"

"The parties to the alliance."

The weary breath Her Majesty drew escaped with an audible sign.

"Why?"

Gwen told her exactly what Harrison had explained to her.

"I have no idea how long it will take," she concluded a moment later. "He didn't say. If you only want to give them a half hour, I'll tell him that's what they'll have to settle for. I really think they just need you to put in an appearance."

Gwen must have looked as torn as she felt. As the queen watched her, the quality of her frown seemed to shift.

"How long have you worried about mentioning this to me?"

"Only a couple of hours."

Shaking her head again, looking as if she thought them quite a pair, the queen started walking once more.

"Considering how late it is, I assume the admiral badgered you into asking me this tonight?"

"He was actually quite flexible about that. He was rather civil about all of it," she conceded, grateful for her friend's understanding. "He even served me a very nice wine."

For the first time in days, a spark of light entered the eyes of the woman who ruled Penwyck. "Of course he did," she murmured.

Dismissing what she clearly thought a joke, that light died in the next blink. "All they need is my assurance that the agreements will go through?"

"That's what he said."

A fair amount of resistance remained visible beneath

the weariness. "You know that I will do what I must. If there is anything I understand, it's duty. But please tell him that I will not be drawn into a negotiating session. I will continue to rely on you to act as my intermediary, if you will allow me. Especially when it comes to dealing with the admiral."

"You know I'll do whatever you wish."

"You weren't serious about the wine, were you?"

Still confused by the earlier events of the evening, Gwen slowly nodded. "He had me taken to his home. He called it his 'quarters.'" As hard as he so often seemed, she wasn't sure the concept of home was one with which he was even familiar. "I had the feeling he was fitting me in between a meeting and before a telephone conference."

"He's behaving himself, I hope."

"He's my problem, Marissa. Don't worry about it."

"That can only mean he's not."

"No. He is," Gwen insisted "He's..."

Her automatic defense put the spark of interest back in the queen's keen eyes. "He's what?" she asked when Gwen's voice trailed off.

"Confusing," she finally decided to say. Confusing because there seemed to be a true sense of compassion beneath his hardness, a sense of compassion she wondered if he even realized he possessed. Confusing because he looked at her, touched her, as if he wanted her. Yet, he clearly didn't want the attraction his own actions encouraged.

Disquiet for her friend momentarily overrode all else that troubled the queen. "Are you attracted to him?"

Absolutely, Gwen thought. "Maybe," she murmured, a little disturbed by the immediacy of her mental response. "I don't think he's as ruthless as he wants everyone to believe."

"Or maybe he truly is," the queen pointed out, caution heavy in her quiet tone, "and whatever he's doing with you just proves it."

"What do you mean?"

"One of the reasons the king always sought his advice is because Monteque inevitably knows how to control a situation. He'll do what he must to best serve his purpose."

In other words, Gwen thought, he'd do what he had to do to make her easier to work with. The thought had occurred to her, too. She'd even called him on it after he'd shared the details surrounding her husband's death.

"Do you think he's trying to manipulate me?"

"I wouldn't presume to speak for him. But unless you're interested in something quick and discreet, I do think he is a man a woman needs to be careful around. He's the first man you've shown any interest in, in all the years I've known you," she reminded her, sounding as bewildered as she was impressed by that fact. Of all the eligible and interesting men her friend had been exposed to, Harrison was clearly not one she would have considered a match. "I just hope you'll be careful, Gwen. I don't know that any woman could ever get a commitment out of our admiral. He's escaped far too long."

They were words of warning, well intentioned, protective. The words of a friend who cared. The doubts they nurtured were even doubts Marissa probably knew were already there. But all Gwen could think about as they continued down the hall, talking now about the soup Gwen was going to heat and Marissa was going to eat, was that the man she'd been warned about was the same one who had been totally up-front with her about what he wanted from the moment she'd walked in his door. And not once had he said he wanted anything from her beyond a truce and her cooperation.

She was still trying to figure out if there was any comfort in that fact as she walked with the queen to her meeting early the next afternoon.

The scene outside the conference room near the king's office was far less chaotic than the press conference that had taken place only two days ago. Here, with the diplomatic business of the kingdom being conducted as usual, quiet dignity reigned.

Her father wouldn't have had it any other way.

Ambassador Charles Worthington was the first to notice the arrival of the queen and her small entourage when they stepped into the hall from the side door leading from the tunnel entrance. Leaving the group of dignitaries and diplomats gathered outside the conference room doors, he hurried toward them, his polished Italian leather shoes silent on the royal red carpet.

Tall and trim, his snow-white hair swept back from his patrician features, he carried his sixty-five years with enviable ease. His pinstriped suit was impeccably tailored. So were his blinding white shirt, burgundy silk tie and the tuft of matching silk in his pocket.

"Your Majesty." Every inch the dignified, distinguished diplomat, he met them halfway and bowed deeply from the waist. "I am at your service."

With Gwen at her side and guards flanking them both, the queen offered a regal nod. "Thank you, Ambassador. Is everyone here who needs to be?"

"I will check with Admiral Monteque. It was he who made the arrangements."

He gave another bow, stopping short of clicking his

heels and finally acknowledged his daughter. "Gwen-dolyn," was all he said before his forehead furrowed at the length of her skirt and he turned away.

He'd never approved of her wearing skirts above the knee. But then, after she'd embarrassed him by not marrying the man he'd chosen for her, he'd never approved of much about her, anyway. The fact that she served the queen redeemed her only on the surface, since her appointment reflected well on him. But he never asked how she was, or said it was good to see her. And heaven forbid, Gwen thought, that he should ever do anything so plebian as give her a smile.

Not that she ever expected him to do such a thing. But thinking about her father's apathetic attitude toward her kept her mind off the man whose glance burned a path from the clip restraining her hair to the hem of the taupe suit skirt that had just earned her father's frown.

Harrison stood tall and dignified himself among the small knot of men fifty feet away. From where she remained with the queen and their escort by an enormous potted palm, Gwen watched him dip his head to hear what her father asked him. As ambassador to the United States, her father's role in the business taking place was as prominent as anyone's. But it was the man in the admiral's uniform who held her attention as he broke away from the group and accompanied her father back to them.

As her father had, Harrison immediately addressed and bowed to Her Majesty. Unlike him, he then turned to Gwen with a nod and a respectful, "My Lady."

"Admiral," she replied with the polite nod protocol required.

From the way Gwen's glance suddenly faltered, Harrison suspected that his own had lingered a few moments longer than it should have. But she had never looked more like the ice maiden to him than she did at that moment. Cool, utterly poised, and with every true emotion she possessed locked beneath her exquisitely polished facade.

He'd watched that facade crystallize the moment her father had approached the queen. The ambassador had been the epitome of regard toward Her Majesty, and while Harrison had seen him warmly greet the delegation from Majorco and the United States ambassador only minutes ago, he hadn't detected so much as a hint of warmth or affection toward his daughter. He'd acknowledged her presence almost as an afterthought.

Remembering what Gwen had told him of her parents, he suspected now that the lack of affection they'd displayed toward each other had extended to her, too.

At the thought, the unfamiliar sense of protectiveness he'd felt last night stirred inside him once more. He knew exactly how it felt to live with that cold distance. He'd just never considered how much a person could shut herself down to escape it.

Feeling something uncomfortably familiar about the phenomenon, he directed his attention to the queen. "Everyone is here except the president of Majorco and Prince Broderick. They are crossing the lower courtyard now. Do you wish to enter or wait until everyone has arrived?"

The thought of having to make small talk clearly did not appeal to the woman in the stark black coatdress. "I'll wait." The toll of another long night visible in her pale features, she immediately turned to the woman standing sedately beside her.

"You will come in to tell me if there is any news whatsoever of Owen."

"Absolutely," Gwen quietly replied. "The very moment I hear," she promised.

The queen's wan smile turned resigned at the murmur of voices ahead of them. Hearing them himself, Gwen's father glanced over his shoulder to see who had arrived, then swept his hand outward with another bow. "I believe we can proceed, Your Majesty."

Beyond them, a brawny gentleman in an ascot and the red sash of a Penwyckian dignitary emerged from the opposite end of the corridor with a guard and the black-suited president of Majorco. As the other men filed into the room after greeting him, he stopped alone outside the doors and bowed to the queen himself.

Every time Gwen saw Prince Broderick, she felt as if she were seeing a ghost.

Every time Harrison saw him he got the sense of a fox watching the henhouse. At the moment, however, he was more interested in the slender woman crossing her arms over the leather-bound notepad she carried. As the queen started forward, Gwen's father dropped back a step and lowered his voice.

"If there is news to deliver to the queen, Gwendolyn, it will be more appropriate if you just come to the door and ask for me or Sir Selwyn to deliver the message. The matters we will be discussing in there are privileged."

The hint of condescension in his voice made it sound as if she probably hadn't realized that. But it was the impression he gave that she was too far beneath the importance of the others who would be present that had Harrison stepping forward the moment he noticed Gwen's grip on her notebook. To her credit not an ounce of poise had drained from her face, but her fingers had nearly gone white.

"Of course," she murmured, looking as if she were

too focused on blocking the unpleasant emotions the man elicited to bother with anything else.

"With all due respect," Harrison said, having no problem with that himself, "there isn't anything that will be discussed in there that your daughter doesn't already know about. Her security clearance is higher than yours."

The man gave a choke of disbelief. "She's a lady-in-waiting," he said, as if the title itself should dispute the claim.

"As far as you know," Harrison returned evenly.

The tips of the ambassador's ears turned the same deep pink as the roses in the garden. But skilled as he was at saving face, his recovery was commendably quick.

Jerking his glance from the second most powerful man in the kingdom, his frosty expression fell back on his daughter. "Then, you will do as Her Majesty directed, of course."

A muscle in Harrison's jaw jerked. "She knows her job, sir."

Lethal. That was the only way Gwen could possibly describe the look in Harrison's piercing eyes as her father took an offended step away, his back ramrod straight, then turned to catch up with the queen.

The guards that had accompanied Her Majesty fell into step behind them. When they reached the doors of the conference room, those guards joined the others to position themselves along the length of the hall. For a moment, the only sounds were the decisive thuds of the doors closing and the muffled thump of rifle butts hitting the floor.

Those sounds echoed to silence in the long seconds before Gwen could even begin to think what to say. Harrison had jumped to her defense like a wolf protecting its mate.

"I've been told I have trouble with diplomacy some-times," he muttered.

Incredulous, touched, grateful, she could only shake her head. "Why did you do that?"

He wasn't sure he wanted to answer that question. He wasn't even sure if he'd done it for her or himself. Not caring to figure it out, he went for the reason that appeared the most obvious. "Because you wouldn't.

"So how is she doing?" he asked, changing the subject with the nod of his head toward the closed doors.

He was right that she wouldn't have said anything, she thought. She never wasted her breath on what her father wouldn't hear or respect. But she didn't tell him that. Harrison seemed no more interested in discussing his gallant defense than he did explaining why it mattered whether she defended herself or not. And, unlike him, she wasn't about to push.

"Not as well as she appears," she replied, wondering if his response hadn't simply been instinctive. The way it had been when he'd thrown his jacket over her in the rain. "She would rather be in the chapel. Or at her husband's side," she continued, feeling a dangerous tug in her heart at his innate need to protect. "In the past couple of days, those are the places she's spent all but the few hours she's managed of sleep."

Studying her profile, seeing the faint lines of fatigue around her own eyes, he almost asked how much sleep she'd managed herself. But the thought of her sleeping evoked an image of her restrained hair loose and spilling like spun gold over his pillow, so he let the topic go.

"Duke Logan said he told you this morning that we're still analyzing the voice on the tape."

"He did. And I passed that on to the queen." Clutching her notepad like a shield, she looked up at the hard, chiseled lines of his face. "Thank you for that."

"For the information?"

"For what you said to my father." Even if he didn't want to discuss it, she needed him to know that she appreciated what he done. Now that she had, she'd let it go, too.

"You're the one running the show," she said, nodding toward the doors as he had done. "Shouldn't you be inside with Her Majesty and the suits?"

Dangerous. The way she looked at him, her eyes luminous with gratitude, had him thinking of her and the pillow again. And a bed. And tangled sheets. "I'm not running anything. I just got it organized."

Holding his beret loosely by its rim at his side, not trusting the direction of his thoughts, he gestured with his free hand toward what she gripped in front of her. "What's left on your schedule today?"

The easy way he dismissed his own importance caused her to overlook the fact the he needed something again. This was a man who commanded Penwyck's entire navy. He headed the RET. At the moment, Penwyck's one million citizens were at the mercy of his advice to the queen. She couldn't imagine that he regarded all that power as simply doing a job.

Yet, that was exactly the impression she had as he waited for her reply.

"I have an appointment to check the silver for Saturday evening."

"How long will that take?"

"Two, maybe three hours."

"To check silver?"

"We have settings for five hundred," she explained. "Each fork, knife and spoon, each caviar knife, every candelabra, serving platter and salt cellar has to be inspected to make sure there is no trace of silver polish or tarnish.''

"Can someone else do it?"

"The queen usually supervises herself. I promised I'd take care of everything."

Of course she had, he thought. There wasn't much of anything that wasn't landing on those slender shoulders at the moment. "After that?"

"I have a meeting with the florists doing the table arrangements and one with Mrs. Ferth about the seating. And I want to stop by to congratulate Monsieur Pomier. I heard he tracked down enough champagne."

"He was short?"

"It's a long story."

Part of him actually wanted to hear it. The other part, the part he was more familiar with, insisted he get to his point. "The seating is what I want to talk to you about. We need to add fifty guests."

The look she gave him said he had to be joking.

The look he gave her back said he was dead serious.

With a slow blink, she tipped her chin. "Do you have any idea what that will do to the seating arrangements?"

"Change them, I imagine."

"You have a gift for understatement," she murmured dryly. "Who would these guests be?"

Other than the guards, they were the only ones there. But he wasn't about to take any chances on being overheard. Curling his fingers around her arm, he moved her away from the huge bushy palm and farther down the hall. Beneath his hand he was aware of the quick tension in her small, supple muscles. Mostly he was aware of the freshness of her scent and the quiet breath she'd drawn when he'd reached toward her.

Lowering his hand as well as his voice, he murmured, "Security."

She stood in front of him, her blue eyes guarded, her notebook between them. The coolness he'd seen before was gone, but not the propriety their surroundings demanded.

There was passion beneath that decorum. The thought of discovering just how deep certain of those passions might run conjured images of slowly stripping away the clip from her hair, her jacket from her shoulders, her skirt from her hips. She favored lace. He remembered that because it was the delicate fabric edging her bra that had distracted him in the queen's drawing room only days ago.

Remembering what he'd done to conceal it, and how soft and firm her flesh had felt, he sucked in a breath of bated frustration.

"I'll need a chart of the seating arrangements myself. We'll have to change whatever the seating plan is now to accommodate personnel. Don't worry," he muttered, suspecting his voice sounded as tight as his body suddenly felt. "They'll look like guests."

He didn't doubt that, a few short days ago, Gwen would have thought his request totally unacceptable and probably, promptly told him so. It was a clear indication of how far they'd come that her expression revealed little beyond concern. "We can't just arbitrarily move the invited guests. There is an order at each table. By rank and title," she hurried to explain.

"That's where you come in." The thought of having his hands on her refused to go away. But it felt safer than thinking about the empathy he still felt for her. Desire he could understand. The other simply felt dangerous. "I have no idea what that protocol is, but we know you do."

Distance, he thought. That was what he needed. "You can help with the new arrangements."

It had taken days to put the original chart together. To rearrange the whole thing now would have given Gwen a headache of monumental proportions had she actually been thinking about the work involved. With Harrison's focus intent on her mouth, she was having trouble thinking at all.

As his glance drifted down her body, it was almost as if he were imagining how her body would fit his.

"Admiral. Sir." A young member of the Royal Guard bounced his self-conscious glance from her to his superior's profile. "Pardon the interruption, but you said to let you know the moment your car arrived. It has, sir."

Harrison's eyes remained on hers. "Thank you, soldier. Tell my driver I'll be right there."

"Sir," came the acknowledging reply.

"So," he said, as if he hadn't just mentally stripped her bare. "Do you want to set up a time now or call my assistant later?"

"I'll have to call her later." Her forehead pinched. "Fifty?"

"Fifty."

"This could take all night."

That was what he was afraid of.

Chapter Nine

Gwen had been under the impression that she would be working with the RET on the seating arrangements. With Colonel Prescott, perhaps, since he was in charge of intelligence. Or with Duke Logan, since he was a member of the Royal Guard. She thought for certain she would be working with Harrison and had found herself looking forward to the possibility with more anticipation than was probably wise—until she called his assistant and realized that nothing about the little project was as straightforward as it had seemed.

Harrison had failed to mention that the chart couldn't remain where it was. He'd also failed to mention that she would be knocking heads with the hard-nosed and humorless General Franklin Vancor, Commander of the Royal Guard, who was in charge of all palace security.

The general had a definite problem with the concept of teamwork. It was as apparent as the annoyance in his beady brown eyes that he hated having to defer to her, a mere lady-in-waiting, when it came to where he could and could not put his personnel. He knew where he wanted his people. Yet he refused to tell her why a particular position at a table was so important. She, on the other hand, generously offered reasons for why such placement wouldn't work—explanations that had earned her either a snort or a look of barely restrained disgust.

Mercifully, the man she'd been sentenced to work with had just left for dinner. A very late dinner, he'd pointed out, making it sound as if it were her fault the project was taking so long.

As she stood in the tunnel conference room where she had met the RET just yesterday, all she cared about at the moment was that he was gone.

The bad news was that he'd be back.

In the meantime she needed to figure out where to put the other half of his guards.

The seating chart for the state dinner to be held Saturday evening measured four feet by six feet and was actually a map of the ballroom. Positioned on that map were cutouts to scale, representing ten long banquet tables, and five hundred small white cards on which had been written a number and the name of each guest.

The cumbersome chart had been removed from the ladies' office late that afternoon, and now took up most of the mahogany table.

Her first task had been to reconstruct the whole thing.

Ignoring the headache brewing behind her eyes, she contemplated her handiwork. The tables had been lengthened to accommodate the security personnel, and seating cards had been replaced according to the notes Mrs. Ferth had meticulously taken before Gwen had allowed the

chart to be carted away. Security personnel were represented by small red squares.

Twenty-six of those markers had been placed between
guest cards. The twenty-four squares in her palm still
needed a home. But noting everything she'd already
noted solved nothing, she thought—and tried not to groan
when she heard the click of the security latch on the door
behind her.

If it was Vancor she was going to cry. She really didn't
want to have to deal with his chauvinism anymore tonight. By comparison her father was a feminist, and Harrison had been the epitome of cooperation since day one.

The thought of Harrison had no sooner entered her
mind than the hairs on the back of her neck prickled with
recognition. Even before she turned, she knew it was his
glance moving over her back.

When she did face him, she found his carved features
remote despite the ease of his manner.

"The guard told me you were still here." Looking as
if he'd rather be anywhere else, he closed the door with
a muffled click. "I thought you'd be at dinner by now."

Her life seemed to be crawling with men destined to
make her uncomfortable. The thought that this particular
one had come when he figured she might be gone had
her turning self-consciously back to her task.

Of all the options she'd contemplated, she hadn't considered that the reason she'd been working with the head
of security was because Harrison had wanted to avoid
working with her himself.

"I want to get this finished. I'm expecting a call from
Amira tonight and I don't want to miss it." She'd thought
his defense of her that morning might actually have
meant something. Feeling foolish because she'd actually
hoped it had, she absently rubbed her temple and tried to

focus on her task. "We still have twenty-four personnel to position."

"That's what Vancor said. I just ran into him." Walking up to where she stood at the table, Harrison casually picked up a lone red square that had fallen from her stack and slanted her a glance. "You must be giving him a hard time."

Gwen almost choked. She'd been beyond polite to the man. She'd been downright tolerant. "He told you that?"

"Not exactly," he conceded. "What he said was that he could have had this finished in no time if he didn't have to work with you."

Harrison expected her chin to come up, her expressive eyes to flash. Instead, he was struck by the dullness in those liquid blue depths when her fingers fell from her temple.

"I think he's having trouble accepting that he can't just arbitrarily seat people wherever he wants them."

She looked tired, he thought, and frowned back at the chart. He didn't want to notice things like that about her. More than that, he didn't want it to matter.

Mostly, he really wished she hadn't been there. Or, that he didn't have to be.

"I don't doubt that. Trying to make personnel unobtrusive at an event like this always hamstrings an operation. But I'm pretty sure he was thinking more along the lines of how you're distracting him from what he's trying to do."

Give me a soldier to work with, the guy had grumbled. *Give me someone in a uniform. Give me someone I can swear around,* he'd groused.

"I'm not trying to distract him from anything," she insisted, oblivious.

"I didn't say you were."

"What I am trying to do is get him to understand that protocol is just as important as security. He's the one who isn't being cooperative," she defended, praying she didn't sound as cranky as she felt. She was as tired as everyone else. Having missed dinner, she was also hungry. Neither contributed to a placid disposition.

Aware of the vague distance in Harrison's manner, she wasn't exactly feeling welcome at the moment, either.

"The man doesn't explain anything."

"That's because he's accustomed to issuing orders rather than taking them. The men he commands do what he says, no questions. You," he concluded, checking out the little white cards, "ask questions."

"I can't do my job without information." Truly at a loss, she shook her head. "Unless he's insinuating that I'm trying to interfere with placement of his people," she ventured, trying to imagine the workings of the man's mind, "I can't see how he regards questions as a distraction."

From the corner of his eye, Harrison glanced toward her profile. She looked exasperated and bewildered, and completely innocent of how easily she could crawl under a man's skin.

"Is that it?" she quietly asked, apparently taking his silence for confirmation. "He thinks I'm trying to sabotage this by not letting him put someone I know nothing about between an earl and his wife?"

"Gwen." Harrison's tone went as flat as the floor. He had no idea how the female mind worked, but hers was getting her farther off base by the second. "That's not the kind of distracting I'm talking about. He's just not accustomed to working with someone like you." She was a beautiful, desirable woman. Interesting. Intriguing. She elicited all manner of feelings in a man, everything from lust to the need to defend. None were comfortable.

Hesitation entered her voice. "'Someone like me?'"

He wasn't about to go into detail. "He's accustomed to dealing with his men. Not civilian women."

"Oh," she murmured, and glanced back to the chart.

Harrison frowned back at it himself. He didn't care for the odd knot curling in his gut. He had nothing against Vancor. He just didn't like the thought of the old goat finding her as distracting as he did. He didn't like that he'd left her there alone with the guy for the past five hours, either.

Possessiveness was definitely new to him.

"I take it that these red things represent security personnel?"

"They do."

"We need at least two there."

"That's what the general said," she replied, his displeased expression making her cautious. "But everyone there carries a title. I haven't been able to figure out who we can put a stranger between or who to move to another table."

"They're all couples?"

"Not all. That's making it a little easier to work in your personnel, but it would be a lot easier if I knew how you're planning to explain these people. I can't put just anyone between a crown prince and a president, but the general wouldn't tell me a thing."

"They'll all use a cover of diplomat. Their story is that they're part of Penwyck's diplomatic corps."

For the first time since he'd walked into the room, Gwen turned to look up at him. Her eyes looked as blue as a summer sky, her expression completely devoid of the caution that had been there from the first moments he'd closed the door.

"Why couldn't he have told me that?"

"He doesn't want their cover blown."

"I wouldn't do that."

He knew she wouldn't. He also knew that standing there staring at her was not a good idea. Not as alone as they were. "He doesn't know you the way I do," he said, and turned back to their task.

"Why don't you move these two?" He tipped his head to see the writing. "Lord and Lady Ashcroft," he read. "There are open spaces at the table next to them."

His confidence in her had been spoken as a simple matter of fact. Something that simply was. That same practical approach marked his manner as he tried to make sense of what she was doing with all the little cards.

Determined to be as focused as he was being, she considered the spot he was talking about. "We can't put the Ashcrofts there. The lord likes his champagne, and the couples that would be on either side of them never touch a drop."

"So he needs to stay at a party table," he concluded.

She couldn't help the hint of relief she felt. Partly because his considering expression removed some of the distance from his handsome features. Partly because his reaction hadn't been a snort.

"What are the green dots for on some of the cards?"

"Green dot designates a vegetarian."

"And the blue one over there?"

"That's the Duke of Rothbury. He's diabetic. They'll replace the lemon sorbet that will be served as a palate cleanser with a sugarless version for him and leave off the chocolate-dipped strawberry to be served with the puff-pastry-and-crème-fraîche swan for dessert. It's easier

on his wife than her having to nag at him not to eat it."
She shook her head, her pity for the poor duchess evident.
"He gets to visiting and will eat everything in front of
him," she confided, "including the garnishes. He's really
not very good about his diet without her."

"Would it be a problem moving the Ashcrofts over
there?"

"Oh, we couldn't possibly do that. That would put
them between their oldest daughter's ex-in-laws and the
parents of the baroness who stole her husband from her."

Beginning to understand another reason Vancor had
become so frustrated, he muttered, "I see." She'd probably defeated every change the general wanted to make.
"I don't suppose that would be politically correct."

"No," she agreed, more grateful than he could imagine at his grasp of the situation. "Unfortunately, it
wouldn't. We really do need to keep them at this table."

"So who can you move?"

Reaching past him, she picked up a white card and
replaced it with a red one. "Now that I know what role
the security personnel are playing, I can slip them in just
about anywhere. Here." She held out some of her
squares. "Find Ambassador and Mrs. Bingham and Monsieur and Madame Lebeau at table three. We can put one
between them. We'll move the negotiators from Majorco
in with some of the gentry from England. That should
keep them from talking about the alliance all night and
allow space for a security person."

Harrison took in her quiet assuredness as she spoke.
The chart, he realized, was actually a carefully designed
battle plan not at all unlike something he and his commanders would organize and strategize over during training games. As he studied the neat rows of markers, he

began to appreciate the logistics behind every decision she made.

Gwen's understanding of the needs, personalities and personal quirks of the guests was undoubtedly indispensable to the queen. Had it not been for the way she was leaning across the table, he might have considered just how valuable it was to him at the moment, too.

She'd reached to move a square, but he wasn't watching where she put it. His attention had fixed on her narrow waist where her jacket stretched snug with her reach, and the gentle roundness of her hips.

Realizing where he was staring, even more aware of what the view was doing to certain parts of his own body, he silently swore to himself.

"What time is your daughter to call?"

The question had her pulling back to glance at her watch. "In an hour. If you can okay the placement of your personnel, this shouldn't take but a few more minutes."

He could do that. It was what he'd come to do, anyway. Get in. Get the job done. That had been his goal tonight. It still was.

Determined to distract himself in the meantime, he located the cards he was searching for. "How is she?"

"I've only talked to her once since they arrived in Scotland, but she's so excited to be there." Genuine pleasure slipped into her expression. It lit her face, her eyes. "It's her first trip away," she explained, putting another square into place. "But you probably already know that. The men who interviewed me about Prince Owen needed to account for all occupants of the palace, so where she is went into their report."

He hadn't read those particular reports himself, but

he'd heard where her daughter was. "You have to be relieved that she's not here right now."

"Enormously. With all that's going on, she's much better off where she is."

Lifting a white marker, he arched his eyebrow to silently ask if it was okay to move. He'd never been any good at small talk. The sooner they finished, the better.

Nodding to indicate his choice was okay, her brow pinched.

"You don't have a child, do you?"

As small talk went, he couldn't honestly say her question qualified. But with her focus back on the chart, which was where he kept his, she seemed simply to be making conversation, too.

"No," he told her. "I don't."

"Did you ever want one?"

"I never had reason to think about it."

The only real thought he had ever given to children was to prevent having any of his own. His idea of torture was to be trapped into a relationship he didn't want. His idea of hell was to have a child he'd have no idea how to raise. The only experience he would have had to call on was his own, and he wouldn't wish his childhood on anything with a soul. "I was in military school. Then the academy. Then the navy. I was never exposed to any."

"You were never around children at all?"

"Not since I was a kid myself. My mother died when I was six. A month later, my father put me in military school." Contemplating the lack of security near the entrance door indicated on the chart, his forehead creased in a frown. "We need four personnel at the ends of all these tables," he muttered, indicating the problem areas. "Do you want to move everyone or just add more seatings?"

"Add more seatings," she replied, far more interested in him than in what they were doing. "Is your father still alive?"

"He was the last I heard." Satisfied, he scrutinized the area by the service entrances. "He retired as vice admiral ten years ago and moved to Belize."

"I take it you have no siblings."

"Only child."

"Is that why you went into our special forces?"

"How did you know that I did?"

"You're wearing the ribbon."

She nodded to the five-inch-wide row of service ribbons on his chest. As schooled as she seemed to be with everything else, he shouldn't be surprised that she would know what most of them represented.

"That probably had something do with it." Bracing his hands on the table, he scanned the chart. It was getting harder by the second to ignore the old knot of resentment beginning to churn in his gut. But ignore it he would, just as he always did. After forty-six years, a man should be over the fact that nothing he did, nothing he accomplished would make his father notice him. So what if he'd been shipped off as a kid and forgotten about? At least he didn't have to still face that indifference the way Gwen did. "Did Vancor tell you we're putting personnel on the kitchen staff?"

Gwen blinked at the carved lines of his strong profile. Moments ago, there hadn't been anything about him that didn't seem focused on their task. Outwardly, he still was. But his hands had curled into fists against the table and, despite the ease of this tone, his features had turned to granite.

"No. He didn't," she replied, struck by the enormity of what he'd revealed with such seeming indifference. It was no wonder he'd become as hard as he was, she thought. He hadn't been able to help it. He'd had no mother. No sister. No softening female influence at all as a child. He had been raised by a father far more unfeeling than hers, a man who had put a grieving, undoubtedly lost little child into a system that focused on discipline and the strict rules of the military.

The thought of him as a motherless little boy nearly broke her heart.

The thought of the man he had become reminded her to be wary.

The parts of his heart that hadn't been battered as a child would have turned to stone in his training. She'd heard that the men accepted into Penwyck's special forces were turned into machines. They were the specialists, the men trained for covert operations. Those were the kinds of jobs given only to single men with no ties because men with ties could hesitate and jeopardize an operation if they had to think about family who depended on them.

It was so easy now for her to see why he'd appeared to express so little sensitivity toward the queen. He'd been exposed to so little of the trait himself. Yet somehow his more redeeming qualities had survived the abandonment, the indoctrination. Over the past few days she'd seen totally unexpected hints of kindness and empathy. That empathy had been there last night when he'd told her about Alex. Again today, when he'd refused to let her father belittle her.

"What about a wife?" she asked carefully. "Is that something you never thought about, either?"

Incredibly, his hands relaxed. His long blunt fingers stretched out once more on the polished mahogany. As he turned his head toward her, she could even see the tension drain from the hard set of his face.

"I wouldn't know what to do with a wife," he told her, his eyes holding hers. "I'm lousy at relationships, Gwen. I always have been."

He was warning her. She should appreciate that, she supposed. And she did. Or would, when she let herself think about it. At the moment, though, she was more drawn by his honesty than put off by it. Something about his admission had struck very close to home.

"I don't think I'm very good at them anymore, either," she murmured, thinking of what Marrisa had pointed out last night. With her head bent, she absently flicked her nail along the edges of the cards she held. "I've been out with a few men over the past ten years. Friends of friends," she explained. "I'm a convenient single female to pair with an extra male guest at a diplomatic function, but I haven't gotten beyond a date or two."

A soft smile touched her mouth as she glanced up. "Now that I think about it, I was pretty lousy at them before I was married, too."

For a moment Harrison said nothing. He'd had women. More than he could remember. And with every single one of them, he made it clear from the beginning that he wasn't looking for anything serious. That was what he'd been doing a moment ago with her. Letting her know that if anything happened between them, it would mean nothing beyond the moment.

He just couldn't remember a single one of those women looking at him the way she was doing now, with what he could swear was understanding.

Drawn by that, by her, he forgot all about making sure

she understood that he never played for keeps. "Why haven't you gotten beyond that second date?"

Beneath the simple lines of her suit jacket, her shrug appeared deceptively casual. It was her darkly lashed eyes that gave her away. She couldn't meet his. "I've never thought about it."

She was thinking about it right now. He was certain of that as he slowly straightened. She had as much as told him that she hadn't been with a man in ten years. She might as well have told him, too, that before and since her husband she simply hadn't been attracted to any of the men she'd met.

Yet, with him, he could swear he'd seen her eyes darken at his touch and heard the telltale hitch of her breath.

"You know, Harrison," she murmured, her weary smile turning rueful as she turned to face the table again, "this isn't getting the job done. You said you want four at the end of each table?"

Clearly evading, she pondered the chart once more, trying to recall where they'd left off.

Taunted by what he'd just realized, he couldn't help thinking that getting the job done could wait.

"Both ends if possible. I want all the exits covered."

"Maybe it would be easiest if you put your markers where you need them and I'll just work around those."

Reaching in front of her, his hand closed over the cards she held. Without a word he slipped them from between her fingers.

Had she stepped back or seemed at all uncomfortable that he was so close, he would have moved away.

She didn't do anything but glance up.

"All you had to do was ask for them," she said, her tone faintly chiding.

The markers landed on the table. "Maybe they're not what I want."

Gwen's heart jerked against her ribs as she felt Harrison's big hand slip around the back of her neck. His eyes dark on hers, he tugged her forward slowly, as if giving her time to pull away if that was what she wanted to do.

It never even occurred to her to try.

She touched her fingertips to the hard wall of his chest. Before she could even begin to question the wisdom of what she was doing, he lowered his head and covered her mouth with his.

She felt herself go still. Warmth shimmered through her, little shocks of electricity darting to her breasts. His lips were far softer than anything that looked so hard had a right to be. His hands, big and strong as they were, felt incredibly gentle on her skin when he turned her toward him and his thumb traced the side of her jaw.

The warmth enlivened every nerve in her body. The gentleness of his touch disarmed her completely.

With a sigh that felt far too much like longing, she opened to him.

His taste filled her, hot and flavored faintly of spearmint as a groan sounded deep in his throat. The guttural sound rumbled through her, drawing her closer as his hands slipped down her back to coax her nearer himself.

Somewhere in the back of her suddenly befuddled brain, common sense battled with her senses for priority. The skirmish was embarrassingly quick. Before she could begin to warn herself of all the reasons she should be protecting herself from this man, her senses won. Inside, she could feel parts of herself melting. Parts that had nearly withered away from neglect. Parts he'd teased before, but now brought completely to life with the touch of his hand to her side, to the curve of her breast.

Need shot through her, liquid and desperate, weakening her knees, silencing defenses.

Fisting the wool of his lapels in her grip, she pulled up, meeting the blatantly sensual thrust of his tongue, encouraging the way his hands roamed her body. The moment she did, his hands drifted lower to press her to the hardness straining against her belly.

For an instant his body didn't move. A heartbeat later, gentleness turned insistent, and she was holding on for dear life because the raw hunger she felt in him was feeding a need inside her that she hadn't even known existed.

That hunger clawed at Harrison, digging its tentacles deep. He wasn't sure if he'd been testing himself when he'd reached out, or if he was testing her. All he'd known when he'd seen the question slip into her luminous eyes and he'd heard her shuddery intake of breath was that he needed to feel her, to taste her. He wanted to know what it was about her that kept drawing him to her when everything about her should have told him to back away.

That was what he thought he wanted, anyway. Now all he wanted was more.

And more was exactly what he shouldn't take.

The knowledge jerked hard.

So did the fact that torturing himself any longer with the feel of her would only make it harder to let her go.

Gritting his teeth against the demand of his body, he slowly lifted his head. As he did, she pulled back far enough to see his eyes.

She was even more beautiful when her skin was flushed. "I wasn't going to do that," he said.

Beneath his palms, he felt the quick tension enter her supple muscles.

"When you put it that way, I rather wish you hadn't."

"Gwen."

"Why did you?"

She watched him search her face, his eyes glittering on hers.

"Because I can't seem to keep my hands off you," he admitted. "Because I want you," he continued, with that amazing blunt honesty of his.

He skimmed his fingers down the smooth skin at the side of her neck, coming to rest at the hollow at the base of her throat. Beneath his fingers, her pulse leaped.

"I want you in bed," he said, making sure she had no doubt about his meaning. "I want to feel you. All of you. I want to taste every inch of you," he murmured, certain she understood. "I want to be inside you."

Her breath shuddered a moment before her glance fell.

With the tips of his fingers, he tilt her chin back up. "You asked why, Gwen. And I told you. But just because I want something doesn't mean I take it. I'm not sure either one of us needs any more complications right now."

It might not have sounded like it to her, but he was being the voice of reason. If she had any idea how tired he was of that role, she might have realized how easy it would be at that moment for her to tell him reason didn't matter and he would believe her. She had a way of making him abandon the ruthless control he'd always maintained over himself. She made him question why it was even necessary. But more than anything, she made him need.

That wasn't a feeling he was terribly comfortable with.

His hands fell from her arms. As they did, she stepped back and picked up the markers scattered on the table.

"How much longer will this take?" he asked, picking out red ones himself.

Gwen kept her focus on the table, trembling inside. He'd left her totally rattled by that kiss. But she'd never been so shaken by a man's words in her entire life. She wasn't entirely sure how she felt at that moment. *Unsettled* was high on the list. So was *confused*. He wanted her but he didn't. He pulled her close only to push her away again.

"Not long," she murmured.

"Let's get it finished, then. Your daughter will be calling soon."

"What if the general wants to make changes?"

"I'll take care of the general," he promised. "You just get your call."

Chapter Ten

Yesterday Harrison had watched the sunrise from his desk. Tonight the late-August sun was setting as he stood at the window, taking the first break he'd allowed himself all day.

He'd been in meetings since seven o'clock that morning. At the Admiralty, with the RET, with Penwyck's ministers, with the royal physician.

The king's condition remained critical but stable.

The prince still hadn't been found.

Clamping his hand over the muscles knotting in the back of his neck, he pulled a deep breath and slowly blew it out.

On his massive desk behind him were piles of reports from the various battleships, submarines and aircraft carriers for which he was ultimately responsible. He had to review an operating budget that rivaled the national debt of some small nations. There were UN communiqués to read about cooperative maneuvers coming up next month and a stack of correspondence to sign that Lieutenant Sotheby had put in his in-box before she'd gone home two hours ago—after reminding him of an early breakfast for one of his most trusted commanders, who was deserting him by retiring next month.

The man was entitled to retirement. He was pushing sixty-five.

Harrison felt as if he, himself, were pushing a hundred.

Being tired to the bone wasn't what had him frowning at the slit of pink below the gray evening clouds. It was the conversation he'd had with the reporter who ruined his morning three days ago. He'd spoken with the man the day the story had broken. He'd spoken with him again a few hours ago.

The reporter, a seasoned veteran of the press named Cartwright Alger, had given the same report both times. He said that he'd received an anonymous call to meet someone who claimed to have intimate knowledge of an illness within the royal family. When he'd met with the caller near a secluded bench in Penleigh Park, he had been given the details he'd put in the paper about the king's illness and resulting coma.

During both calls, Alger had insisted that his source was irrefutable. He'd also maintained that he couldn't name him because he feared what would happen to him if he did.

His editor stood behind the decision to protect his source.

Behind his editor was Penwyck's own law that guaranteed a free press.

Watching a sailing sloop navigate the breakwater in the dimming light, Harrison conceded that the reporter had, at least, eliminated females as possible leads since he'd consistently referred to his source as masculine. But the fact that the man sounded genuinely fearful of the threat was what interested Harrison the most. That and the way the headline had been worded. The reporter claimed that his source had insisted on the particular wording to be used: King in Coma; Prince Broderick in Power.

To Harrison, the caption sounded like something Broderick himself would want—which was why Harrison couldn't help but wonder if the king's twin hadn't called the reporter himself. Broderick was certainly vain enough to want everyone to know he was there. Yet he'd had far more perceived power when he'd been playing the king than he did now.

The puzzle had him shoving his fingers through his hair, frustration piling on top of fatigue and a growing sense that there was no end in sight.

"Harrison?"

At the hesitant sound of his name, he dropped his hand as he turned around. Gwen stood in the open doorway, that same uncertainty on her face as she studied him across the wide expanse of navy-blue carpet.

"The door was open and your secretary is gone," she explained, motioning to the empty office behind her. "The guard at the main door said I could come up."

"It's fine." He'd known she was coming. His assistant had said she'd called that afternoon needing to see him.

Seeing her now, aware of the quiet concern in her eyes, he wasn't sure being alone with her was especially wise.

Having no choice, given the nature of their meeting, he motioned her inside. "Come on in."

"Am I interrupting?"

"No. No," he repeated, because his thoughts hadn't

been getting anywhere, anyway. "I just didn't realize how late it was."

Puzzled by his claim, Gwen crossed her arms over the jacket of her cobalt-blue suit and ventured into his official domain. He'd been staring out the window, the last gasp of the sunset clearly visible, and he hadn't realized the time?

The question only added to the sense of uncertainty she'd felt when she'd first seen him standing there, his white-shirted back to her, his neck bent. Never before had she seen him looking anything less than his confident, capable self. But as he'd stood, framed by the high, arched window, what she'd seen was fatigue and something that looked very much like dejection.

When he faced her now, the dejection had vanished. But the fatigue stayed etched in the sculpted lines of his face. It deepened the creases fanning from the corners of his eyes and the masculine creases bracketing his sensual mouth. That weariness almost seemed tangible to her as he motioned to one of the two burgundy leather wing chairs facing his huge desk.

"Please, sit down." He'd tossed his uniform jacket over the nearest chair. He moved it now to the one beside it.

"I don't know that I'll be that long," she replied, wondering if he realized how dim it was in the office. The only light came from the brass lamp in the leather conversation grouping at the other end of the room. It was as if he'd turned off the overheads to watch the sunset, then totally forgotten his purpose.

"I just wanted...the queen wanted," she corrected, "to know what's being done to find Prince Owen. We've had no word today." She glanced behind her, into the empty outer office. There was a cleaning crew in the hallway. She'd run into them on her way in. "Is there nothing to tell, or should I close the door?"

Harrison's expression was a study in stone as he ran his fingers through his hair once more. "Close the door."

She'd barely turned after the latch caught, when she saw him push aside a pile of documents on the corner of his desk.

The desk itself overflowed with papers, files, charts. The wall and credenza behind him were covered with aerial photographs of battleships at sea, pictures of crews crouched in front of aircraft and the certificates, commendations and royal decrees that proclaimed him the accomplished and powerful man that he was.

Of everything surrounding him at that moment, it was his fatigue that impressed her the most. She truly doubted he thought that fatigue was visible, but as she crossed back toward him, taking in the tall flags flanking the credenza, the young men in the photographs, the sheer volume of work on his desk, she realized that the responsibility she'd seen him bear the past few days barely scratched the surface of what he carried on his broad shoulders every single day.

"There isn't much," he said as she stopped beside the chair he'd cleared for her. "Our trace of the call Prince Broderick received the day before yesterday got us as far as northeastern Majorca before it petered out. The voice prints don't match anything in any of our intelligence files or any on the international criminal registry. Our best shot at the moment is Gage Weston."

"You've called him?"

"I'd put a call in for him before you suggested it," he told her, hitching the fabric at the knee of his slacks as he rested his hip on the corner he'd cleared. "So we were already on the same wavelength there." They actually shared that wavelength on a lot of things, he realized. Far more than he would have ever imagined. Even on those occasions when their approaches seemed diametrically opposed, they were after the same end result. "He just couldn't get here until this afternoon. He's searching the prince's apartments now."

"Have you heard if he's come up with anything?"

His hand clamped the back of his neck again, his fingers kneading at the hard muscles there. "Not yet," he muttered, the furrows in his brow doubling. "I'll call Pierce in a while."

He sounded frustrated. He looked exhausted.

Something about that combination looked very familiar to Gwen. Watching his shoulders rise when he took a deep breath, she realized there had been something familiar, too, about the sense of dejection she'd glimpsed when she'd first seen him minutes ago. She'd seen it before, the morning he'd claimed to have avoided the complications of caring.

She wondered now if what she'd seen hadn't been dejection at all. If what she'd seen then, and what she was seeing now because he was too tired to hide it, was simply loneliness.

"Do you want me to do it?" she asked, unable to imagine how he survived. The burdens he carried, he'd chosen to carry alone, with no one to share that strain at the end of the day.

He shook his head slowly, as if to conserve what energy he still possessed. "Thanks, but I'll do it," he said, still kneading. "There are a couple of other things I need to talk to him about, anyway."

She took a step toward him. "Is there anything else I can do?"

Four feet of carpet separated them. Across that short

distance Harrison lifted his glance from the long length of her shapely calves, past the slim knee-skimming skirt and trim jacket and met the blue of her eyes. There was concern in those intriguing depths. He recognized it because he'd seen it there before, for the queen, for the queen's children. He'd seen it for her own daughter.

On occasion he'd seen it for himself.

Her concern for him had just never seemed quite so obvious as it did now.

"Would it help to talk?" she prompted.

Talking was the last thing he wanted to do. "Probably not. But thanks."

He couldn't imagine dumping the burdens of his job on anyone. He couldn't imagine anyone being worried about him, either. But she was. There was no doubt in his mind of that as she stepped closer, her troubled glance sweeping his face.

The knowledge that she cared touched something inside him that refused to be denied.

Too weary and discouraged to fight it, he found himself craving her caring to the depths of his soul.

"It's been a long day," he explained, trying to deny it anyway. "I'm just..."

She stepped closer when he said nothing else. "Tired?" she ventured.

"That, too," he muttered, not trusting the need building inside him.

"Can you just leave all this and go upstairs? If you're waiting for a call or a delivery or something, I can stay here and get it for you."

"Gwen. Don't."

Confusion clouded concern. "Don't what?"

"You don't have to run interference for me."

"I just wanted to help."

He knew that. That was what was tearing at him. She wanted to make things easier for him.

She was only making them more difficult instead.

The golden light from the lamp behind her made a faint halo of her pale hair. She wore it smoothed back and clipped at her nape, the soft strands fairly begging to be freed of their confines. Her lush mouth was glossed with something that left her lips looking natural and soft.

She was close enough for him to see the chips of turquoise in her eyes. Close enough for him to breathe her scent—that impossible combination of gentleness and seduction.

Close enough to touch.

At that moment that was what he needed very much to do.

With his eyes locked on hers, he snagged her waist and slowly tugged her to him. She took the step easily, looking far more worried about him than with what he was doing when he lifted his free hand to her face.

She had a tiny cleft below her mouth. He touched it lightly, then skimmed his finger to the point of her chin. Intent on the motion of his hand, he slowly traced the delicate line of her jaw to where fragile bone met the pea-size gold ball piercing the small lobe of her ear.

Her skin felt warm to him and soft, like the petal of a rose—though he couldn't honestly say he'd ever stopped to appreciate the beauty of that particular flower before. He was appreciating beauty now, though, he realized, and let his exploration drift down the side of her graceful neck to her collarbones. In the hollow space between them, he felt her pulse skip wildly beneath his touch.

His touch drifted lower, his knuckles brushing the porcelain skin visible between slashes of cobalt linen.

When his fingers slipped beneath that fabric and

stroked the gentle swell he'd brushed once before, her lips parted, a tremulous breath slipping between them.

Gwen said nothing. She couldn't. She couldn't even move. His hand at her waist rested as lightly as the brush of his fingers against her skin. Yet, he might as well have shackled and bound her. Raw need shadowed the sculpted angles and planes of his face. A kind of hunger that made her ache inside even as he sent little licks of fire racing along her nerves. She couldn't have pulled from him had her next breath depended on it.

His hand slipped to the top button of her jacket.

It was only then that his glance drifted up. That same hunger was in his eyes, turning them diamond bright as they locked on hers.

She swallowed and stayed right where she was.

The gleam in his gaze turned feral, but the motion of his fingers remained unhurried as he slowly flicked open one button. Then, another. And one more.

It wasn't until the front of her jacket was open that he let his glance move from her face. When he did, he slipped his hands between the sides of the deep-blue fabric, moving them back to expose the ivory satin camisole she wore beneath it.

She had no idea what made his features go so taut just then. But what he did made her throat go tight. Flexing his fingers against the sides of her hips, he pulled her nearer and rested his forehead between her breasts. His broad shoulders seemed to sag when his breath leaked out in a long, relieved sigh.

Caution filled her as she lifted her hand and touched it to the back of his head. She couldn't believe how defenseless he suddenly seemed, or how exhausted he had to be to expose such vulnerability to her. The way he held her, with his arms snug around her hips, his head leaning against her, made it almost seem as if he were seeking comfort.

She didn't know which pulled at her more profoundly. The thought that he truly needed solace or the thought that he wanted it from her. The fact that he needed it at all had her threading her fingers through his surprisingly soft hair, cradling her to him as she would a tired, lonely little boy. Except the little boy in him had long ago ceased to exist. And the needs of the grown man were creating needs in her that she had long denied.

There was so much about this powerful, complicated male that she never would have suspected, so much about him that drew her closer. In so many ways he'd touched her heart. As he nuzzled the slick fabric of her camisole with his cheek, all she considered was how he was touching her body.

Slick fabric slid against her as his lips edged to the curve of her breast, his mouth seeking bare skin. He found it just above scalloped lace. The feel of his lips and his warm breath on her flesh sent delicious little shivers racing through her in the moments before he tugged the silky fabric from the waistband of her skirt. A uneven heartbeat later, his hands were under that fabric and he pushed it up to trace a trail of heat over her stomach to the filmy barrier of her bra.

The pads of his fingers tightened against her as he sought her through the sheer fabric. Hot and moist, his breath penetrated the thin piece of lingerie, sapping the strength from her knees. He threatened to buckle them completely when he found her nipple.

Her fingers slipped from the back of his head. With both hands, she gripped his solid shoulders to keep herself from sinking to the floor.

Stark need sculpted his features when he finally looked up.

For a moment he remained silent, his hands still holding her hips. His touch was measuring, as if he might be imagining how she would fit against him.

"You know what I want, Gwen."

Her heart already felt as if it were bruising her breastbone with each beat. His husky statement threatened to pound it right out of her chest.

She definitely knew what he wanted. He'd told her. In explicit detail.

Heaven help her, she wanted it, too.

"I believe you made it fairly clear," she whispered, her stomach muscles quivering inches from his thumbs.

"Only fairly?"

A heady glint of challenge flashed in his eyes. Sliding one hand to the bare skin on her back, he tapped a small pad by his telephone and rose up over her. Behind him the lock of his door tumbled into place. Behind her the tall curtain of navy-blue drapes rode across the wall to cover the window.

The electric hum of the curtain mechanism gave way to the pounding of her pulse in her ears as he slipped the clip from her hair and lowered his head.

"Then, let's see what I can do to make you completely certain."

Anticipation shot through her as he captured her mouth and pulled her against him, fitting her the way she imagined he'd considered only moments before. His erection pressed her stomach. His tongue felt as hot as his hands.

She clung to him, melting inside at the feel of his hard, honed body seeking hers. With each passing day he had awakened feelings she'd forgotten, sensations that had lain dormant and dying.

Those feelings rushed back with a vengeance, compounding themselves when he slowly slipped off her jacket and eased the thin straps of her camisole and bra over her shoulders. A quick flick of his fingers, and the bra was on the floor, the satin at her waist. The coolness of air against her skin had barely registered when he sank back with her to the desk, his mouth still devouring hers.

She was wrong. It was more than reawakening she experienced beneath his touch. He electrified nerves she didn't know she possessed when he cupped the aching fullness of her breast and trailed his lips down her throat. Teasing, taunting, he overwhelmed her with sensation when he found her turgid peak once more. Then he soothed her, caressed her, molding his hands to her sides, tasting the flesh of her stomach, her ribs.

Her eyes drifted shut, her head falling back at the exquisite weakness coursing through her. With her throat exposed, he carried his exploration there, and caught her behind the neck to bring her mouth back to his.

He'd said he wanted to taste all of her body. When he tugged down the zipper on the side of her skirt, the thought that he actually intended to do just that drew a faint moan of longing. He drank that sound like a man dying of thirst, a groan of his own rumbling from deep in his chest.

He'd robbed her of sensibility the moment he'd rested his head against her. Now, he was crumbling barriers, destroying any possible defense and shredding any hope of sanity.

Her skirt had been tossed to the chair when he moved her hand from his shoulder to his tie.

"You wanted to help." His husky words vibrated against her lips. "How are you at untying knots?"

Feeling tied in knots herself, she murmured back, "I think I can manage."

"Then, please," he growled, before he closed that negligible distance "don't let me stop you."

She wasn't sure how she accomplished the small task with his hands busily stripping away her slip and pantyhose. But the knot came undone, along with the buttons on his shirt. As he had with her, she slipped her hands between the sides of the fabric to push them apart. Unlike him, her touch was less certain as she explored the sculpted muscles of his beautiful chest, the corded strength of his biceps.

She couldn't believe that she was free to caress him, that she could make him tremble as easily as he did her. He was a man of such control, such discipline. Yet she made his breath snag with the light brush of her fingers over his flat nipple, caused it to hitch again when she leaned forward to touch it with her tongue. She loved that she could do that to him. She loved the way his eyes stayed closed when she kissed the silvering hair at his temple, the lobe of his ear. She loved the low, guttural way he growled her name when her hand ventured low over the washboard ripples of his abdomen. Mostly, she realized, she loved him.

It wasn't wise. It wasn't rational. It wasn't even sensible, considering all that she knew about him. But the knowledge was there, as sure and as certain as anything she'd ever felt in her entire life.

His heart was thundering beneath her palm when his arm slipped behind her thighs. His other locked around her back an instant before he rose and swept her off her feet.

Like a primitive warrior claiming his mate, he carried her to the leather sofa and lowered her to stand beside it in the buttery glow of the room's only light. Her feet had barely hit the ground when he bent to her neck, kissing the sensitive flesh behind her ear while he propped his foot on the sofa to untie his shoe, then toed off that one to do the same with the other. The faint clink of metal as he unbuckled his belt joined the intimate sounds of their breathing and the warning rasp of his zipper.

"I want you," he murmured, peeling off his shirt, ridding himself of his pants. "I want you now."

She was like a drug in his body, each taste of her making him crave her more. And the more he craved, the more he needed to touch, to explore, to learn every inch of her.

His flesh felt on fire as he caught her to him, lowering her to the soft cushions, covering her with his body. The passion he'd suspected in her was definitely there. But even now, naked in his arms, she wasn't letting that passion completely go. He wanted her to feel the same urgency clawing at him, the same need that had him damning restraint because he'd never needed any woman the way he needed her at that moment.

Daring her to hold back, he kissed his way down her stomach, stroking her thighs, teasing the very heart of her femininity.

"Harrison."

His name was a thin, ragged whisper on her lips.

"Say it again," he murmured, his voice a dark rasp as she jerked beneath him. "My name. Say it again."

She did, the pleading sound of it inflaming him as much as the feel of her clinging hands.

He'd intended to wait. To drive her mad with the same desire he felt before caving in to it himself. The way she reached for him, her fingers digging into his flesh to pull him closer, her mouth seeking his, destroyed the thought completely.

Leather squeaked as he pulled her under him. She urged him closer, wrapping her legs around him, making it impossible for him to remember why it had been so important that he retain that last bit of control. All that mattered was that he get inside her.

Then, he was, and he wasn't sure he was thinking at all. His existence narrowed to nothing but sensation. The feel of her welcoming him. The rightness of being exactly where he was as he thrust forward wanting to get as close as he humanly could. Then he was aware only of the need to take her with him before his mind blanked and he spilled himself inside her.

Awareness returned by degrees.

His labored breathing began to slow. His thundering heart worked down to a steadier beat. The thin sheen of perspiration on his body cooled the heated skin of his back. But his first awareness was of the warm, sweetly shaped woman in his arms.

Her supple muscles had been utterly relaxed, as spent and limp as his own. With her body curled around his, he could feel a fine tension beginning to thread its way through her limbs.

Still holding her, he angled his weight to the side as much as he could on the narrow sofa and slipped his fingers through her hair. He had the feeling reality was trying to tug her back, too. But the way she'd tucked her head against his shoulder made him think that she wasn't quite ready to emerge from the protective little island of intimacy they'd created.

That was fine with him. He wasn't ready to let go of it himself. She felt too good in his arms. Later he could deal with all the reasons why he shouldn't have caved in to his need for her. Right now he just wanted to absorb the strangely peaceful feeling of her lying against him, and hold off the world for as long as he could.

The thought had barely registered when the electronic ring of the telephone mercilessly tore through the intimate silence. Reality jerked hard. In the space of a heartbeat he felt her limbs tense, and all the reasons he should never have reached for her lined up in his mind like a battalion of good little soldiers.

"I need to answer that."

She blinked up at his chin, caution shadowing her lovely face as she shoved her hair from her eyes.

His jaw tightened as the electronic summons sounded again. Pulling his body from hers, he groped for the telephone on the table at the end of the big sofa.

"Do you want my shirt?"

"Please."

The awkwardness Gwen felt was undeniable as he sat up, answered the phone with a flat "Monteque" and snatched his shirt from the floor. He didn't seem the least self-conscious about his nakedness as he handed the garment to her. He didn't even seem particularly conscious of hers when he picked up his pants and pulled them on while holding the receiver to his ear with his shoulder.

"Sure," he said, shoving his fingers through his hair on his way to his desk. "I can be at the palace in ten minutes. Where do we meet?"

Quickly stuffing her arms into his sleeves, Gwen looked from Harrison's magnificent back to the clothes draped over the arm of the wing chair and scattered over the carpet. She couldn't believe how completely she'd abandoned herself to him. Or how uncertain she was feeling now that she was no longer in his arms.

The vulnerability she'd sensed in him was nowhere in evidence. The need for her was gone. He was once again completely in control, and she had no idea where that left her.

She picked up her underwear, slipped them on and looked around for her bra. Spotting it puddled by the nearest wing chair, she headed there, snaring her stockings on the way.

She'd just picked up the filmy lace along with his tie when he hung up and turned to face her.

Before he could say a word, she skimmed a glance up his powerful chest and held out the long strip of black fabric. "Can I get a ride with you?"

Holding out the camisole he'd picked up himself, he traded lace for gabardine. "Of course you can."

Frowning, he caught her by the chin when she started to turn away.

He regretted the interruption that had pulled him so rudely from her. He wasn't terribly proud of the fact that he was grateful for it, too. It gave him no time to consider why he should have kept his hands to himself.

Having blown it already, he threaded his fingers through her thoroughly tousled hair. She looked like a lovely fallen angel, he thought, and brushed his lips over her lush mouth.

"Are you all right?" he asked.

No, she wasn't. Not with him looking so anxious to leave. "I'm fine," she lied, and gave him a faint little smile to prove it.

"Good." Seeming perfectly willing to believe her, he pulled back and handed her her slip. "We need to go. Gage found something."

Chapter Eleven

The ride to the palace in the back of the black sedan took all of five minutes. Harrison spent most of that time on the cell phone asking Carson Logan to meet him and Pierce outside Prince Owen's room and taking a call from Sir Selwyn who was apparently already there.

Gwen spent it nursing the knot of nerves in her stomach.

She had pulled herself together as best she could in the small private bathroom in Harrison's office, then hurried with him down to meet the car. Despite the fact that she'd combed her hair into its sleek, low ponytail after she'd found her clip and had smoothed most of the wrinkles from her suit, she felt totally thrown together.

She was missing an earring.

It was a stupid thing to obsess about. The small gold-colored ball that matched the one she'd taken off and put in her handbag wasn't even a good piece of jewelry. But thinking about it was preferable to beating herself up over falling in love with a man whose idea of commitment probably meant sticking around for the weekend.

She didn't fault him for the hurried departure. Whatever Gage Weston had found had to be important for the entire RET to be converging on the prince's apartment. She didn't even have a problem understanding that Harrison was a man consumed by duty and dedication, and that duty had been and always would be his first priority. It was all he'd really ever had.

She understood the circumstances. She'd just had no practice having an affair. Beyond absolute discretion, she had no idea what the protocol was. There were no manuals or rules that she was aware of, and it wasn't the sort of thing she could ask her friends about without raising questions that canceled the discretion part.

She wasn't even sure what Harrison wanted from her now. He'd threaded his fingers through hers and curled them together between them in the seat, but he hadn't said a word to her since they'd entered the car.

Even his glance told her nothing. His focus remained mostly on the back of their driver's head.

"We're past the main gate," she heard him say to Sir Selwyn, his thumb absently rubbing hers. "I'll be upstairs in about three minutes."

The reassuring warmth of his palm seeped into her. She couldn't believe how grateful she was for the small contact. Or how relieved she was that he wanted it himself. Hating how vulnerable she felt, determined not to let him know it, she glanced toward the side portico that led to the private residence. As they approached it, she could see Colonel Prescott pacing between two of the large columns waiting for the admiral to arrive. Whatever news he had was apparently too significant to wait.

The cell phone closed with a quiet click. In the dusky light from the lampposts they passed, Harrison's rugged features looked carved of granite.

"You'll tell me what they found?" she asked, knowing it was more necessary at the moment to focus on what they were doing now, rather than what they had done.

"I imagine we'll hear together. Prescott looks like he's ready to pace out of his skin."

"He does seem rather anxious."

His eyes glittered on hers as the car came to a stop, his expression unreadable in the shadows. But he said nothing else in the few seconds that passed before he gave her hand a little squeeze and pulled his away.

His driver had already climbed out and was opening his door.

Her door swung open an instant later.

"My lady," came the greeting from her side.

Harrison was already at the back of the car. Colonel Prescott stood with his hand extended, waiting to help her.

"Lady Corbin," he greeted, polite as always. "I didn't realize you would be joining us."

Smile, she coached herself, and managed a commendable one as she rose to stand beside him.

"I'd gone to see if there was anything to report to Her Majesty about Prince Owen," she told him, enormously grateful for the preoccupation that had him barely smiling back. "The admiral kindly allowed me to ride with him when you called."

She should have felt more awkward. She was sure she would have, too, if Harrison hadn't come up her behind just then and flattened his hand against the small of her back.

"I think she should come with us." He guided her

forward, the gesture appearing more courteous than personal to anyone watching. "It will save having to repeat what she needs to relay to the queen."

The colonel seemed to appreciate the logic in that. Falling into step beside her, he also seemed as aware as Harrison was of the others around them. Both men fell silent as they headed past the sentries flanking the French doors under the portico. Another set of guards stood post inside at the arched entry to the long colonnade.

Gwen was aware of those other ears, too. But she was far more conscious of the proprietary feel of Harrison's hand as he guided her into the marble-pillared walkway, and a vague sense of loss when he no longer had an excuse to touch her and that reassuring weight fell away.

"So what did Gage find?" he asked, his voice low.

Under the echo of their footsteps, Pierce spoke just as quietly. "A handmade weapon. It was wedged between the leg and headboard of the prince's bed. It's a five-sided throwing device. We've already had it finger-printed."

"A throwing device," Harrison repeated, his brow furrowing. "Like a ninja star?"

"Exactly."

Gwen frowned in incomprehension.

Harrison must have noticed.

"It's basically a couple of inches of metal disc with points or blades that give it a star shape," he told her. "It's small, convenient and silent. A master can throw one into the neck of his target from a hundred feet away and you'll barely see his hand move."

Gwen gave a small shudder. Charming, she thought.

"I've only known one man who could do that." His tone turned forbidding. "He was Royal Guard until he disappeared a couple of years ago."

"Gunther Westbury." Pierce gave a grim nod. "The device had the same inverted *W* on the end of each spike that was Westbury's trademark. It also had his prints on it."

His name had actually once been Sir Gunther Westbury. Gwen remembered him because his departure had been such a scandal. No one knew why the good and powerful knight had suddenly resigned his commission, returned the sword of his knighthood and deserted his country, but King Morgan had been wounded to the core by his defection, and absolutely furious.

The thought of such a traitorous action clearly did not please Harrison, either. But finally having a solid lead definitely did. "Given the time he spent in the corps, he would certainly know the layout of the grounds and the routines of the guards. Once it was out that the king was ill, he would have known security would be lighter around the king's apartments because he wasn't there. With Prince Dylan gone, that left only Owen in that wing."

Pierce had reached the same conclusion. "We figure he didn't go after him right away, though. We know Westbury had no problem entering the king's apartments. Since he used the king's stationery and computer for the ransom note, he would have gone there first, then headed off to get Owen."

"Who put up a fight," Harrison said, continuing the scenario. "That would explain why the weapon was in such an odd place. It isn't something Westbury would have used at close range, so it must have come off him during the struggle and been kicked under the bed."

The golden threads in Harrison's beret medallion caught the light from the wall sconces as he drew to a halt. On his shoulders the stars of his rank gleamed against navy blue. "Back up to the stationery," he muttered, suddenly looking troubled. "He would have gone into the king's apartment and used that to show how vulnerable the royal family is. Do we have any idea how long he was in there?"

"The man trained for covert ops. He can move like a shadow. It could have been anywhere from minutes to an hour." Pierce's voice went flat as he concluded. "I take it you're thinking the same thing we are."

"So what's being done about it?"

"The dogs are in there now."

"Where are the royals?"

Pierce's first thought was obviously for his fiancée. "Meredith is at my flat with her bodyguard. Princess Megan is being guarded at her home with her husband. Princess Ana is with the queen in the queen's apartment. We ran the dogs through their wing first."

Gwen clutched her handbag a little tighter. They had come to a stop not far from the foyer with its wide stairway separating the two wings. The usual red-jacketed soldiers flanked it. As she had listened with growing trepidation to the men's exchange, she had been vaguely aware of the guards. Only now did she notice two men in army uniforms conversing with each other at the top of the stairway. One leaned over to check the underside of the stairway banister.

She wasn't totally sure what was happening. But she was growing more apprehensive than she cared to let on. "Excuse me, Colonel. The dogs you're speaking of. What exactly are they looking for?"

The young commander's glance cut to the man beside her. "Any sort of incendiary device," Pierce replied at Harrison's faint nod. "Or anything that might harm a person when he opened a door or drawer or that sort of thing. But the queen's wing is clear,'' he hurried to remind her. ''A special team went in right after the dogs.''

''My room was searched, too?''

''Yes, ma'am. You weren't available, so we had to go in without you. I assure you, we disturbed as little as possible.''

She understood the necessity. She was glad they'd done what they had. Still, the thought of booby traps, and strange men going through her private space left her feeling vulnerable in ways far different than she had only minutes ago.

There were advantages to focusing on obligations. Wondering if that might not be why Harrison devoted his life to the responsibilities he'd chosen to accept, she forced her attention to the queen. If bomb-sniffing canines had been through the royal apartments, there was no doubt in her mind that the queen was wide awake and pacing the nap off the antique carpets in her rooms.

''Did you speak with Her Majesty?''

''Sir Selwyn did. About half an hour ago.'' The steady beat of footsteps drew Pierce's glance behind him. After noting the approach of one of the men from the stairs, he turned back to her. ''All she's been told is that we needed to search the wing as a precaution. She and Princess Ana were sitting with the king at the time. They were safe in the tunnel, so we kept them there until the search was completed.''

And while all that had been going on, Gwen thought, she had been safe in the arms of the man beside her.

It didn't occur to her to question that she had felt completely secure when Harrison held her. Something about him had made her feel protected from the moment he'd thrown his jacket over her shoulders and pushed her in from the rain. In his position and in his soul, he was a man of principle. A noble man. A defender to the core of his being. She could trust him with her very life.

She just couldn't trust him with her heart.

"Then, she doesn't know of the weapon Duke Weston found?" she asked, suddenly aware that she'd actually inched closer to Harrison as Pierce had spoken. "Or, what made you conduct the search?"

"No, my lady." Apology entered the younger man's tone. "If you'll excuse me for a moment?"

The captain who'd approached stopped a discreet distance behind him. Turning on his heal, Pierce took a step to see what the problem was, only to turn right back with a frown carved into his face.

"There's one more thing," he said to Harrison. "The weapon has a black sword etched into it. It looks as if Westbury might have joined the Black Knights." Looking as matter-of-fact as he sounded, he nodded to her, then glanced back at his colleague's equally impassive expression. "I'll see you upstairs."

To Gwen, Harrison's implacable features gave away nothing as Pierce and the other officer headed for the wide marble stairway. Like the other morning when he and the others had been informed of the call from the kidnappers, Harrison's thoughts seemed to remain solely on what needed to be dealt with at that moment.

What he needed to deal with at that particular moment was her.

"What should I tell Her Majesty?" she asked, certain from the way he glanced after the men that he was anxious to go. "I'm not sure I understand what's going on."

He wasn't, either. The information about Westbury was huge. He just needed time to digest it. "Tell her we have reason to believe the prince's kidnapper was in the palace long enough to have sabotaged certain areas. The princes' rooms and the king's apartments in particular. That's why the dogs were brought in.''

"She's going to want to know why that wasn't done before.''

"Not if you don't bring it up.''

The look she gave him was remarkably level.

"So why wasn't it?''

"Because it first appeared that the kidnapper's goal was only to take the prince hostage. Since nothing looked disturbed anywhere other than the prince's room, no one had reason to suspect any other motive.''

"Except to prove how vulnerable the royal family is by using the king's personal stationery,'' she reminded him. "And maybe,'' she speculated, easily accepting his touch when he took her elbow to walk her to the queen's drawing room, "to prove how good he is himself.''

"I don't doubt that.'' Letting his thoughts follow her lead, distracted by it, he unconsciously started to slide his hand to her back. Catching himself because there were guards ahead of them, he dropped his hand completely. He hadn't even realized what he was doing until he was doing it, and he was standing too close to her to make the gesture look casual. "He was known to master everything he took on.''

Seeing his considering frown, Gwen hesitated.

"What are you thinking?'' she asked, a moment later.

"That the Knights apparently always dress in black.''

Her expression mirrored his. "It would be a practical color. Pierce just said he moves like a shadow. Black would just make him less visible.''

"It's also the color of the ninja.''

The information seemed significant enough to Harrison to deepen his concentration. It meant nothing to Gwen. All she knew about ninja was that she'd once bought pajamas with ninja turtles on them for Mrs. Ferth's grandson's birthday. The child had apparently been crazy about the militant-looking little reptiles. "And the weapon he uses is theirs, too?"

They passed the guards, their voices as hushed as their footsteps as they turned into the wide, richly carpeted hallway.

"I think he might be into the whole philosophy. The ninja practice a form of martial art called ninjitsu. The original form was banned in Japan a few hundred years ago, but back then they were masters with their bodies and with weapons. They were also practiced at using bombs and poisons."

Intrigued, disturbed, she searched his profile. His fatigue was still there, but the weariness was gone. The adrenaline of discovery had replaced it. "By poison are you thinking of the encephalitis?"

Light glinted in his eyes as he glanced at her. "I hadn't gotten that far," he admitted, "but that would fit, too. I was thinking more of what this could tell us about the Black Knights. *Ninjutsu* means *the art of stealing in.* Another way to put it is *espionage.*

"But *espionage* means *to spy* or *obtain information.*" She was lost again. "How does that fit?"

He didn't know. He didn't like that, either. But he was feeling close to something major. If he trusted anything, it was his instincts.

"I just know it does," he concluded, and stopped because they were nearly at the guards by the queen's door.

"I'm going up to see what else they have."

"You'll let us know if you find out anything else?"

The play of emotions over her face tugged hard at something deep inside him. He wasn't going to worry now about what that something was. He wasn't going to worry, either, about why he was suddenly feeling so cheated by the timing of Pierce's phone call.

An hour passed before word came that the king's wing was secure. A guard brought the news to the drawing room door. There were no other messages, however, and though the news relieved Gwen, the queen and Ana enormously, the information wasn't enough.

Within minutes of the young officer's departure, Ana had said good-night to seek escape in sleep, and Marissa was back to pacing restlessly across the room.

Within fifteen minutes Gwen was ready to pace with her.

"Why don't you go to bed, Marissa? It's late. I'm sure if they find anything else significant, the admiral will make sure you know first thing in the morning."

"I couldn't sleep if I tried. All I can think about is that people we've trusted keep turning on us. And that awful little weapon. I hate thinking of Owen fighting that horrid man. I hate thinking that he's hurt and no one's helping him." She turned, her arms snugged tight around her middle, her voice a raw whisper. "I hate all of this."

"Marissa, stop," Gwen urged, feeling totally helpless. She wished desperately that there was something she could do for her friend. She just had no idea what that something could be. "You're going to make yourself sick."

"I am sick." Tears streamed down the weary woman's cheeks, silent testimony to pain she no longer knew how to deal with. "I'm sick to death of not knowing what's happening. I want to know everything those men up there know. I want to know what they're going to do with the information. I don't want them to wait until they get all their clues put together or whatever it is they're doing. I want to know what they're doing *now*."

Considering the number of people involved in the investigation, it would be nearly impossible to track down what each of them was doing at that particular moment. Gwen didn't bother mentioning that to the distraught queen, though. As she stepped into her path and touched her arm, she was thinking only that she'd just found a small way to help. "I'm going to get Ana to stay with you until I get back."

"Where are you going?"

"You just said you wanted to know what they're doing. I'm going upstairs to see what else I can find out."

Marissa had only been venting. Gwen knew that. But there was no mistaking the relief that swept the woman's tear-stained face. "Thank you, Gwen," she murmured. "But, please, don't bother Ana. I'm all right. Really."

Gwen didn't believe the queen for a moment. Marissa wasn't all right and she wouldn't be until some semblance of normalcy returned to her life. But if she didn't want her child disturbed, then Gwen would abide by her wishes. There was no point in upsetting her further.

There was also no point in denying how ambivalent she felt as she hurried toward the one man on all of Penwyck she should be running from. In a matter of days Harrison had turned her small, tidy world entirely upside down. He made her feel emotions she'd somehow buried. He made her want all the things she'd come to believe she could live without. He made her want *him*.

For years she'd lived her life through and for her daughter and her queen, and somehow that had always been enough.

Now she knew it would never be enough again.

It was with that unsettling realization that she offered a strained smile to the guards in the foyer and started toward the wide stairway that curved upstairs.

Because she was known to them, the guards at the foot of the stairs let her pass. Since her apartment was down past Princess Ana's rooms, the upstairs guards knew her, too. It was only when she headed toward the opposite wing that one of them stopped her.

The lanky soldier appeared to be half her age, a fresh-faced young man life had yet to rob of his innocence. "I'm sorry, ma'am" he said, his voice a few octives from real authority. "This area has been secured."

She wondered if Harrison had ever appeared that young.

The sudden thought gave her pause. She truly doubted that he had. A man robbed of his childhood would have grown up feeling very old inside. Old and unwanted.

"I need to speak with Admiral Monteque." She really didn't need Harrison messing with her heart right now. What she needed was simply to find him. "I understand he's in Prince Owen's rooms."

"He's not here, ma'am. He left about half an hour ago."

"What about Colonel Prescott?"

"He left with him."

"Then, Duke Logan or Sir Selwyn?"

"I'm sorry," he repeated. "They aren't here, either."

Behind him, she could see a few men conversing in a knot near the end of the long burgundy-carpeted wing by Prince Owen's rooms, but without a single member of the RET around, she had no hope of gaining information from any one of them.

The fact that the entire RET had suddenly left gave her pause.

"What about a rather-dashing looking gentleman with black hair and green eyes?" she inquired, thinking of the enigmatic man they had turned to for help. "He's not military."

It was doubtful that Duke Gage Weston had been introduced to anyone. Or, that either of the decidedly youthful men respectfully keeping her at bay would know who he was. International spies tended to keep low profiles.

"I don't know about the dashing part," the soldier qualified, frowning at the term, "but a civilian with dark hair left with them, ma'am."

"With whom?"

"The admiral and the colonel."

A black gun strap slashed his red jacket. Clipped to it at his shoulder was a small communicating device. She nodded toward it. "Can you reach either one of them on that?"

"I'd have to go through the security office, but I could get a message to them, ma'am."

"Would you do that, please? Just tell Admiral Monteque that the queen has a question."

The young man was most obliging. In a matter of minutes a call came back.

"He sent a message asking you to meet him in the foyer."

"Thank you…Corporal," she said, double-checking his insignia to be sure of his rank. "You've been very helpful."

Gwen didn't stop when she reached the foyer. Instead she crossed the expansive space, turned into the alcove and slipped behind the false column obscuring the door to the underground tunnel the royals used. She didn't know how many relays her call had taken to get through to Harrison, but she had the feeling it had been several. It was doubtful that a cell signal would reach into the depths of the tunnel. Considering all of the high-tech equipment she'd seen behind the glass guard-wall, the signal probably would have been blocked, anyway.

At the bottom of the stairs, the door gave way with a faint squeak. In the small space separating her from the door ahead of her, she reached for the handle of the second one.

It opened on its own.

Her heart gave a startled jerk. It bumped her ribs again when she saw Harrison blocking her path.

His dark eyebrows jammed together. "How did you know where I was?"

The craggy lines of his face revealed far more curiosity than displeasure. "It just made sense," she replied, dropping her hand from her heart. "You were all together with Duke Weston and the tunnel is the closest secure place for all of you to talk."

Holding the big door open with one hand, he quietly scanned her face. She studied his just as openly. The light from the overhead bulb was bright and unforgiving.

"Where do you want to talk?" he asked.

"Wherever you want," she replied, curling her fingers to keep from touching the haggard lines carved by his mouth. "The queen just needs to know everything you've come up with."

"Everything?"

"That's what she said."

"Does she want to see me?"

She shook her head, wishing now that she hadn't interrupted him. Her request only added to the demands weighing on him. But the reason for her request was to ease the mind of the queen.

Torn, she murmured, "You can just tell me and I'll pass it on."

He looked as if he were running on nothing but sheer will as he reached for her hand. "Then, let's talk right here," he said, and tugged her through the doorway.

They wouldn't be overheard here. They wouldn't even be seen. There were no people. No bugs. No cameras. Considering that, Harrison wearily leaned against the old limestone wall and pulled her to him. He was too tired to wrestle with why he wanted her in his arms. He just knew that he did.

She came willingly, her body going soft against his.

"Everything," he repeated, smoothing his hand over her hair to coax her head to his shoulder. He breathed in her scent, felt himself stir in some places, relax in others. Interesting, he thought, the range of effects she had on him.

"You were told the wing is secure?"

"We were." She nodded against his chest, her voice soft, calming. "But that was all."

"I didn't want to send any more information by guard," he told her. "We didn't find any evidence of sabotage, but while the team was searching for planted devices we did discover that the king's apartments had been searched. By a pro," he added, more interested at the moment in how good Gwen felt than the unforgivable breach in security. "Nothing appeared disturbed on the surface. That was why the security team that checked the area after the prince's kidnapping didn't look further.

"But we got Selwyn in there with Gage a while ago," he continued, liking the easy way she snuggled against him. "Since Selwyn is the king's private secretary, he had a good idea of what was kept where. Between the two of them, it was apparent that someone went through pretty much everything looking for something.''

She tipped her head back, curiosity locking her eyes on his. ''Any idea what?''

''None.''

Curiosity faded. ''I'm sorry.''

He heard regret in her tone. He could even see it in the fragile lines of her face. But that regret didn't seem to be so much for the lack of information as it was for the disappointment and frustration that lack brought him.

He wasn't accustomed to that sort of caring. The sympathy touched him, but the caring brought a hint of need he forced himself to ignore in order to concentrate.

''We also might know where they're keeping Owen. We know Gunther Westbury lives in a villa on Majorco,'' he told her, aware that her entire body had just gone on alert. ''Gage knows the place, but it's practically inaccessible because of the way it's situated above the ocean. We think the Black Knights may have Owen there.''

''How will you find out for sure?''

''That's what we're working on now. We need surveillance first to see if we can spot him, or anything that looks as if a particular area of the place is being guarded. If we do, we'll take it from there.''

Gwen fell silent. She just stood in his arms, her hands flat on his lapels and her eyes searching his face.

He had no idea why the concern crept into her expression, but he now recognized her look as easily as he would his own face in the mirror.

''Then, you need to get back to your meeting,'' she finally said.

She understood his priorities. She knew that his obligations demanded his attention. He'd never known a woman who'd appreciated how little choice he had when it came to responsibilities. But then, he supposed, she *would* understand. Duty was her life, too.

Reluctance had him drawing a deep breath. "I know," he murmured, and slipped his hand around the back of her neck.

He'd thought he'd been relieved when the phone had interrupted before. But he realized now that he'd been robbed of this. This chance to simply hold her.

Edging her closer, he lowered his head. "I should have thought of meeting you here myself."

He brushed his lips over hers, thinking just to taste her and let her go. But that small contact wasn't enough. So he pulled her closer, drank more deeply and felt his body jolt with the memory of being inside her.

Gwen felt his body harden, felt the muscles in his chest and thighs go deliciously tight. It hadn't been her intention to seek privacy with him. At least the thought hadn't been a conscious one. She'd just wanted information to take back to Marissa and she had wanted it as soon as she could get it.

Any further thought of her purpose dissolved under the gentle assault of his kiss. His scent was familiar to her now. Citrus aftershave and warm male. The combination mingled with the taste of strong coffee and the feel of his hand pressing the small of her back. He fitted her to him like old lovers, seeking her softness, altering her breathing, weakening her knees.

His own breathing seemed a little ragged when he finally lifted his head and settled his hands on her shoulders.

"We both need to go," he murmured.

Looking sorely tempted to kiss her again, he eased her back. For good measure he dropped his hands and opened the door so she would leave.

Later, he told himself, as he watched her give him a little nod and murmur, "Good night." Later, he repeated, when she walked past the door he held and disappeared behind the one beyond. That was when he would think about what he was doing with her.

Right now he needed to find the prince.

Chapter Twelve

"We have a profile shot of the prince through one of the windows on the cliff side. Looks like a storage room. Bars on the window. No balcony. No visible exterior access. The villa is walled and guarded by at least a dozen men. There are probably more, but that's all we can count in the photographs."

Pierce slid the sheets of reconnaissance photographs across the mahogany conference table. Low clouds and fog had hung over the island of Majorco all day, making recon shots impossible until the weather had finally given them a break an hour before sunset.

Harrison and Sir Selwyn stood shoulder to shoulder, studying what had come off the intelligence satellite feed only minutes ago.

"Look here." Harrison pointed to a shot of another storage room. "This second window. You can see racks of guns and boxes of ammo."

"Here, too." Pierce indicated another barred window. "They have a regular arsenal."

Harrison scanned the photos, sweeping past some, studying others more closely. "Then, we'll take an arsenal with us, too. I'll get an RNS team in here to go over these with you, Colonel." The Royal Navy SEALs were the only men for the job. "They're going to need maps of that end of the island. Land and underwater. That shoreline looks too rocky to get in close with an amphibious launch. They can scuba in from an air drop, but they won't be able to bring him out over those boulders. Especially if he's injured. We need to coordinate a chopper pickup or stuff a vehicle back in the trees to get them to a pickup point. It'll depend on the weather and how the team captain sees his options."

"Are you going to try for a rescue tonight?"

Harrison hesitated. In theory the rescue could be put together in a matter of hours. "We have good teams here we could use. But the best of the best is training off the Hebrides." He glanced at his watch. "If I send for them now, it will be 2:00 a.m. before they can get here. It could be daybreak before they'd be ready to go. We need the cover of darkness for this."

Pondering his colleague's conclusions, Sir Selwyn straightened. "Are you saying you want to wait?"

"I'm saying I don't want to blow this. The extra time will allow us to get my best team onboard and put back-ups in place. We have one shot to rescue the prince. The more contingencies we plan for and the more information we can gather about what's going on in that villa, the better chance we have at success. If we can get it put together tonight and have time before dawn, then we go for it. If not, we wait."

As if starting a mental clock, Selwyn gave a slow,

considering nod. "The treaty is being signed at the banquet. Right about eight."

No one was more aware of the time factor than Harrison was. "Then, that means if we don't get in there tonight, we have until just after dark tomorrow."

He wouldn't rush if he had a choice. Mistakes were made when an operation was thrown together. Critical points could be overlooked. Had this information not been discovered until tomorrow, then he would have had no choice but to act with what they had. But there was a choice, and whenever he had options, he inevitably chose the one guaranteed the greatest chance of success—even if success meant taking a calculated risk.

Selwyn and Pierce both knew how his mind worked. They also knew he was a master of logistics.

"I'll get someone on those maps," Pierce said, tacitly agreeing to the plan as he turned toward the door. "We could use some night-vision shots of the villa, too. That's the easiest way to get a body count to see how many men our guys will be up against."

Running through a mental check list, Harrison absently pushed his hand into his pants pocket. His knuckle rolled over a pea-size metal ball. "I'll get a jet up."

"Will you inform Lady Corbin?" asked Sir Selwyn.

The metal ball had a stem. Rolling it between his fingers, Harrison considered the question for all of two seconds. "I need to call in the team and scramble another plane to get those night shots," he replied, letting the stem go. "It would be better if you do that."

"I'll be glad to. It was just that she asked about you when I told her that the surveillance planes had been sent up this morning. Since you've been working so closely together, I thought perhaps you might want to see her yourself."

Harrison couldn't imagine Gwen saying anything that would give the king's secretary reason to look at him with such speculation. Unless, he thought, the curiosity was there simply because of the circumstances. The entire RET knew the two of them had been thrown together a lot lately. They also had to be aware that the initial friction between them no longer existed.

What they couldn't possible know was that the relationship had turned into something it shouldn't have.

Keeping his tone deceptively disinterested, he stepped toward the phone on the credenza. "She asked about me?"

"It was actually more of a comment," the very proper gentleman admitted. "She said she hoped you'd managed to get some rest last night."

"We could all use that."

"Indeed. Well," Selwyn said, his speculation fading at Harrison's less than enlightening response. "I'd best go find her, then."

"Thank you."

"No thanks necessary. Speaking with Lady Corbin has been one of my more pleasant duties lately."

His, too, Harrison thought solemnly, and watched Selwyn follow Pierce from the room.

The door closed automatically, but he didn't pick up the telephone as he'd intended. Instead, he pulled the little gold ball from his pocket by its gold stem and held it in his palm.

He'd found the earring in the center of his desk blotter this morning. The cleaning people had obviously come across it and put it there.

It was Gwen's. He recognized it because he'd noticed her wearing it last night. Thinking he would return it to her when he gave her an update for the queen this morning, he had slipped it into his pocket. But the more he'd thought about seeing her and the more he thought about what had happened between them, the greater had become his need for distance. So, he'd sent Selwyn to see her instead.

He had no business being with her.

He had no business wanting her.

He understood sex well enough. There wasn't anything terribly complicated about the human sex drive. It was everything else she made him feel that he didn't comprehend. Or trust. He had never craved softness before, or felt a need like he had in the moments before he'd first reached for her in his office. He'd begun to feel that same need when he'd held her during those stolen moments in the tunnel. He'd felt it again when he'd awakened that morning.

There was something about her that seemed almost necessary to him. It felt unfamiliar to want anything that badly. Unfamiliar, and more than a little threatening.

He turned to the phone, punched in a couple of numbers. There was nothing complicated about how he dealt with threat, either. His defenses simply slammed into place. But even with the excuse of a rescue mission allowing him the distance he needed for the moment, he knew he couldn't put off facing her forever. The problem was that when he did see her, he had no idea what he was going to say.

Gwen wasn't the sort of woman for a quick affair. She was a lady with a reputation to protect. Yet he wasn't prepared to offer her anything more.

Gwen had fallen asleep on the sofa in the queen's drawing room sometime after three o'clock in the morning. She awoke a little after seven to the light rap on the main door.

Her first thought was that it had to be news of Owen. Sir Selwyn had told them that he had been sighted and that there was a slight possibility of a rescue last night. Her second thought was that it would be Harrison bringing that news.

Her heart was beating a little too rapidly as she tossed off the cashmere throw blanket she'd borrowed from the queen's salon. Anxiously pushing back her hair, she slipped on her shoes, tugged her sweater over her slacks and headed for the door.

She had no idea how late Harrison had stayed up with Gage and the RET the night before last. Since she hadn't seen him at all yesterday, she assumed that the leads they'd developed had kept him swamped. She just hoped that somewhere during all of that he had found time to get a few hours of sleep. She didn't know how long he would stay in her life. She wasn't even going to think about it right now. She just wanted him to be all right— and hoped that they had found the prince safe.

With a click of the latch, she opened the door. An instant later, the expectation and worry in her face met the weariness in Colonel Pierce Prescott's.

Expectation stuttered to disappointment.

The worry remained.

With his beret tucked under his arm, the head of Royal Intelligence gave a polite nod. "May I enter, my lady?"

"Of course," she replied, hastily masking that disappointment as she stepped back. "Please, come in. You have a message for the queen?"

"I do." He stopped six feet into the room, turning to face her as she closed the door. "I won't keep you but a minute," he said, generously overlooking the obvious fact that he'd awakened her. His manner was polite as always. It was also a bit cautious, as it tended to be when they encountered each other alone. "We thought Her Majesty would want to know that the operation was postponed until tonight."

"They didn't get him?"

"They didn't try. As Sir Selwyn relayed to you, it was only a slight possibility last night. By the time the team got in this morning and they had their plans in place, it was too late to start the operation. They will rest today and be in place at nightfall."

Gwen didn't know what time the queen had gone to her bedroom. The last she'd seen of her, she'd been sitting in the chair by the window, staring out at the blackness, waiting.

The possibility Sir Selwyn had mentioned had been her greatest hope in days.

"I'll tell Her Majesty."

"Thank you, ma'am."

He looked relieved to be going. Aware of that, knowing exactly why that was, she reached for the door. A moment later she dropped her hand.

Harrison had told her that the conversation they'd had about the night her husband died was to remain between the two of them. She wasn't about to break that confidence. But that didn't mean she couldn't let Meredith's fiancé know in some small way that she bore him no ill will for his inability to answer the question she'd once asked of him.

"If you'll forgive me for bringing up the subject," she began quietly, "there is something I need you to know."

Caution immediately shadowed his impossibly blue eyes. "My lady?"

"About that night. The one you and I were never permitted to talk about to each other,'' she explained, though she could tell from his expression that he was already aware of that. Every time he saw her, he seemed to be reminded of it.

''I'm not asking you anything about that night now,'' she continued. ''I understand there are things you can't say. I just want you to know how it has relieved me to know that Alex wasn't alone when he died.'' She paused, the words sounding hopelessly inadequate for the comfort the knowledge had brought. ''I've always been grateful to you for being there.''

For a moment the handsome young officer didn't seem to know what to say. He just looked at her as if he would rather be anywhere else than where he was at the moment—until he slowly realized what else she was saying. She wasn't blaming him for what he couldn't tell her. She held nothing against him for not having been there an instant earlier to help her husband, or for not being the one to take the bullet instead.

His shoulders rose with his deep breath, then dropped as if some awful weight had finally been lifted from them. Some of the shadows even seemed to leave his eyes.

With a bow, he took her hand. ''It was my privilege,'' he said, and gallantly touched his lips to her knuckles before he stepped back.

''Thank you, Colonel.''

''It's Pierce.''

She smiled. Incredibly, with everything else he had to have on his mind, he smiled back.

Meredith was truly a fortunate young lady, she thought, watching him depart. But thoughts of Pierce and how relieved she was to have put to rest the last ghosts of that long-ago night gave way to an entirely different sort of uneasiness within seconds of closing the door.

It seemed that Harrison was avoiding her.

The suspicion lodged as a hard knot under her breast-bone. Since yesterday he had sent Sir Selwyn twice with updates. Today he was sending Pierce. Always before, information had come from him.

The knot seemed to grow. Crossing her arms over it, she tried to will it away. She knew he was busy. She'd been thinking of that only moments before Pierce had arrived. But what seemed logical as fact didn't work as well in terms of an excuse. He couldn't be any busier than he had been all week. He wasn't even that far away. She knew from Sir Selwyn that he'd been in the tunnel most of yesterday. Considering what Pierce had just told her, he'd undoubtedly been there most of last night, too.

The thought that she had just become a one-night stand had her tightening her grip on herself as she started across the room. She wouldn't go there now. The thought was too demoralizing. Aside from that, she truly didn't have the energy to cope with the awful possibility with everything she had to do.

She needed to deliver the RET's update to the queen. She then had an hour to shower and get back to coax Her Majesty to try on the ball gown in case it needed adjustment before the signing. There was also a rather large state dinner planned for that evening she had to oversee—which meant she needed to run down to the ballroom after she checked on the gown to make sure the flowers had been delivered and the candelabras put in place, then get back afterward to make sure the tables were being set properly and that everything was going well in the kitchen.

Those were the things she needed to concentrate on.

So that was what she did.

Within the hour, however, all of her priorities changed. She had been right on schedule, too. She'd spoken with the queen, hurried upstairs to get herself ready for the day and had come back down with her hair in a neat chignon and wearing a simple slate-gray suit. When she'd knocked on the queen's bedroom door again, she had expected to find Marissa showered and Mrs. Westerbrook helping her with her wardrobe.

Instead, she found that the queen had sent her wardrobe mistress away—and that the queen refused to sign the alliance.

When she told Gwen why, Gwen didn't even try to change her mind. She simply left the room and headed straight for the telephone on Mrs. Ferth's desk—only to hesitate the moment she touched the receiver.

Her first thought had been to call Harrison. She knew that duty came first, that her obligation to the Crown should outweigh any uneasiness, embarrassment, hurt or discomfort she might personally be feeling toward the head of the RET. But she had no desire to confirm that he really didn't want to see her by telling him what was going on and having him send someone else to get the details from her.

She called Pierce instead. Attempted to, anyway. She reached his office through the main number for Intelligence and left an urgent message asking him to call her as soon as he could.

His secretary wasn't nearly as accommodating as Harrison's always was. Since Gwen couldn't tell the woman what was so urgent or otherwise describe the nature of the call without causing possible panic in the diplomatic circles, she hung up and called the number Harrison had given her. It was his office number, and though his assistant wasn't there on the weekend, the call patched through to a human who had no problem taking her message asking Colonel Prescott to call. If the young man thought it odd that she was leaving a message for the colonel rather than the admiral, he said nothing about it. He just said he'd get word to the colonel as soon as possible.

It was Harrison, however, who called her back.

"What's urgent?" he asked, sounding totally uninterested in the fact that she'd called his colleague rather than him.

"There is a problem," was all she said. "I need to tell someone about it."

Harrison was heading up the colonnade for the foyer when she reached the foyer herself. Even from twenty feet away he looked better than the last time she'd seen him. The lines around his eyes were less pronounced, the weariness seemed to be gone. There was nothing at all to detract from the aura of power he radiated with every long stride.

She had no idea what he noticed about her as he scanned her face in the moments before he stopped in front of her. "What's the problem?" he asked, motioning her into the colonnade.

They started back the way he'd come, walking as they talked as they so often had before. "She isn't going to sign."

Harrison canceled his next step. Taking her arm, he turned her toward him, only to realize when she stiffened that touching her was not a good thing to do.

"She what?"

"She's not going to sign the treaty," Gwen repeated, her calm tone camouflaging most of her caution. "This is one thing I'm not going to be able to talk her out of, either.''

Considering what she had just told him, what the ramifications would be if that alliance wasn't signed, he shouldn't even have noticed how tightly her hands were clasped, how uneasily she held his glance.

"Did you try?" he asked, noticing anyway.

"No."

His eyebrow shot up. "Why not?"

"Because she feels as if she would be signing her son's death warrant.''

There should have been more concern in her eyes, more worry evident about her friend the queen. Knowing her as he did now, he knew that when she cared about something it showed. It was only when she felt threatened that she tended to mask whatever she was feeling.

A fist of guilt caught him square in the gut. Given the wary way she watched him, that threat undoubtedly came from him.

They needed to talk. He knew that. Now just wasn't the time. Not with the little bombshell she'd just dropped.

He turned on his heel. "I'll go speak with her myself."

"She won't see you."

He turned right back, frustration bumping into the guilt and a few other reactions he didn't want to deal with just then. "Then, what do you suggest I do?"

His tight demand would have had anyone else backing up. All Gwen did was unclasp her hands and cross her arms.

"Maybe you could have Broderick sign. I was thinking about it on the way down the hall," she said, her stance clearly protective, her manner all business. "Royals do things by proxy all the time. She won't put a pen to the alliance during an official ceremony. It's not a cause to celebrate for her, and that's what it will be for everyone else. But she might agree to sign a proxy for the king's brother to do it.'' She hesitated. ''Would that work?''

The tension tightening his jaw slowly changed quality. ''It might,'' he conceded, carefully considering her suggestion. He just as carefully considered her. The concern he'd expected was finally leaking through. It entered her voice, her eyes. ''What reason would we give the delegates for her not signing it herself?''

''She truly doesn't feel well,'' she said, sending a troubled glance in the direction of the queen's wing. ''She isn't sleeping or eating. Between that and the stress, she almost always has a headache. Just tell them the queen has a migraine.''

He'd told himself once before that he needed her for her mind. Now he could have kissed her for the way it worked. Since there were any number of reasons that wouldn't be a good idea at the moment, the least of which were the guards in the distance, he focused only on the disaster she could help him avert.

''Go talk to her. Please,'' he amended, not wanting it to sound like an order. ''Call me when you have. All right? You don't need to go through Pierce.''

He watched her glance flicker from his. She'd gone through Pierce because she'd thought he didn't want to talk to her. He was sure of that. But she was only partly right. It wasn't that he didn't want to talk. He just didn't want to talk about how she made him feel.

''If that's what you want,'' she replied, and started to turn.

He caught her by the arm. He shouldn't have. He should have just let her go and been happy with the fact that she was still cooperating. But he knew what it was like to have her on his side, and he needed her there now.

Beneath his hand he felt her muscles tense as she slowly drew away.

"It is what I want. We work well together," he reminded her, focusing on that rather than the disquieting way it felt to have her pull from his touch. "And you're our only link to the queen right now. We need you."

We, he'd said. Not *I.*

If he'd hoped to restore the ease they'd once managed with each other, he'd failed miserably. "I'll do my duty, Harrison," she said quietly. "I always have."

He had the decency to look apologetic. "I didn't mean to imply that you wouldn't."

He was spared the chance to explain what he did mean. Pierce strode into the colonnade from the alcove and started for the foyer. Spotting them, he immediately changed direction, bearing down on them like a tank and so preoccupied with whatever it was on his mind that he didn't notice the strain in either of their faces.

"We just received another message from the Black Knights," he said the moment he stopped in front of them. "The call went to Prince Broderick again, but it didn't come from Majorco this time. It was traced to a phone kiosk in town. The gist of it is that if the alliance is signed, they're going after another royal because the Crown didn't take them seriously."

She truly envied Harrison's ability to take such news with little more than a blink. "They're upping the stakes," he concluded flatly.

"It appears so."

Gwen forcibly masked her alarm as her glance shot to Harrison. "Do I need to tell the queen this?"

His response came without hesitation. "I can't see that there would be anything to be gained by it. Security is as tight as it can get here and around Princesses Megan and Meredith. Since the queen won't be going to the signing that actually eliminates one risk situation.''

Pierce blanched. ''She what?''

Thinking that the RET seemed rather limited in their response to that bit of information, she offered Pierce a faint smile. ''The admiral will explain it. If you'll excuse me, I need to talk with the queen about an alternative.''

She hurried away, aware of the hushed and fading tones of their deep voices. She was also aware of the prickling sensation of eyes on her back and the certain feeling that Harrison was watching her in the moments before she forced her thoughts from her raw nerves to the idea she needed to present to her queen.

She truly felt that Marissa would be all right with the idea of the proxy. It would break the queen's heart to have to sign that document herself, but Gwen knew she understood that caving in to the demands of subversives wouldn't stop them from demanding more.

When Gwen proposed the plan a few minutes later, Marissa remained silent for what seemed like forever— then responded with a spiritless ''fine'' before sending her off to make the call to Harrison.

All Gwen had to say to him was, ''She agreed,'' and within the hour the proper document along with Sir Selwyn, who brought the official seal and the two ministers required as witnesses, arrived at the queen's drawing room door. Seeing Her Majesty as pale and drawn as she was, the entourage also provided excellent witness to the reason for her failure to attend the signing herself. No one with a functioning brain would think that the woman looked well.

Sir Selwyn whispered words to that effect to Gwen on his way out.

He also mentioned to her after the alliance had been

signed that the queen had proved less of a problem than Prince Broderick.

Gwen was in the banquet hall that afternoon checking the massive floral arrangements by the orchestral stage and the smaller ones lined ten to a table when the king's secretary passed on that the king's twin had come up with half a dozen excuses about why he shouldn't sign—everything from the legality of it, to a last-minute claim that he would be jeopardizing the life of his beloved nephew and he couldn't do that to either Prince Owen or the queen. Apparently, it wasn't until he had been reminded of his public promise to help in any way he could, advised of how humiliating it would be for him to have the leaders and diplomats of three countries angry with him because he was personally responsible for the collapse of the agreements, and assured that his signature would be entirely legal and binding with the proxy, that he'd finally, reluctantly backed down.

It seemed to her that everyone was having one of those days. As Sir Selwyn left to join the security team prowling the room and she turned to the next elaborately set table, she found that twenty place settings had the butter knife in the wrong position. Twenty on the other side had fish forks where the salad forks should go.

Rather than track down someone to switch things around, she corrected the error herself and was surveying the results when she noticed that one of the cleaning staff at the far end of the room had stopped to pick up something. As the girl did, she balanced herself against the huge sheet of bullet-proof glass that protected a display of the crown jewels and the royal thrones.

Certain that her hand had left a smudge, Gwen stopped another of the staff running a vacuum around the perimeter of the gold and red carpet. A smile and a request to have the window cleaned and the smudge had disappeared by the time Gwen was checking the last table.

The details were what the queen depended on her to oversee. And Gwen tended them as best she could. But in the back of her mind the entire time was the thought that the rescue operation would begin in a matter of hours—and an unrelenting awareness of the big man in the admiral's uniform.

As busy as she'd been, she hadn't seen Harrison arrive. It was only when she began to feel that telltale prickle on her neck that she realized he was there. And that he was watching her.

He had obviously come to do a last-minute check of security measures with General Vancor and the members of the RET. The five of them moved from entrance to entrance, pointing this way and that. Every few minutes she felt that tingling chill.

It unnerved her to be that sensitive to him. She tried to ignore the sensation, holding out until she felt as if she were ready to crawl out of her skin. Yet each time she could no longer bear it, and she turned in his direction, he held her glance only long enough to make the knot in her stomach tighten before he deliberately glanced away. It was almost as if he were studying her, trying to figure out what she expected of him. Or maybe, he was considering which approach to take; whether he should let her down gently or be his usual blunt self and tell her it had been an interesting week and maybe they could get together again at his place sometime.

She gave up. She couldn't take any more of his presence or her own thoughts. The minute she'd inspected the last table and decided that the queen would have been pleased with the elegant and sparkling results, she headed out the nearest door to see how Marissa was holding up.

From across the vast room with its enormous chandeliers and long tables of flowers, china and gleaming crystal, Harrison watched her go. He'd seen grown men buckle under less stress and responsibility than she'd been under lately, yet she'd moved through the huge space with quiet poise and confidence. He hadn't been able to help being impressed by both her dignified manner and the obvious respect others had for her as she'd issued orders and requests with the calm efficiency of a fleet commander.

He couldn't help, either, the odd tug of concern when she disappeared from his sight.

"General," he said to the pugnacious head of the Royal Guard. "Put a bodyguard on Lady Corbin. She just left through the east entrance."

"On the lady? Why? She wouldn't be a target."

"The queen holds her in regard. She'd make a good hostage if they can't get a royal."

The man with the ruddy jowls puffed up like a bullfrog. "No one's getting in here tonight. Not under my command."

"It was under your command that the prince was kidnapped. She's all over this palace by herself, General." Harrison's eyes narrowed to slits, his voice dropping ominously low. "Do you have a problem putting a guard on her?"

General Vancor turned the color of the crimson roses in a nearby centerpiece and opened his mouth, only to promptly shut it when he caught the dangerous edge in Harrison's expression. Without another word to him, he headed for one of his men to do as he'd been instructed.

Harrison didn't bother to consider what he'd done. Or why. He was feeling torn and guilty and he needed to bury anything he thought or felt about the woman who'd distracted him from the moment he'd walked into the room. There were too many details to concentrate on right now, and he didn't want her wrecking his concentration. In an hour he would meet with his special forces team for a weather update and to go over the contingency plans once more. In two hours the operation to rescue the prince would be set in motion—just as the guests for the dinner were scheduled to arrive.

Dusk was slowly giving way to darkness when Gwen made her final trip from the ballroom to the residence. She had wanted to take one last peek from the balcony as the guests arrived to make sure the string quartet was playing, that champagne was flowing, that the tapers on the tables had been lit.

When she'd seen Prince Broderick arrive in all his finery amid the elegantly gowned and tuxedoed guests, she had slipped out of the ballroom complex. He would be the only Penwyckian royalty present. He was the only one the RET would allow.

There was nothing more for her to do now.

Nothing but wait.

Her footsteps echoed lightly on the ancient travertine. A heavier beat echoed six feet behind her. The square-jawed hulk in the Royal Guard uniform had followed her everywhere for the past couple of hours.

"I was ordered to protect you," was the only explanation the young corporal could give her. That, and that his orders had come from General Vancor.

Figuring it was just part of the heightened security, silently grateful for the reassurance it provided about the safety of the royal family tonight, she moved into the quite corridor leading to the chapel.

The queen's guards flanked the arched chapel door. Princess Ana's bodyguard stood opposite them.

Her own guard joined the ranks as Gwen slipped inside the dimly lit and peaceful space. Ahead of her the queen knelt on a narrow kneeling bench in front of the small altar, her head bent and her hands clasped. Princess Ana knelt on the bench beside her.

In the flickering candlelight, Gwen quietly slipped into the last pew and knelt down herself.

They all knew that the team Harrison had sent to rescue Owen would be positioning themselves right now. In a matter of hours the rescue would be over. One way or another.

Adrenaline flowed like an electric current beneath the professional calm in the tunnel's command center. On the large electronic wall screen, concentric circles were superimposed over an outline of Majorco's northern shore. Little pea-green dots indicated the six members of the Royal Navy SEAL team.

The men had just been dropped into the ocean a quarter of a mile from Gunther Westbury's villa with its protective wall of cliffs and boulders. Night-vision photos had revealed dogs and armed men patroling the front borders of the property. Entering from the road or forest would have been suicide. Getting out wasn't going to be a walk in the park, either.

Monitors beeped. A technician spoke into a phone. Another called off coordinates in a quiet monotone. As Harrison stood like the commander he was in the sea of sophisticated electronics and the military personnel monitoring them, the only thing that should have been on his mind were the dots on the screen and how those dots were progressing. But standing there willing everything to go as planned wasn't going to make it happen. At this point his faith had to be in his men, not his own will.

The problem was that the moment he stopped thinking about the mission, thoughts of Gwen crept in.

He stuffed his hand into his slacks pocket, absently toying with her earring. He knew she had a guard. He knew as well as anyone involved that every possible measure had been taken to ensure the safety of everyone inside the palace walls. He would even concede that Vancor had a point, that she probably wouldn't be a target herself. But simply being with the queen could put her in harm's way.

As he had off and on for the past couple of hours, he tried to divorce himself from that knowledge, to compartmentalize it as he did the 101 other worrisome details shifting through his mind. He had men bobbing around in the ocean. He had troops on training exercises in submarines powered by nuclear reactors. On any given day he had people in danger simply because they were using heavy equipment, learning to fly at supersonic speeds or working with all manner of explosives.

She was safe. He knew that. But try as he might, he couldn't seem to separate himself from the person and the situation. He could do it with anyone else. He always had. As he stood watching the impersonal dots move closer to shore, he realized that he just couldn't seem to do it with Gwen.

He couldn't bear the thought of anything happening to her.

At the admission, something oddly painful squeezed his heart. The unfamiliar sensation stilled his fingers in his pocket, drew his brow low beneath his navy-blue beret.

Sir Selwyn walked up beside him. "How long will it

be before the team reaches the storage room where the prince is being held?''

"At least half an hour.''

"Would you like me to tell Lady Corbin the operation is underway?''

Twenty four hours ago, Harrison would have told him to go ahead. He had a mission to oversee. But with the announcement from beside them that the team had just made landfall and that radio communication was going to silence, he knew the present situation was now completely out of his hands.

There was another, however, he needed to salvage.

"I'll go."

Though the smartly dressed nobleman's focus remained on the large circular screen, his eyebrow arched ever so slightly. "They're not in the queen's apartments," he advised, clearly wondering at his colleague's inconsistency where the lady was concerned. "They're in the chapel.''

Gwen had no idea that large men could move so silently. The big hand that lightly touched her shoulder caused her to jump an instant before she realized it was Harrison drawing back to press his finger to his lips.

Holding out his hand to help her up, he tipped his bare head toward the door for her to follow him.

She hadn't even heard the door open. Apparently, neither had the queen, who was still kneeling. Or Ana, who was now reading from her prayer book in the first pew.

Since Harrison's actions clearly indicated that he didn't want the queen to know he was there, Gwen moved as quietly as he did, her heart still knocking against her ribs, and slipped out of the chapel behind him.

He held the door with one hand, guided it silently

closed with his other and nodded to the guards. "Which one of you is responsible for Lady Corbin?" he asked.

The hulk stepped forward, saluted as he and the others undoubtedly had done when they'd first seen the admiral, and said, "I am, sir."

"I need to speak with her alone. Follow us as far as the colonnade. If anyone comes looking for either of us, we'll be in the rose garden."

With the polite touch of his hand to her elbow, he nudged her forward. As he did, the corporal executed another smart salute and fell into step behind them. She didn't know if he'd come with a progress report, or if something had gone wrong. Though his expression remained carefully guarded, tension coiled around him like smoke.

He didn't say a word as they moved down the corridor into the colonnade. She could understand his reticence with the guard so close. But even when he pushed open the nearest door to the garden and they stepped into the cool evening air, all he said was, "Let's go over there."

He guided her from the light spilling from the tall arched windows, away from the building and into the shadows of a rose arbor. In the distance, the faint strains of a Viennese waltz drifted from the ballroom.

"What's happening with the rescue?" she asked, growing more uneasy by the second.

He stopped in front of her, his broad shoulders blocking her view of the distant floodlit walls, his face a study of hard angles in the faint light.

"The team is below the villa and moving into position. There won't be any more contact with them until the operation is over."

A breeze rustled the leaves around them. Slipping her

arms around the middle of her jacket, she shivered, partly from the chill, mostly from nerves.

"How long will that be?"

"It'll take them a while to get up there. If all goes well, I'm hoping we'll hear within the hour that the chopper has picked them up."

"I'll tell Her Majesty."

"I'm sure she'll want to know."

"Is there anything else?"

She thought he might tell her that was all for now, and that he would let them know as soon as he heard anything else. As she shivered again, she also considered that he could have told her all of this inside, where it was warmer, but the thought got lost in the sudden silence.

In that quick and disturbing quiet, the tension radiating from his body snaked around her, making it hard to breathe. She knew part of that tension grew from the huge responsibility he bore at that moment, and from all the other problems he was dealing with because the king had still failed to show any sign of improvement.

She also suspected part of it was because, to him, she had become a problem, too.

Her heart hurt at the thought. There was no doubt in her mind how she felt about him. They were so alike in so many ways. In so many ways they completed each other. It wouldn't have made sense to anyone else that she would fall so hard and so fast. But she had. She had been in love twice her entire life, and both times she had fallen in less than week.

Next time, she swore she would take longer. At least with Harrison, she didn't have years worth of memories to make the parting worse. All she had to do was see him at some official function every once in a while and face the reminder that she had meant nothing to him.

Marissa had warned her. Harrison had warned her himself.

The lengthening silence grew awkward. His jaw working, he glanced at his watch and took a step back.

She stepped with him, stopping him before he could turn. She couldn't make him care about her, but she could try to make their future encounters a little less uncomfortable.

"Harrison, please. I can't stand this." Her glance barely met his eyes before it fell to the double row of buttons on his jacket. "Would it help if you knew that I don't expect anything from you? Because of what happened the other night," she clarified, her surge of courage failing her. Her voice dropped. "In case you were afraid I did."

She'd obviously thought he was about to leave. What he'd been about to do was pace, because what he was feeling had him agitated and uncertain and half a dozen other things he wasn't accustomed to dealing with.

Now he froze, caution creeping over him as he studied her face in the shadows. He should have taken her where there was light, where he could see what she was trying to hide. But his only thought when he'd left the operations room had been to get her away from everyone, and the garden had been the nearest place.

"Is that really what you want from me, Gwen? Nothing?"

Even in the dim light, he could see her sudden uncertainty.

"If it is," he said, "then we can end it right here."

"Isn't that what you want?"

"No."

The utter conviction in his reply had her drawing a deep breath.

"No," he repeated, feeling more certain of that by the second. "I thought it was," he admitted, wanting to touch her, afraid she'd pull back. "You threw me, Gwen. I've never felt...I mean, I don't want..."

He shook his head as his voice trailed off, his eyes searching her face, looking for hope, looking for help. He could command a navy. He could express exactly what he wanted when it came to any aspect of his duties. Yet, he had no idea how he was supposed to tell her how he felt. He'd never expressed such things in his entire life. All he knew was that the threat he'd felt with his need for her was nothing compared to what he felt at the thought of her no longer being part of his life.

"You don't want what?" she asked cautiously.

That was easy. "To lose you."

For a moment Gwen could have sworn everything around them went still. The words hung in the air between them, the admission seeming to strip him bare of defense. She held his earnest glance, afraid to believe what she was hearing, wanting desperately to believe it. Harrison wasn't a man to make himself vulnerable. Yet, he just had. He was admitting she mattered to him. That he cared.

The few defenses of hers that he hadn't already destroyed turned to dust. "Maybe you don't have to."

Something shifted in his expression, something that made his eyes glitter on hers as he slowly lifted his hand to her cheek. His touch was almost tentative, as if he didn't quite believe what he was hearing, either.

"I don't?"

"No," she murmured, touching her fingers to the back of his hand. "You don't. I just didn't think that what I wanted mattered."

"What is it you want?" he asked, drawing closer.

"I think I'm afraid to say."

With a touch as light as air he brushed her cheek with his other hand, then slipped it to the back of her neck. "Don't be." He moved closer still. Lowering his head, he brushed his lips over hers. "What is it you want?"

He already knew what she wanted. She was as certain of that as she was of the plea in his eyes when he raised his head.

"You," she murmured.

The plea turned to relief, then to something vaguely feral in the moments before his head came down once more and he claimed her mouth with his.

Harrison drank her sigh, gathering her closer as her body melted against him. He couldn't believe how badly he'd wanted to hold her, or the strength of the need he'd felt so compelled to deny. Breathing in her scent, filling himself with the taste of her, he had no idea how he thought he'd be better off letting her go.

She'd once asked him if he'd ever been sick at the thought of what a person might be going through, or what his life would be like without that person in it. He'd told her, and himself, that he didn't let himself get involved that way, just as he'd told himself all week that he was simply using her to get a job done. He hadn't realized, until he'd thought of his life without her, that he'd been falling in love with her since the moment she'd first tipped her chin up at him in the queen's drawing room.

Feeling as if he'd just run a marathon, he kissed her cheek, her temple and pressed her head to his shoulder.

"I told you I was lousy at relationships," he reminded her.

"I think you just need practice."

"Practice would be good."

She tipped her head back, her eyes smiling into his, her voice a little breathless. "Can I help?"

"How long are you available?"

He saw her smile falter. She was still wary of him, he realized. Hating that, needing her not to be, he edged her back and dipped his hand into the pocket of his uniform slacks. Pulling out her earring, he lifted her palm and placed the small gold ball in it.

"I want to replace these with diamonds. It seems like an appropriate engagement present," he explained, watching her eyes as she lifted her head. "When this is all over, I'm going to ask you to marry me. I love you, Gwen." He hesitated, realizing the absolute truth to the words. She'd shown him that he needed more than duty in his life. She made him realize that he wanted more. That he wanted her. "I really do."

Her heart leaped, her chest feeling oddly tight. Closing her earring in her fist, she swallowed hard. "I love you, too," she murmured, and slipped her arms around his waist. "And when this is all over, I'm going to say yes."

She felt as if she were coming home as he wrapped her in his arms, enclosing her in his strength, weakening her knees with his smile. She had never seen him smile before.

The effect was devastating.

"Why don't you just say it now?"

Everything she felt must have been reflected in her eyes when she smiled back. "Yes," she whispered, and rose to meet his fierce kiss.

In the distance, music drifted on the breeze.

In the chapel, the queen was still on her knees.

The king was still ill. And the rescue team would be trying to free the prince at any moment. But in the precious minutes before the guard at the door started toward them, wrapped in each other's arms, duty was the absolute last thing on their minds.

* * * * *

*Will Prince Owen return
safely to the Royal Palace?
Find out next month when*

CROWN & GLORY

moves to Silhouette Romance with

HER ROYAL HUSBAND

by Cora Colter (RS #1600).

**Where royalty and romance
go hand in hand...**

The series continues in Silhouette Romance
with these unforgettable novels:

HER ROYAL HUSBAND
by Cara Colter
on sale July 2002 (SR #1600)

THE PRINCESS HAS AMNESIA!
by Patricia Thayer
on sale August 2002 (SR #1606)

SEARCHING FOR HER PRINCE
by Karen Rose Smith
on sale September 2002 (SR #1612)

And look for more Crown and Glory stories in
SILHOUETTE DESIRE starting in October 2002!

Available at your favorite retail outlet.

Beloved author
JOAN ELLIOTT PICKART
introduces the next generation of MacAllisters in

The Baby Bet:
MacAllister's Gifts

with the following heartwarming romances:

On sale July 2002

THE ROYAL MacALLISTER
Silhouette Special Edition #1477
As the MacAllisters prepare for a royal wedding,
Alice "Trip" MacAllister meets her own Prince Charming.

On sale September 2002

PLAIN JANE MacALLISTER
Silhouette Desire #1462
A secret child stirs up trouble—and long-buried
passions—for Emily MacAllister when she is reunited
with her son's father, Dr. Mark Maxwell.

And look for the next exciting installment of
the MacAllister family saga, coming only to
Silhouette Special Edition in December 2002.

*Don't miss these unforgettable romances...
available at your favorite retail outlet.*

Where love comes alive™

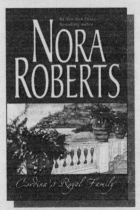
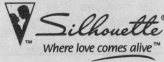

If you enjoyed what you just read,
then we've got an offer you can't resist!

Take 2 bestselling love stories FREE!
Plus get a FREE surprise gift!

Clip this page and mail it to Silhouette Reader Service™

IN U.S.A.	**IN CANADA**
3010 Walden Ave.	P.O. Box 609
P.O. Box 1867	Fort Erie, Ontario
Buffalo, N.Y. 14240-1867	L2A 5X3

YES! Please send me 2 free Silhouette Special Edition® novels and my free surprise gift. After receiving them, if I don't wish to receive anymore, I can return the shipping statement marked cancel. If I don't cancel, I will receive 6 brand-new novels every month, before they're available in stores! In the U.S.A., bill me at the bargain price of $3.80 plus 25¢ shipping and handling per book and applicable sales tax, if any*. In Canada, bill me at the bargain price of $4.21 plus 25¢ shipping and handling per book and applicable taxes**. That's the complete price and a savings of at least 10% off the cover prices—what a great deal! I understand that accepting the 2 free books and gift places me under no obligation ever to buy any books. I can always return a shipment and cancel at any time. Even if I never buy another book from Silhouette, the 2 free books and gift are mine to keep forever.

235 SEN DFNN
335 SEN DFNP

Name	(PLEASE PRINT)	
Address	Apt.#	
City	State/Prov.	Zip/Postal Code

* Terms and prices subject to change without notice. Sales tax applicable in N.Y.
** Canadian residents will be charged applicable provincial taxes and GST.
  All orders subject to approval. Offer limited to one per household and not valid to
  current Silhouette Special Edition® subscribers.
  ® are registered trademarks of Harlequin Enterprises Limited.

SPED01   ©1998 Harlequin Enterprises Limited

Where Texas society reigns supreme—and appearances are *everything.*

Coming in June 2002
Stroke of Fortune by Christine Rimmer

Millionaire rancher and eligible bachelor Flynt Carson struck a hole in one when his Sunday golf ritual at the Lone Star Country Club unveiled an abandoned baby girl. Flynt felt he had no business raising a child, and desperately needed the help of former flame Josie Lavender. Though this woman was too innocent for his tarnished soul, the love-struck nanny was determined to help him raise the mysterious baby—and what happened next was anyone's guess!

Available at your favorite retail outlet.

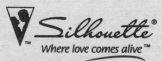

COMING NEXT MONTH